Praise for Legacy of Lies

"Shawgo does it again. This next installment of Archidamus is as exciting and fast-paced as its predecessor thanks to well-written characters and strong story arc. The reader feels both the growth and struggles of her protagonist. I believe this latest book is her best one yet!"

—*Angelina Assanti, Award-Winning and Best-Selling Author of* **Thank God I got Cancer…I'm Not a Hypochondriac Anymore.**

"Twists and turns keep you on your toes as you peek around each corner with protagonists on the run. A tale of revenge and redemption, lightning strikes twice with Janet Shawgo's latest thriller, Legacy of Lies!"

—*Michael Byars Lewis, Award-Winning Author of the* **Jason Conrad Thriller Series**

"Legacy of Lies, a sequel, to the thriller Archidamus. It is even better than the first one. This story will not let you put it down, with its twists, turns and action.

A great, great read. Kudos to Janet Shawgo for another fine example of mayhem."

—*Mike Hartner, Award-Winning Author of the* **Eternity Series**

"Shawgo has done it again with this suspenseful mystery circling around the infamous ghost of Aaron Caydon."

—*Michelle Rene, Award-Winning-Author, of* **Hour Glass, Chanticleer's Book of the year 2017**

"Janet Shawgo moves onto the bestseller list with this entertaining thriller of intrigue and espionage at its finest. A cryptic opening turn into a full-fledged manhunt as our heroine struggles to stay one step ahead of the men determined to end her life at all costs. Can the ghost of her brother save them from certain destruction? Five guns up for this story! I read it cover to cover and couldn't put it down."

—*John Yarrow, International Award-Winning author, of* **The Future's Dark Past**

PRAISE FOR ARCHIDAMUS

"I was absolutely entranced by the uniqueness of each and every character. Such a rich cast. There is nothing cookie-cutter about this thriller."

—Michelle Rene, award-winning author of *I Once Knew Vincent*

"Janet Shawgo weaves an intricate tale of espionage and suspense that draws you in and puts you in the driver's seat! Hang on, this romance writer is about to rock your world with her new thriller!"

—Michael Byars Lewis, award-winning author of *Surly Bonds* and *Veil of Deception*

"Janet Shawgo is a talented writer who possesses a vivid imagination and the ability to create complex characters and interesting story lines that draw readers in and leave them longing for more."

—Kaylin McFarren, RWA Golden Heart® Finalist for *Flaherty's Crossing*, and author of the multi-award-winning *Threads* series

PRAISE FOR THE *LOOK FOR ME* SERIES

Look for Me

"Janet's story line was captivating, and it beautifully illustrated the wonderful profession of nursing, which has no boundaries. After reading this book, anyone thinking of joining the nursing profession will have a solid conviction to pursue that career path."

—Christopher Walker, MD, FACOG, FICS

"Shawgo captures the true essence of what nursing is all about. Her first attempt at novel writing is an inspiration to the writer in all of us."

—Patricia Hensley, BSN, RNC

"A wonderfully written, heroic saga of a woman's determination, strength, and resourcefulness in giving unselfishly on the battlefield while putting herself in danger."

—Rosemarie Masetta, BSN, RN

"I found the book engaging and difficult to put down. I felt like I was actually there."

—Melanie Reis, CNM, ARNP

Wait for Me

"As a lover of historical and medical fiction, I found it a special treat to find the combination done with such skill. The characters in Shawgo's first novel helped me to remember the true reason why I chose a vocation of healing. These characters also made me proud to be a woman. This second novel does not disappoint, and it more than reinforces these sentiments. I challenge you to try to put it down!"

—Elizabeth Hutcheson, MD, FACOG

"I find Janet's writing style very compelling, leaving the reader to wonder what will be found just around the corner. This is a tribute to all females who sacrifice their lives in the service of others."

—*Christine Leblond, Colonel, United States Army, (Ret.)*

"*Wait for Me* catches your attention from the very beginning. Janet has shown the courage of women during a time of war. They answered the call to serve their country, and went where the need was greatest."

—*Pamela L. Little, Captain, United States Air Force, NC*

Find Me Again

"I have read and enjoyed all of Janet's books, and after reading the first few pages of *Find Me Again*, I know I'm in for another great ride. Janet writes strong and wonderfully self-sufficient women, and she captivates her readers with powerful story lines that flow without friction. I am a huge fan and will continue to be for years to come. Bravo, Janet!"

—Neeley Bratcher, author of The Victoria Childs series

"Janet does it again with the final book in the *Look for Me* trilogy. Set aside plenty of time to read, as you will not want to put this one down. There is a larger sense of the paranormal element in *Find Me Again* than in the others. The love story was brought to a wonderful ending with a great lead into a spin-off series. I can't wait to see what else is in store for us from this wonderful indie author!"

—Stephanie Shaw, Steph's Book Club

"Janet has done it again—a wonderful story from the first to last paragraph."

—Michael Cacciatore, MD OB/GYN

AWARDS AND HONORS FOR THE LOOK FOR ME SERIES

Look for Me

Winner, Romance Division, 2012 International Book Awards

Winner, Historical Fiction Division, 2012 Chanticleer Book Awards

Four-Star Review, 2012 Chanticleer Book Reviews

Finalist, Historical Fiction Division, 2012 International Book Awards

Finalist, Romance Division, 2012 Next Generation Indie Book Awards

Finalist, Mainstream Division, 2012 Chanticleer Book Awards

Finalist, Laramie Awards, Historical Fiction Division, 2013 Chanticleer Book Awards

Finalist, Romance Division, 2013 USA Best Book Awards

Historical Novel Society acknowledgment, 2015

Wait for Me

Winner Chaucer Award 2013 Women's Fiction WWII Chanticleer Book Awards

Winner Beverly Hills Book Awards 2015 Military Fiction

Silver Medal Back List Feathered Quill Silver 2018

Five Star Review 2014 Readers Favorite

Four Star Review 2016 Chanticleer Book Reviews

Finalist Chatelaine Romance 2013 Chanticleer Book Awards

Finalist Romance Division 2013 Next Indie Generation Book Awards

Finalist Best Design Fiction 2013 Next Indie Generation Book Awards

Finalist Romance Division 2013 International Book Awards

Finalist Readers Favorite 2015 Military Fiction

Finalist Beverly Hills Book Awards 2015 Historical Fiction

Find Me Again

Grand Prize Winner 2014 Chanticleer Book Awards Chatelaine Category Romance

Winner Chatelaine Awards 2014 Blended Genre Chanticleer Book Review

Winner Mystery and Mayhem Romance 2014 Chanticleer Book Review

Winner Beverly Hills Book Awards 2016 Romance Category

Winner Independent Press Awards 2017 Adventure Category
Winner NYC Big Book Awards 2017 Adventure Category
Winner Feathered Quill 2018 First in Back List
Five Star Review 2014 Chanticleer Book Review
Five Star Review 2015 Readers Favorite Adventure Category
Finalist Romance Division 2014 Next Indie Generation Book Awards
Finalist Action/ Adventure 2014 Next Indie Generation Book Awards
Finalist Romance Division 2014 International Book Awards
Finalist Murder and Mayhem 2014 Chanticleer Book Review
Finalist Chatelaine Awards 2014 Chanticleer Book Review
Finalist Clue Awards, Suspense/Thriller 2014 Chanticleer Book Review
Finalist Paranormal Awards for Supernatural
Fiction 2014 Chanticleer Book Review
Finalist Somerset Awards for Literary and Contemporary
Fiction 2014 Chanticleer Book Review
Honorable Readers Favorite 2016 Fiction Intrigue
Finalist Romance 2017 Indie Excellence Book Awards

Archidamus

Winner Chanticleer Book Review 2016, First
in Category Paranormal/Thriller
Winner Beverly Hills Book Awards 2017 Best Cover Design
Winner Independent Press Awards 2018 Suspense
Silver Medal, Mystery Category FAPA 2017
Five Star Review Readers Favorite 2017
Five Star Review Chanticleer Book Review 2017
Finalist Best Cover Design Fiction 2017 International Book Awards
Finalist Clue Awards, Suspense/Thriller 2016 Chanticleer Book Review
Finalist Paranormal Awards. Thriller 2016 Chanticleer Book Review
Finalist Somerset Awards, Thriller 2016 Chanticleer Book Review
Finalist Beverly Hills Book Awards 2017 Suspense
Distinguished Favorite Independent Press Awards 2018 Cover Design
Finalist National Indie Excellence Awards 2017 Suspense
Finalist National Indie Excellence Awards 2017 Cover Design

LEGACY OF LIES

LEGACY OF LIES

JANET K. SHAWGO

Published by:
Five Ladies Press
John Davis Rd, Galveston, Texas 77554

ISBN-13: 978-1-7334045-0-1
Ebook ISBN: 978-1-7334045-1-8

Printed in the United States of America

Cover Photography by, Heather Eubank-Westerfield, Sweet Jeans Photography

Irish translations by, Professor Sean Dwyer, Western Washington University

Cover and Interior Design by Jaad at JaadBookDesign.com

Eric Acklin cover model

Dedication

In memory of…

Les Constable, winemaker and owner of Brushy Creek Vineyards, a man who believed in the honor of a handshake. Thank you, for your friendship and support over the years.

George Deeb, my apologies this book was not completed before you were gone.

Rest well gentlemen, you will be missed.

Acknowledgement

I wish to thank my early Beta Readers, editors, friends and family who continue to support me with every novel. You are wonderful, amazing, and patient individuals. I love you all!

This sequel was not planned. It appears there were too many questions left unanswered in Archidamus. The demands to have those questions answered were received loud and clear.

It's time to lock the door, obtain your favorite beverage, and enjoy Legacy of Lies.

Once you enter into the service of Aaron Caydon, you will never truly be free…

Dr. Gordon Morres

PROLOGUE

Boston, Massachusetts
June, 2004

A well-dressed man waited in the back of a stretch limousine; his right hand caressed the package at his side. A few moments passed; he pressed a small button to indicate his desire to exit. The driver opened the door and waited. The passenger's hands trembled as he picked up the item to be delivered. The warm weather greeted him when he stepped into the sunshine. He was unsure if the sweat that ran down his back came from the summer heat or the fear of being watched.

"This will not take long," the man said.

"Yes, sir," the driver said.

He walked to the single-story home, in what was considered an upscaled neighborhood outside of Boston. The bicycles and toys indicated children were in the house. The smell of freshly cut grass and flowers assaulted his senses. He could not understand the desire to live in the suburbs. The man held an oblong wooden box, with a rose carved on the lid, tightly as he approached the entry. He rang the bell, stood back, and waited for an answer. As the door opened, he focused with a professional sincerity. The sound of children's laughter, and small dogs yelping greeted him.

"Sorry about all the barking," she said.

He was not prepared for the woman who greeted him. She appeared more as a teenager than an adult and her lavender colored eyes caused him to hesitate.

"Caren?"

"Yes, can I help you?"

"I have a delivery from your brother."

"Aaron?" Caren said, and looked towards the limousine, then back to him.

"Yes. He has entrusted this box to you, with his blessings," The man said and held it out to her.

"Thank you," Caren said and took the box from trembling hands.

"It has been my pleasure."

The man turned away, walked back to the limousine, and was quickly driven away.

●

Caren closed the door, took the box into the kitchen and opened it. Inside were two envelopes. The first contained a handwritten letter.

My dear sister,

I regret that I cannot be there to share this great joy with you, but I must leave for an unknown amount of time. I have finally found love and happiness. I want you to know that you will always be in my heart.

Aaron

Caren opened the second envelope and removed the slim piece of paper. Her hands began to tremble when she realized it was a cashier's check for ten million dollars.

"Stephen! You need to see what my big brother has given us!"

Her husband walked into the kitchen. She handed the check to him.

"Who delivered this?" he asked.

"A courier, in a limousine."

"That's a little strange?"

Caren laughed. "It's Aaron's way."

"Where did he get this kind of money?"

"Aaron is a businessman, it could be from property sales, investments. Ask him next time he's here."

"I'm going to place this in the safety deposit box until we can talk with Duncan."

"Our accountant, why?"

"This amount of money could cause problems. I really think you should contact Aaron."

"No, he'll call or show up one day like he always does."

CHAPTER ONE

octor Gordon Morres walked home from the local clinic where he volunteered four days each week. The small mountain town had been his solace for the last eight almost nine years. He enjoyed the change of seasons, peace, and simplicity of his life. He turned the corner and stopped at the sight of a familiar face. The man sat on the steps of his house. Gordon began to check his surroundings. He knew the arrival of this individual could mean only one thing. Aaron Caydon was in need of his services. Gordon approached his home, faced the man and looked at the package.

"Marcus."

"Doc."

Gordon sat down next to Marcus.

"Do you have work for me?"

"Not sure, Doc."

"I assume that is from Aaron?"

"Yes."

"When?"

"It's from the last job we did together in Virginia."

"Any contact with Aaron since that time?"

"No, and that's why I'm here. Aaron's last instructions to me were to locate you and deliver the package if I hadn't heard from him by January of 2012. You weren't the easiest person to find."

Gordon smiled at Marcus then rubbed his forehead.

"I intended for it to be difficult. I moved here, cut that long gray braid off, and updated my credentials. A new identity, birth certificate, professional information, all take time and a large sum of money.

"Anyone you know seen Aaron?"

"No."

"Aaron's either dead or in hiding," Gordon said.

"He didn't leave me any way to contact him. The only thing I know for sure is once in the service of Aaron Caydon, always in his service."

Gordon nodded.

"The last time I saw Aaron he released me from his service, but I will always be in his debt."

"I've been sent here to help you." Marcus said.

"Let's see what job Aaron left us to do. I assume you still fly?"

Gordon picked up the package.

"There's no other way to travel is there, Doc?"

Gordon took keys from his front pants pocket and opened the door. He turned to see Marcus checking the area.

"Marcus."

"Sorry Doc, old habits die hard."

Gordon heard the door lock and grinned.

"It took me a long time before I stopped looking over my shoulder."

"Beer?"

Gordon pointed. "In the fridge."

Marcus opened the door, took one out and held it up.

"Local brewery?"

Gordon nodded then turned and began to remove the paper wrapping around the package. He opened the box and began to take out photographs, letters and files. The silence became heavy between them.

"What's on your mind, Marcus?"

"Doc, it's not any of my business."

"You might as well get it off your chest. If there isn't trust between us this job will become more difficult."

Marcus hesitated for a moment. "You look the same."

"I'd say you haven't changed either. You're still fit. Just a sprinkling of grey in that black hair."

He turned the bottle over in his hand and finished it before answering.

"I meant to say, you haven't aged."

Gordon took two bottles of beer from the fridge and handed a second one to Marcus.

"Let's talk."

They walked into the main room where Gordon motioned for Marcus to sit down.

"Doc, I didn't mean to pry. It's not my business."

Gordon held his hand up.

"It's fine Marcus, I knew this day would come. It's not possible to hide forever."

"Doc, I'm not following you."

"I've known Aaron Caydon a very long time. Our friendship began as children. In my college years, I was involved in a skiing accident. I was dying. Aaron appeared at the hospital one day and transferred me to a private facility. I received an experimental treatment that saved me."

"What type of treatment?"

"A unique blood transfusion. I miraculously recovered with unusual side effects."

Marcus seemed puzzled.

"Are you saying you don't age?"

"I age, but not like you."

"What you are describing doesn't seem possible."

"I understand this can be perplexing."

"Well, I'm glad you're still around."

Gordon smiled. "I'd rather tell you the truth, so there will be trust. How have you survived all this time?"

Gordon motioned for Marcus to follow him back into the kitchen, where he focused on the contents of the box.

"Doc, you know Aaron always paid us well. I knew eventually the jobs would end one day and made investments. I live comfortably and out of view."

"I thought I had accomplished that until today. This information is going to take me some time to go through."

"Doc, I have no place to be."

"The bedroom across from the bathroom is yours. I didn't see a car; how did you get here?"

"I parked it on the next block."

"You need to bring it here; folks get nervous when people park cars in front of their houses."

Marcus took a set of keys from his pocket and opened the front door.

"I'll be back in a minute. Doc, if you don't mind me asking whose blood was it?"

"Aaron's."

•

One Week Later

Gordon misjudged the time needed to review all the information contained in the box. He thought about the conversation and confession to Marcus that first day. He had omitted detailed information about his and Aaron's childhood association, on the same military base. They went to the same school, played together and spent time in each other's home. One evening Gordon had been invited to dinner at Colonel Caydon's home, where he made the mistake of asking a question about his best friend.

"Colonel Caydon, sir?"

"Yes, Gordon."

"Why isn't Aaron growing like me?"

Two weeks later their family was transferred to another base. Gordon lost all contact with Aaron until his junior year in college. After several days of drinking and renewing old friendships, Aaron made an offer of financial assistance if he would change his major to pre-med. Gordon was hesitant in the beginning and requested a few days to think about the offer. Aaron sweetened the deal with an apartment and monthly cash for expenses. The offer was just too good to pass so he accepted not realizing the consequences of his decision.

The accident happened a year later. Gordon survived, thanks to Aaron, returned to the university, and became a physician. His four years in New York at a major trauma center only enhanced what would be needed in the service of Aaron Caydon. His friendship and loyalty were tested over the years. The continuous calls of medical needs, most outside the normal and legal standards of care forced him to leave the hospital setting. Gordon heard the front door open and Marcus enter.

"You got a nice little town here, Doc. People are really friendly."

"Yes, they're good people here. I'm going to hate to leave it."

"Sorry, I thought this was something I could do on my own. I should have known."

"The day you arrived; I knew I'd have to leave."

"What's the job?"

Gordon handed Marcus a file marked Caren.

"Did you know he had a sister?"

"No."

"It appears there is a contract out on Caren and her family." Gordon said.

"A contract? On Aaron Caydon's sister. Who would be that insane?"

Gordon shook his head.

"We're to collect all family members and take them to these coordinates."

Gordon handed a map to Marcus and waited for him to assess the information.

"This is going to take quite a bit of preparation on our end. We need to hire someone to make contact and remove the family. If we are to make these deadlines we need to leave. I need time to train the individual we hire."

"I'll call the clinic in the morning and close up the house. We should be able to leave in two days."

"I can make arrangements today to have the plane ready for us. I know a couple of men who might be interested in this job."

"You may want to wait on contacting them. Aaron left a name, number and two words."

"Let me guess, payment due."

Gordon nodded his head and handed Marcus the information.

"I know this number."

"Make the call."

"The bastard is too old for this job," Marcus said.

"Aaron must feel he can help, who is it?"

"Ferrell Mallone and you're correct. He will know the perfect individual to assist us."

Gordon could tell by the conversation there was an issue between them.

"If there is a problem between you two, put it aside. Make the call now!"

Marcus laughed. "I bet Ferrell never thought this day would come."

"Marcus, all debts owed to Aaron come due. As I have learned from experience it is always at a most inopportune time."

He walked to the front closet and removed a large duffle bag. Gordon could hear Marcus as he paced the floor, holding the paper and his cell phone.

"Marcus, what's the problem?"

"Doc, what do you think?"

Gordon reached for a large medical bag on the top shelf of the closet.

"Think about what, Marcus?"

"Do you think Aaron made it out of that last job alive or are we working for a dead man?"

Gordon stopped and turned slightly towards Marcus.

"Does it matter?"

CHAPTER TWO

Ferrell Mallone held the cell phone that had arrived almost a week ago with the words, *Payment due* attached to it. It had been left on his doorstep in a small box with only his name written on the paper wrapping. He had prayed year after year to the virgin to intercede for his sinful acts over the years. The rumors of Caydon's death had been met with some trepidation. The years passed and he became complacent where his debt was concerned. The mistakes men make in their younger lives tend to return at some point and demand retribution.

He took the bottle of Jameson, poured a drink and waited as he had each day since the bloody thing had arrived. As he raised the glass to quivering lips the phone began to ring. Ferrell closed his faded eyes and answered.

"Ferrell Mallone?"

"Aye, ye know it is."

"Your account has come due."

"The devil is dead! Let me and mine be!"

"Ferrell, we are all accountable. I know of your debt to Aaron."

"Marcus?"

"I see your memory hasn't failed you."

"Aye, but my body has, I'm too old for such adventures."

"You have kin available, the one you attempted to hide him from Aaron."

"Ye bloody bastard, he's my sister's only son."

"His life belongs to Aaron, or you can forfeit yours."

"I'll need time to find him, where do ye need him to be?"

Ferrell waited, and began to write.

"You'll not speak of your debt to him."

"What would I tell him? I sold my soul and his to Satan? He'll be there!"

He threw the phone against the wall and scattered plastic pieces across the floor. The hurried footsteps to his location made him wished he'd not been so brash.

"Daideó? (Grandpa)"

"Lass, I'm fine, too much Jameson."

Ferrell held up his glass.

"Aye, ye like the drink."

She smiled and began to pick up the pieces.

"I need ye to drive me to Skerries tomorrow. Are ye free?"

"Aye, I can take ye."

"I've had difficult news."

"Another of your friends gone?"

"Aye lass, and this time I must go in person to give my respects."

●

Belfast

Ferrell waited at the door of an abandoned building, outside of the city. He knew the little bastard was in town and had lowered himself all but begging for an audience. A war was coming, and the people would need strong leaders, men who were capable of making the hard decisions. Conor Kelly and his illth couldn't lead an ass out of this barn.

The sounds of footsteps made the hairs on his neck rise. He began to believe someone had betrayed him.

"Ferrell Carrick Mallone, are you armed?"

"Aye, ye bloody fool, I am."

The man covered by the darkness sounded American.

"Place it on the ground for now." He demanded.

"Is he here?"

"Unless you place your weapon on the ground, he will not meet with you," he said.

Ferrell held his hands up, then slowly removed and placed his weapon on the ground.

"Where is he?"

"I'm behind you."

Ferrell turned and held his light up into the face of, Aaron Caydon.

"I thank ye for coming."

"What do you want, Ferrell?"

"I'm only asking for what is rightfully mine."

"Conor feels the same," Aaron said.

"I knew he'd contact ye, I hoped to be the first," Ferrell said.

"You weren't, but I'm listening," Aaron said.

"Ye know where Ireland is headed and soon. My country will need leaders not men with no ballocks. I'll give or promise ye whatever is requested," Ferrell said.

"You'll give me anything?"

"Aye, if ye help me," He said.

"The cost will be high."

"I'll have money, arms…"

"I don't need your money or weapons," Aaron said.

"What bloody fool doesn't need or want money?"

"Money, I have, a blood debt you'll owe. One that can be called due at any time, present or future," Aaron said.

"Name it then," Ferrell said.

"You will be called into my service to complete any job I may need," Aaron said.

"Done!"

"I'm not finished," Aaron said.

"Did ye change your mind about the money?" Ferrell said and laughed.

"If you are unable to fulfil that obligation a male family member will be sent."

"I say done, the Mallone's will honor this debt to the end of our blood," Ferrell said, and grasped Aaron's hand.

"I never forget what is owed to me, do you understand, Ferrell?"

"Aye."

"You will have all that has been asked and more. Long life to you and to your heirs," Aaron said and left the dingy dwelling.

Ferrell followed Aaron to the door and watched as a company of ten maybe fifteen men disappeared into the black night. He picked up his weapon, found the bottle and poured a glass of whiskey to celebrate. He had no male heirs at this time and cared not what would happen in the years to come. His greed and wish for power were placed above his life and family yet to be born. Years passed with many a lass brought into the Mallone family. Ferrell thought he would never see a lad to carry the name until Declan Carrick Mallone was born. He was the last of the Mallone blood line.

"Daideó, Daideó."

Ferrell opened his eyes. "Aye, lass."

"We're in Skerries, at the pub. Do ye need me to stay?"

"No, I'll be fine."

Ferrell watched as his granddaughter's car disappeared before he entered Joe May's pub. He wasn't a stranger here, which meant there wouldn't be questions to his presence in town. He removed his cap and waved to the bartender on the short trip to the far end of the bar.

"What brings ye here, Ferrell?"

"The need for a pint and some adult conversation. The chatter of children and women are not good for an old man."

A glass was filled to the brim and slid to Ferrell.

"There'll be nothing but lies and beer for ye here." the bartender said.

Ferrell heartily drank his beer and thought about the promise he made years past.

"Another beer?"

"Aye, and can ye tell me where a ship called, *The Glory* is docked?" Ferrell asked.

"Just down the way, it might be twenty minutes from here. What in the name of the virgin do ye want with that old rust bucket?"

"Old friends and memories are on that old bucket."

"Aye, Ferrell, we all have them in one place or another."

He left the pub without change from the bill that was left and entered the liquor store four doors down. He spent extra money to get a good bottle today. Good news or bad was better served with whiskey, but Ferrell knew it was the latter he delivered today. He thought about Marcus's comment concerning his attempt to conceal Declan. The only soul who knew that information was Conor Kelly. He would make a special trip *to Friar's Bush* in Belfast, find that bastard's grave and take a piss.

The Glory was docked in the correct location, but it no longer honored the name, now covered in barnacles and rust. He raised his head to heaven.

"Forgive me, sister."

He was responsible for Declan's situation, this despicable place he hid, involvement with the IRA, and debt to Caydon. Ferrell wiped the tears from his unshaven face, walked aboard the ship not caring about the noise he made. The entry into the bow of the ship was met with a gun pressed to the back of his head.

"Ye nothing to fear from this old man."

He held his hands up, bottle in plain sight.

"Jesus Christ, Uncle, what the hell are ye doing here?"

"I've come to give ye hope, but let's drink first."

Declan put away his weapon.

"How'd ye find me?"

"I may be out of the fight, but I'll always know where my kin are. Even in this rusted piece of garbage."

"Who brought ye?"

"Mary."

Declan stood up. "No, Uncle."

Ferrell held his hand up.

"She dropped me off at the pub and left. I'll go back and call a friend when our business is completed."

"Why are ye here?"

"Can an old bastard get a chair before we go to discussing business? Where are your manners?"

Declan pulled two metal stools up to a small table.

"I'm not used to company and it's been a while where manners were needed."

Ferrell reached and slapped his face.

"That's to remind ye."

"What business do ye have that would bring ye here?"

Ferrell poured whiskey into two tin cups and pointed for Declan to take one.

"I've been contacted about a job in the States. I don't know all the specifics but the money will be good."

"Do ye trust the individual who gave this information?"

Ferrell emptied his cup, and poured another.

"Aye, from a time before ye were born."

"Uncle, if I leave Ireland, I can never return."

"Declan, ye need to leave here. Go find a life where you're not living in filth and hiding in the shadows."

"Aye, the last year has been difficult on all of us. Do ye have the information for me?"

"I do."

He handed Declan the instructions he'd written down.

"A meeting in Scotland, in two weeks."

"I've made arrangements and have money for ye."

Declan raised his brow.

"What if I had said no?"

"Then I would've begged ye on my knees to leave. I'll not see my namesake in prison or worse. Declan, forgive this foolish old man. Who has caused all your troubles?"

"Uncle, I made my own decisions and troubles. Ye cannot blame everything upon yourself."

Declan placed a hand on Ferrell's shoulder.

"Ye have your mathair's (mother's) brown eyes and hair." Ferrell said and wiped his eyes.

"I'll go. Can't have a Mallone crying or begging."

"I'll light a candle and pray the virgin watch over ye while you're gone."

Declan laughed. "Ferrell Mallone in church. The last time that happened was at my baptism."

"I now have a reason to go back."

Declan raised the bottle. "Another drink in celebration."

"Aye, and will ye do me another favor?"

"Anything, uncle."

"I want ye out of here tomorrow. Go bathe, shave that red stubble off your face, and burn those clothes. Ye smell like the gut pile from the fish market down the way."

"Aye, I can do that."

They finished half the bottle of Jameson and talked of days past. Ferrell checked his watch and smiled at Declan.

"I need to be heading back to the pub. It will take some time for my ride to arrive from Dublin."

"Aye, and ye need to call Mary so she'll not worry," Declan reminded him.

"She worries like your mother use to."

"I'll see ye off the ship."

The two men shook hands, then Ferrell embraced him for the last time. He placed his hand on his nephew's face.

"Long life, Declan."

"Be safe, Uncle."

Ferrell walked away, but knew his nephew was close, hidden in the shadows to see him safely back into the lights of Skerries. He could never understand how Declan had been trained to hide his height, but he had become the IRA's best and most feared soldier.

He had fulfilled his payment. Declan belonged to Aaron Caydon or whomever ran the team. The last of the Mallone bloodline had become an expendable pawn and he would eventually face God to explain his sin. Ferrell drank the last swallow from the bottle and discarded it into the dark water.

"Burn in hell, Aaron Caydon. The Mallone's don't die that easily."

CHAPTER THREE

Declan Carrick Mallone left Ireland a few days after his uncle's visit. The money Ferrell had given him made it possible for decent room, bath and new clothes. He had a price on his head which made him fair game to anyone that could prove he'd been eliminated regardless of the location in the United Kingdom. A daylight meeting would be uncomfortable and dangerous for those caught in a crossfire. He shook his head at the phrase that would be used to contact him. Who did that now? The clock next to his bed indicated it was time to leave. It would take almost an hour to drive to Stirling Castle.

Declan's decision to desert his fellow soldiers had been a difficult decision but he no longer wished to see the bodies of children and friends left in the streets. Ferrell was correct, he needed to leave and start over.

He waited in his vehicle until it was closer to the assigned time, then entered with a group of elderly ladies from a tour bus. He stood in a corner, surprised at the large number of tourists and groups of children present. He had been on the tour here as a child. The guides were quite informative about the history and contents of the castle. It seemed most visitors were more interested in the ghosts that walk the hallways.

Declan took his map of the castle and located the great hall where he was to meet Dr. Morres. He could not shake the feeling of being observed, followed. He entered the great hall and began to view the grandeur of this massive room. The throne was elevated with two chairs. The king and queen sat above their subjects as the rays of the sun gleamed through the multi-colored stained-glass windows. The thought of dead kings distracted him from the stranger who appeared suddenly and in his space. Declan turned quickly to see an older man.

"Beautiful work, wouldn't you agree?"

"If you're into such lavishness and waste of good money."

"The sun must have been like gold shining through them."

Declan recognized the phrase to identify his contact. He turned back and faced the man.

"Dr. Morres?"

"I am, and you would be, Declan Mallone."

The two shook hands.

"Aye, could we find another place to discuss our business?"

"Are you hungry?" Gordon asked.

"I know of a place down the road, where the food is good and we can have some privacy," Declan answered.

"Lead on. I'm at your service."

They left the castle and walked to Declan's vehicle.

"Do ye need to get your car?"

"No, I'll ride with you if that's permissible."

Declan thought it was odd the doctor wished to ride with him, but observed the outline of a cell phone. If their meeting did not proceed well, Dr. Morres could make his own arrangements. Declan continued to check the rearview mirror and made several turns to see if they were being followed. He glanced towards Dr. Morres who seemed to be amused.

"You do not need to make any more evasions. The car following us is my associate. He'll be joining us for dinner."

"Ye could have told me and saved some petrol."

"I could have, but it was important for me to observe you first."

Declan pulled into a small pub, and both men exited the car. Gordon walked to the road and waved for a vehicle to pull into the small drive. The men gathered at the Range Rover.

Gordon made the introductions.

"Marcus, this is Declan Mallone."

Both men shook hands.

"You weren't easy to follow," Marcus said.

"I had to be sure I was being followed," Declan said.

Marcus turned to Gordon and nodded. They entered the pub.

"Lass, could we get a table in the back?" Declan asked.

She walked the three men to the far corner of the pub. Declan and Marcus sat on the same side of the table with their backs against a wall. The waitress took out a pencil.

"What can I get ye to drink?"

"Three pints," Declan said.

"I see you have good safety practices," Marcus said.

"I don't like surprises," Declan said.

Gordon picked up some nuts and threw them in his mouth.

"What were you told?"

"The information I was given indicated there was a well-paying job in the States," Declan said.

"You took a chance to come," Marcus said.

"The information came from my kin or else I wouldn't be here. I'd like to leave Ireland. The States suit me fine."

The waitress brought their drinks to the table.

"Do ye want to order?"

"We'd like to have a couple rounds first," Gordon said.

"Just let me know when you're ready for another," she said.

"Go ahead and bring them," Marcus said.

She nodded and walked away.

"What's the job?"

"You will contact, extract and transport a family to a designated safe location. Once there you will be paid and free to leave," Gordon said.

"That's it, transport a family?"

Gordon looked at Marcus.

"There could be issues that might arise," Marcus said.

"Issues? The kind that require a final solution?"

"In this type of transaction there could be a need for such," Marcus answered.

"Your experience placed you above other candidates," Gordon said.

"The fact I have a death sentence hanging over me wasn't a deterrent?"

"It makes you the type of individual we need," Marcus answered.
Gordon slid a folded piece of paper across the table.

"I've been authorized to make a substantial offer for your services."
Declan could not believe what had been written on the paper. He looked at both men.

"Only a fool would refuse what is written here."

"Then our initial business is over. Shall we order?"

Gordon turned to see the waitress headed to their table with beer.

"You'll train with me for a month, possibly longer. Once I feel you are prepared, you'll be sent to the States," Marcus told him.

"What makes ye think I need training?"

"Your past training may have been the best for those you once served, but no longer. Aaron Caydon demands a higher standard for his men," Marcus told him.

"Jesus, Mary!" Declan said.

The waitress became concerned as she delivered the beer at the outburst.

"Are ye okay?"

Marcus placed a large bill on her tray.

"He just received some good news. Keep the change."

She smiled at Marcus.

"I'm fine. Thank ye, lass. We'll order shortly," Declan said.

Gordon watched the waitress leave their area. He turned back to face Declan.

"Is there a problem?"

Declan picked up the paper with the offer and counted the zeros.

"The word is Caydon was killed. How is it possible I'm working for him?"

"That lie has been passed around for the last eight years," Marcus said.

"Did we make a mistake about your ability? Are you going to allow rumors and lies stop you from making an unbelievable amount of money?" Gordon asked.

Marcus pointed to the paper.

"I'll ask you once again. Is there a problem with the offer?"

Gordon waited for an answer.

"No, no problem," Declan answered.

"Good, let's eat. Declan, you order," Gordon said and waved to the waitress.

"What can I get from the kitchen for ye?" she asked.

"We'll have the pub special and bring another round," Declan said.

The special filled the table when the waitress returned about thirty minutes later. Declan ate and continued to observe his employers. He knew there had never been any proof Aaron Caydon had been killed, but the stories continued of his demise. His main concern was to leave Ireland and complete the job. Once he was paid, Caydon dead or alive matter not to him. The three walked out of the pub into the evening light.

"What now?" Declan asked.

"Is the car rental or personal?" Gordon asked.

"Rental."

"Leave it. Get your bag and come with us," Gordon said.

Declan retrieved his bag, and left the keys in the front seat. He threw his bag in the rear of the Land Rover.

"Nice."

Marcus opened a small trunk and turned towards Declan.

"I need your weapon."

Declan felt odd about giving his only protection away, but did as he was instructed.

"You're not about to leave a man without protection are ye?"

Marcus handed a box to Declan.

"The Glock 22 is Aaron's choice of weapon for his men."

"A good weapon, no safety, but extremely reliable," Declan said.

"We start a 0430 every morning and will work until I say we are done," Marcus told him.

"Or ye fall behind," Declan said.

"We'll see who falls behind," Marcus said.

"If you two are through pissing on each other I'd like to leave," Gordon said.

As the three entered the Rover, Gordon's cell notified him of a text message.

"Is that the airport?" Marcus asked.

"Yes, the plane is ready for us," Gordon answered.

"Plane? Where are we going?" Declan asked.

"Does it matter?"

"I don't have a passport," Declan said.

"I have one for you," Gordon said, then tossed an envelope to him.

Declan opened and removed the items. The forgeries he held were outstanding.

"When we get to the airport, go onboard and do not speak to anyone," Gordon said.

"What about the authorities?" Declan asked.

"I've already taken care of them," Marcus answered.

"What..."

"Declan, stop asking questions and start following orders. Once we're in the air I suggest you get some rest. I intend to run your ass into the ground once we've settled in at the chateau," Marcus said.

They arrived at a small airport where Declan followed Gordon and entered the plane as he had been instructed. Ten minutes later Marcus boarded, shut and locked the cabin door.

"We've been cleared," Marcus said and entered the cockpit.

"Declan, you need to sit down and buckle up," Gordon said.

"Is there another pilot?"

"The flight is short, and Marcus is quite capable," Gordon answered.

"A short flight means a close location," Declan said.

"Austria, I'd tell you to take a nap but we won't be in the air long enough. I know you have questions and I promise they will all be answered," Gordon said.

Declan leaned back in the leather seat as the plane began to taxi. He realized the horrors of his life were being left behind. He had a real chance to start over. As the plane took flight Declan fell into a deep sleep.

CHAPTER FOUR

Declan walked down the marble stairs of the chateau and into the granite and stainless steel of the kitchen. He took a moment to French press his coffee and leaned against the counter remembering the day he arrived in Vienna. He had fallen into a deep sleep as the jet he had entered left Scotland. Gordon and Marcus allowed him to rest while they cleared customs or rather paid customs upon their arrival. The three were chauffeur-driven to the chateau, where he had approximately three hours of rest before the inquisition began.

The promise Marcus had made two months ago in reference to his training came to fruition. Declan had been worked beyond what he felt was humanly possible for anyone to withstand. He had spent hours in the gym, running every morning to build stamina then with full military packs for strength. He fired thousands of rounds through the Glock, learned to take it apart and reassemble it in total darkness. Marcus was extremely proficient in hand-to-hand combat, leaving him bruised and stiff. His training had been polished, efficient, and focused. Caydon's men were more than mercenaries they were a private army.

Declan had reviewed maps of the United States and photographs of the family neighborhood, outside of Boston. He memorized the description of the house, vehicles, and each face of the family. He felt that two months of training seemed overkill for a simple extraction of one family. Declan raised his head as Gordon entered the kitchen and poured a cup of coffee from the French press.

"Marcus advised me you're ready."

"I would hope so after he kicked my ass for the last two months."

Gordon laughed and held up a platter. "Croissant?"

"No, thank you."

"Marcus is very impressed with your use of knives."

"I've had a knife in my hand since I was old enough to walk. They are an extension of me," Declan said.

Gordon could see Declan grimace as he moved his neck.

"The masseuse and chiropractor will be here this afternoon."

"I admit the amenities of the job have been extremely pleasant."

"The chateau provided the privacy Marcus needed to train you. The rest is a normal compensation for his men."

"I could become accustomed to this type of compensation," Declan admitted.

"A man of your talents has an opportunity for future or continued employment with Aaron, if you desire."

"I might be interested once this job is completed."

"His men are well paid. I hope you'll consider it," Gordon said.

Declan nodded his head.

"Where's Marcus?"

"I believe he's making arrangements for your flight to the States."

"I understand expenses will be covered. What about car rentals, identifications, passports for me and the family?" Declan asked.

"All being arranged," Gordon answered.

Declan felt it was time to ask details about the family.

"Who are these people? Why are they so important to Aaron?"

"I wondered when you would inquire about them," Gordon answered.

"Normally, I wouldn't care. The extensive training means they are important."

"They are Aaron's family, his sister, her husband and two children."

"Names?" Declan asked.

"Caren and Stephen Johnson, a son, Kieran who is in college, and a daughter Enora. They are being extracted for their protection," Gordon answered.

"Protection?"

"Aaron Caydon made a number of enemies in his life. It appears one has placed a large contract on the family."

"When did ye discover that information?" Declan asked.

"It was confirmed two weeks ago. The reason Marcus pushed you so hard these last two weeks."

"Any information available on that contract would be helpful."

"We'll do our best," Gordon said.

It's difficult for me to believe anyone would chance the wrath of Aaron Caydon. We've all heard the stories."

"Stories or rumors?"

"I would say a little of both, from fools that have never seen the results of his work."

"Declan, are you saying you've firsthand knowledge of Aaron's judgements?" Gordon asked.

"Only once. His enemies die in great pain and never quickly," Declan answered.

Marcus walked up to the counter and picked up the empty press. "Coffee?"

"I'll call Michelle to come," Gordon said and walked to the back room of the kitchen.

"Declan, you'll have one week to survey the neighborhood. You need to be out of the States in forty-eight hours once you have them," Marcus informed him "What about backup if I run into problems?"

Gordon and an older woman returned. She began to heat water for the coffee.

"You'll have four disposable cell phones, one use only. If you lose them the job will be completed regardless," Marcus said.

"I'll be on my own," Declan said.

"You were hired for your ability to react to any situation you might encounter," Gordon said.

Michelle handed Marcus a cup and refilled Declan's.

"I'm not too worried," Declan said and picked up a croissant.

Marcus swallowed hard at Declan's statement. "Why is that?"

"What could possibly go wrong, in a small neighborhood, on America soil?"

CHAPTER FIVE

Boston, Massachusetts
December 23, 2012
6:30 pm

Caren Johnson pulled back the curtains in the family room, and looked at the foreboding skies. The man on the weather channel said there would be several inches of snow across their area tonight. She hoped this might be the year that Aaron would come to visit. It had been eight years since his last contact with her. This was a long time for Aaron to be absent from family. She shivered as she closed the curtain, then checked the automatic setting on the fireplace. A nice controlled fire would keep her warm and toasty. She sat down on the couch and picked up the box of night-time medicine off the ottoman. Caren read the directions, poured the correct amount in the clear cup, and swallowed the green liquid.

"God, what a horrible smell."

"Mom, you are such a baby," Enora said.

Caren looked at her seventeen-year-old daughter and smiled. Her eidetic memory brought sweet memories of Enora as she held her immediately after giving birth.

"Sing well tonight."

"Just like an angel," Enora responded.

Caren was sad to be absent from the church play. Stephen would video it on his new phone. She just didn't want to expose anyone to this cold. Caren grabbed the quilt from the back of the couch and lay down.

"Are you going to be okay?" Stephen asked.

"You need to go or Enora will be late," Caren said.

"We're leaving now," Stephen said.

"Be careful the weather report is not good. I think it starting to snow," Caren said.

Stephen threw the keys to their nineteen-year-old son Kieran.

"I'll let our college student drive."

"Wonderful, no rest for me," she said.

"We've been asked to a late dinner with the pastor after the program," Stephen said.

He leaned down and kissed Caren's forehead.

"I'll be up when you get back," Caren mumbled.

Stephen picked up the box of medicine and laughed.

"I doubt that."

Caren heard the door lock as she pulled the quilt around her shoulders. The dogs were cuddled in their beds near the fireplace. She couldn't remember ever being ill, not even as a child. She guessed her luck had finally run out. The glow of the fire and an inner warmth grew from the green liquid. Caren could no longer keep her eyes open. She smiled; it seemed for once the advertisement was correct.

CHAPTER SIX

Boston, Massachusetts
8:00 pm

eclan glanced at the clock on the dash of the Escalade. The plan was to contact and extract the family, travel to the airport, and be off the ground by ten. Declan had Gordon's letter in his pants pocket. It would explain his presence and reason to flee their residence.

In the first few days of surveillance in the neighborhood, Declan found the need to avoid the nightly watch groups. He noticed these groups began to diminish as families packed and left their homes for the holidays. Each night, with regularity, timers brightened empty residences with the multi-colored lights of Christmas. He shook his head and knew this would never deter any thief.

Declan was relieved all members of the family would be present. He had been concerned the young man would not be home from college, but had arrived on the third evening of his check.

He parked the Escalade on a side street in the shadows. It appeared the family minivan was absent from the house.

"Damn!"

It was Sunday. They must have gone to church services. He could wait, take a chance of being noticed by the neighbors still in the area or return in an hour to recheck. Declan reached for the key to start the Escalade when motion lights over the garage indicated movement.

He left the Escalade and used the shadows to hide his approach to the home. His senses indicated danger was present; instincts forced him to take cover behind a tree and wait. The light went dark, Declan felt it might have been set off by an animal. The explosion caused him to double over for protection. The roof burst into a fireball that sent black smoke and debris in multiple directions.

Declan had to check the house to be positive no one had remained. He checked the door for heat, took a deep breath and kicked open the main entrance.

"Is there anyone here? Are ye hurt?" Declan called out.

He made his way to the back of the house. The family pets had become victims of the roof collapse near the fireplace. He turned to leave the heat and smothering black smoke when her body stopped his retreat. He discovered a pulse and began to shake her.

"Lass, get up!" Declan said.

"Stephen, is that you?"

"Lass! Open your eyes or we're both going to die!"

He couldn't understand why it was so difficult to arouse her.

"I'm so cold. Stephen please turn up the thermostat."

"Jesus, Mary and Joseph," Declan said.

He couldn't wait any longer as the sounds of voices and sirens drew closer. They had to leave now or risk being seen.

"Stephen, did the kids burn something? I smell smoke," she said.

Declan felt her snuggle into the warmth of his body as he carried her away from the black smoke and flames.

•

4:00 am

Declan leaned against the wall and peered out the window of the Motel 6 in Albany, New York. The three-hour drive took almost six hours due to weather and roadblocks he had to avoid. *"How did such a simple job go to hell?"*, he thought and closed his eyes. The plan to return and collect the rest of the family was interrupted by the report of their deaths on multiple news and radio stations. The immediate connection between the explosion and the family involved more than just the local authorities. Homeland Security, ATF and the FBI were either on the scene or in route. He rubbed the back of his neck.

"Jesus! What are ye involved in now?" he said.

Neither Gordon nor Marcus ever indicated he might have to explain the death and loss of everything that mattered in this woman's life. He had let his own selfish interest blind him to what this job actually meant. Anything that involved Aaron Caydon should have been his first clue to turn and run. The individuals involved in this operation tonight were well trained and funded.

Declan stopped at the bed to check on Caren before entering the bathroom to splash cold water on his face. She had been asleep for hours which concerned him. If she had received serious injuries in the explosion, he would be forced to leave her. When he turned to face the bed, she was awake, and Declan could see the terror in her eyes due to the restraints. Explanations must be made and unfortunately, this had been his only option. The letter from Gordon was lost when he rescued his charge. Declan held his hands up as he approached the bed.

"I'm going to remove the tape, but first ye need to know I'm here to keep ye safe, understand?"

He watched as she shook her head no, trembled, and tears ran down her soot covered face.

"I was sent by a friend of your brother."

Declan watched Caren's breathing slow as the terror turned to concern. She looked around the room.

"Please don't scream. I'll answer all that I can, just don't scream," he said.

Declan stopped as he reached for the tape.

"Promise?"

Caren shook her head up and down. Declan slowly pulled the tape from her mouth.

"Water please."

Declan took the bottle on the night stand and gave her a sip. She coughed several times.

"Can you release me?"

"We need to have a conversation first."

"Where do you think I am going to go in pajamas?"

Declan lowered his head, as he heard the trembling voice. He took one of his knives and cut the bonds. She quickly moved away from him and began to rub both wrists. He held his hands up again.

"Twenty minutes, that's all I am asking?"

"If you answer one question first," She said firmly.

"If I can, lass."

"Where's my family?"

CHAPTER SEVEN

A Life Gone

Caren Johnson had no reason to trust a stranger who kidnapped and bound her to a bed. She knew there would be no chance to reach the door before he would overpower her. The main concern was for her family and why she was covered in soot and smelled of smoke. Caren's' memory was not clear after she ingested the cold medicine.

"Who are you? Where is my family?"

"My name is Declan Mallone. I was employed by your brother to collect ye and your family..."

Caren listened in disbelief to the story being told by Declan. Aaron would not send a total stranger to her home. This was a fabrication; this man had kidnapped her for money.

"Where is the letter?"

"It was destroyed in the fire."

"I don't believe you. If it's money you want my husband will give it to you. I beg you, don't harm me. I have children."

She waited for him to tell more lies, but he picked up the remote and turned the television on. The news story being reported was in front of the remains of her home. He increased the volume so she could hear what the woman had to report.

"*That's right Bob this is a tragedy for this bedroom community. The entire neighborhood is mourning for the loss of a family of four. Three members killed in what is being called a freak car accident and the mother presumed killed in this intense house fire. Her body has not been found. According to the fire marshal the temperature of the blaze may have consumed the body. There is an ongoing investigation that will take some time.*"

The next moment a photograph from the church directory was flashed on the television.

"Turn it off, turn it off!"

She screamed and began to sob uncontrollably.

"I'm so sorry."

"Who did this?"

"I don't know, lass."

Caren leaped across Declan and made it to the locked door.

"Please let me go." she begged him.

"I can't, I'm sorry."

Caren felt him wrap his arms around her like a child, as she wept and trembled in grief. She laid in the arms of a man she didn't know or trust. When there were no more tears to be cried at this moment, she pulled away and looked at his tear-soaked shirt.

"I need to go to the restroom."

Caren shut the door and started to lock it but didn't. She turned on the water and took a cold rag and placed it over her swollen eyes. When she opened the door, he was sitting on the bed with his head bent.

"Did you say your name was Declan?"

"Aye, lass it is."

"You said my brother sent you?"

"I was hired by two of your brother's associates to transport everyone to safety."

"Well you messed that part up, didn't you?"

"Aye."

"We need to contact the police and let them know I'm alive. I have to make arrangements for my, my family."

The tears came again as she choked out the words.

"May I call ye, Caren?" Declan asked.

She nodded unable to answer.

"Why weren't ye with your family tonight?"

"I'm sick."

"When I found ye on the floor, ye couldn't open your eyes and could barely speak."

"I took some cold medication."

"Are ye ill often?"

Caren thought about his question.

"I've never been ill in my entire life, until two days ago."

"Did ye eat something different?"

"I received a box of candy from a friend for Christmas. My favorite, I ate several pieces."

"Did ye call and talk to her?"

"No."

"I don't believe the gift was from your friend," he said.

"I don't understand."

"When is the last time ye spoke to your brother?"

"Aaron sent a courier eight years ago with a letter that said he would be out of touch for an undetermined time."

"What do ye know about his work?"

"Aaron worked for the government at one time. He left and began his own business. I would see him once or twice a year. He traveled to other countries quite often. I didn't ask him about his work and he didn't offer information. I love my brother; he's always been good to us."

"Your brother has disappeared. No one has seen or heard from him since 2003. The events tonight have complicated the original plan."

"Why were you sent to collect us?"

"Your brother has enemies. A contract was placed on your lives."

"No, that's ridiculous, Aaron is a businessman. Stephen and I aren't special."

"You are the sister of Aaron Caydon. My job is to see ye delivered safely to him."

"We have to go back, tell the authorities."

"Ye can't."

"I have to bury my family."

"It's not possible."

"I will!"

"The individuals that murdered your family and destroyed your home, believe ye are dead. If ye go back, they will try again. There is not an option to go back."

"I'm a victim, my entire life is gone. You can tell the authorities what happened."

"Caren, if ye remain dead, you're a victim. Alive, a suspect and continued target. I cannot return ye."

"Why can't you talk to the authorities?"

"I am not the type of person the authorities would listen to or believe."

"What would you suggest?"

"We need to find a place where we can stay for a few weeks until things settle."

Caren looked around the room. "I don't want to stay here."

"We can't stay here for much longer."

Caren wasn't sure the next words she spoke would be the best. She knew there were weapons, money and a possible way to escape.

"We have a summer home. It may be difficult to get there due to weather conditions."

"Is it close?"

"No, it's located in the mountains of Maine. I need something to wear besides pajamas."

"I bought a few things for ye, since there was no time to gather anything from the house. I apologize if they don't fit properly."

"I know I haven't sounded grateful, but I am. I don't suppose either of the dogs made it?"

Declan shook his head.

"Lass, I need to step outside for a moment."

Caren nodded, sat down on the bed and looked at the white rag in her hand covered in soot. She should have died with her family, wished she had died. A one-time illness condemned her to a lifetime of pain no one should endure. She cursed the eidetic memory and the torment it would cause in the days to come. The door opened and Declan handed her a couple of sacks.

"I've got to clean up," she said.

Caren stopped and turned back to see him take a protective stance at the door. She stood in the shower until the soot no longer ran down her body. Leaning against the tiles she slid to the floor. It became difficult to tell the difference between water and tears. She wiped the steam from the mirror not recognizing the individual that stared back. She was pleased to have a few simple items, clothes to wear, a comb and toothbrush.

"You wouldn't happen to have something stronger than water, would you?" Caren asked, as she exited the bathroom.

Declan held up a bottle. "Whiskey?"

"A large one please."

She watched him fill the standard plastic motel cup.

"Here ye go, lass."

"Thank you for saving me."

"My regrets lass, I should have saved all of ye," Declan said.

He tipped the glass back and emptied it.

"I'm going to try and rest," she said.

Caren finished her drink and crawled under the sheets and thin bedspread. She faced the wall as Declan turned the lights out and returned to his position at the door.

"Nite, lass."

She had been a strong woman throughout her life but the pain and emptiness were indescribable. Aaron would tell her as a child to be patient, find the strength and search for the answer. Caren began to feel the whiskey, it numbed the pain and allowed her to ignore the ache.

CHAPTER EIGHT

December 24th

Declan continued to guard the door as Caren's breathing became regular, less labored and the tears ceased. *"Thank ye, Irish whiskey."* He hadn't noticed the physical make-up of the woman he saved until she showered and dressed. She was a small lass and did not appear to be the age he had been advised. Declan thought her hair was a dark brown under the black soot, but it was black as the darkest night. Caren's eyes were an unusual color. Not the lavender he first thought in photographs, but a mixture between lilac and light blue. Aesthetic changes would be required to keep her safe and hidden. It had been almost six when Caren went to sleep.

"Morning."

"It's closer to one in the afternoon. How do ye feel?"

"Numb."

"I need to go out for food. Ye shouldn't turn the television on not much has changed from last night. There is a computer I left the username and password on the table."

She shook her head. "I can't do this right now."

"I understand, but if ye change your mind, do not sign on to any family accounts. It will lead the authorities, or someone worse to this location."

"Whiskey."

Declan gave her the bottle.

"I'll be right back. Lock the door."

Caren nodded and followed him to the door. He waited until her heard the deadbolt before the short walk to the Chick-fil-A. Declan purchased enough food for the time he would be gone so she didn't drink whiskey all day. When he returned, the lass all but attacked him for the food as soon as the door opened. He was glad to see she was able to eat.

"Lass, I need to leave again. I'll be gone probably until dark."

"Shouldn't I go with you?"

"Not this time."

"You will come back for me."

"Caren, ye are my responsibility until we arrive at our destination or find your brother."

"Declan, there is another place we could go besides Maine."

"Where?"

"We have a condo in Florida."

"We'll decide when I get back, it is another option."

He motioned for her to follow him to the door.

"I know, lock it, don't answer it."

Declan waited until he heard the deadbolt again, then walked the perimeter of the motel before leaving.

●

Declan requested directions on the GPS to the closest mall. He was not the best with purchasing clothing for women but he needed to buy the lass some clothes and women's items. He hoped the items he purchased would fit and be acceptable. The young woman at the eyeglass store was more than happy to give him several samples of colored contacts with no power to try. He was surprised at the large crowds on Christmas Eve, apparently the stories of last-minute shoppers in the States were true. A corner in the food court allowed him to make a much-needed call to Gordon.

"Declan?"

Gordon's voice was frantic.

"Aye."

"What the hell happened?"

"First the lass is safe."

"We feared everyone had been killed. It's good to hear your voice. Did anyone see you?" Gordon asked.

"I cannot be sure, but I used the smoke and confusion to disappear."

"How is Caren?"

"It's been difficult, she has lost everything. Trust is not something she is willing to give right now. We have another problem with all the legal agencies involved. It will not be long before they realize she didn't die in the fire."

"Do you have a plan until we can meet?"

"We need to disappear for a few weeks and let some of the interest fade. She has two options I think will be acceptable and secure. One is in Maine the other Florida."

"I hate the cold myself, but Maine will be a better option. Notify us when you are ready to be picked up," Gordon said.

"We're going to need a few items."

"Warehouse five, waterfront, nine tomorrow night."

Gordon ended the call.

Declan broke the phone apart leaving it in multiple trash cans in the food court. He stopped and bought a large bag of chocolate chip cookies before exiting the area. One last stop before returning to the motel for whiskey.

●

The Do Not Disturb sign on the outside of the room concerned Declan as he parked the Escalade. He walked the perimeter twice and through the lobby of the motel before returning to the car. As he passed the room, he could see Caren peeking out the curtain. Declan shook his head and removed the sacks from the back of the SUV. He didn't even have the opportunity to knock or identify himself when the door opened.

"Ye weren't to open the door until I knocked."

"I saw you, that doesn't make any sense."

Declan handed her the sacks with clothing, found his plastic cup and poured a drink.

"I did my best, lass."

Caren opened the sacks and pulled out the items.

"I'll make do."

"I wasn't sure, so I bought two different sizes."

"These are all fine."

"Lass, ye cannot be going outside without a disguise. I have several pair of colored contacts without power for you to try."

Declan could see her eyes were swollen and wished he'd not said anything.

"Maybe tomorrow. I've never had a need for glasses or contacts."

"Can ye dye your hair?"

"Unfortunately, my hair will not take the color. I'll use hats and caps until you can purchase some wigs."

"Why is the sign on the door?"

"Housekeeping came by right after you left. I told her we didn't need anything then placed the sign."

"Tell me about these places Maine and Florida."

"The condo is in a large retirement community, and there will be a lot of snowbirds there this time of year."

"Why would there be birds in the condos?"

Caren looked at him and thought about what she had said.

"Not real birds. Retired people who live in the north but go south to stay warm during the winter months."

"They have two homes?"

"Yes."

"If there will be a lot of snowbirds we shouldn't go there," He said.

"I agree, so we should go to Maine, regardless the weather."

"Are there a lot of winter birds in Maine?"

Caren almost laughed at him.

"I'll try to explain it to you later, there will not be many people in the city. If privacy is what we need it will be the place to go."

"It may be several weeks before we can leave. What city in Maine?"

"Caribou."

"Do you know the mileage from here?"

"I've never driven there. Stephen … he was a pilot so we flew."

Caren wiped her face.

"I'll be back in a minute."

Declan walked out to the Escalade and plotted the address Caren gave him.

"How long?" She asked from the doorway.

"Nine plus hours, longer if the weather is bad. Do we have access to snowmobiles?"

He motioned for her to go back inside the room.

"Yes, and you will have to buy supplies unless we get them before driving into Caribou. Stephen and I are known to the people in the area."

"Does the house have winter utilities?"

"Yes, of course it does. We will have access to cash, clothing and weapons."

"We cannot leave until tomorrow night."

"Why?"

"I'm waiting on necessary information for us. I need a shower and some sleep."

Caren turned and looked at the only bed in the room.

"I'll sit up for a while."

"Lass, all I need is a blanket and pillow, the floor will be fine."

Declan took his bag and closed the door to the bathroom behind him. He was thankful for the tall shower and endless hot water. Thirty minutes later he walked out with a pair of sweatpants and no shirt. The bed had been divided for two strangers to share. He could see she was staring at the multiple scars on his back, but tonight was not the time for such a discussion.

"Thank ye lass, but it wasn't necessary."

"I would prefer not to be tripping over you in the dark."

"Why didn't ye leave while I was gone today? It would have been easy to run to the lobby and call the police."

"I had my hand on the door handle a couple of times. The thought you might have killed my family, and kidnapped me to obtain money from Aaron."

"What changed your mind?"

"The realization that if I did leave, I have no proof of being drugged or kidnapped. You would disappear, I'd never find my brother or who did this and why. The food and whiskey helped, but for a moment in my grief, you made me laugh."

"Laugh?"

"I thought everyone knew what a snowbird was in the States."

"I know ye haven't much trust in me, but I'll do my best to earn it."

"Good night, Declan."

"Nite, lass."

CHAPTER NINE

aren stood in the family room with her arms around Stephen. They watched their children open gift after gift. The screams and laughter as they received their list of goodies from Santa. The most wonderful sound a parent could hear was their voices.

She opened her eyes and wiped away the tears as another memory stabbed through her heart. Caren looked around the motel room and wondered if this was to be her life? She knew Aaron would protect her and find those responsible if they could find him. Who was this man that had been hired to save them? The scars on his back left more questions than answers. What had Aaron been involved in that would garner a death sentence for her family?

Caren was worried she revealed more information than needed in reference to the money and weapons in Maine. She had questions to be answered on the road to Caribou. If at any point Declan proved to be deceptive, she would escape and take her chances with the authorities. She walked to the bathroom door.

"What time do we need to leave here?"

"I paid for another night that way we can leave at any time."

Caren separated the clothes from both bags keeping everything in her size. She thought he must have a girlfriend or sisters as he bought a sport bra, underwear and makeup. She took a pair of dark brown contacts, jeans, and a black sweater and waited for Declan to come out. The pull of the chocolate chips cookies was too strong to resist so she relented and complimented them with a bad cup of motel coffee.

Declan walked out as she dipped the cookie.

"Are there any more?"

"A couple."

Caren picked up the clothes and entered the bathroom. Twenty minutes later she exited with the contacts, dark eye shadow, heavy eyeliner and mascara which added to the harsh appearance. The transformation left a surprised expression she noted on his face.

"How do the contacts feel?"

She blinked several times.

"I'll have to adjust and need a supply of colors."

"The overall appearance is what we need to keep from drawing unwanted attention."

"I intentionally over did the makeup. In my younger life, I did the whole Goth thing."

She took a burgundy lipstick and applied it.

"Are ye ready?" he asked.

"I believe so."

"We can't leave anything. I'll take the rest of the clothes and put them in the dumpster."

"I'd prefer we give them to a shelter. I'm sure there will be donation sites somewhere."

She noticed he seemed to be interested in her feet.

"Is there a problem?"

"The boots look a little big on ye."

"I put extra socks on. They'll be fine."

"I'll get ye another pair once we are away from here."

"I have several pair of boots at the house in Maine. Don't waste the money. When can I ask you some questions?"

"Lass, can ye wait until we are on the road? We have some time to waste before we leave.

"If that is what you'd prefer."

She placed a blue knitted hat over her head and prepared to meet the outside world. Christmas should be a wonderful time bright and cheerful, but the overcast, cold and gloom of the New York sky forced the reality of their situation. Caren waited in the doorway as Declan placed bags in the Escalade. As she entered the vehicle, Caren felt lost, alone and disoriented. The only individual she could trust was the stranger next to her.

"Nervous?"

Caren shivered. "Just cold."

Declan reached and turned on Caren's seat warmer.

"I believe we deserve something that doesn't come out of a paper sack. How does that sound?"

"I think that would be nice, do you have a place in mind?"

"The pier."

Caren was surprised he would take a chance, but a hot meal would be a treat. He drove to them to the front door of a small restaurant located on the water.

"I need ye to stay put until I've checked the area."

"I'm not in a hurry, but could you leave the car running for the heater?"

She locked the doors and waited for him to return. Declan knocked on the window. The door was unlocked and a protective arm was placed around Caren's shoulders.

"It's not white linens and champagne, but it's safe," He said.

Caren bit her lip as they entered the building, this was more of a dive or hole in-the-wall. She prayed for decent food and was not disappointed with the shrimp and lobster plates Declan ordered for them. Towards the end of their meal, she began to notice him glancing at the clock above the bar.

"Do we need to leave?"

"Aye."

She watched as he paid for their meal with two one hundred-dollar bills and refused to accept the change.

"That was very nice of you."

"Lass, no one should have to work on a blessed day. It's the least I can do."

Their next location was dark and devoid of life, it made Caren feel ill.

"This doesn't seem like a safe place for us to be," She told him.

"I have a package to pick up for us and if I'm not back in ten minutes ye will need to leave."

"Leave! Why in God's name would I leave you?"

Declan grabbed her arm and placed one of the burner phones in her hand.

"Listen to me! If I don't come back this phone is your lifeline to people who can get ye to Aaron. Ten minutes no longer, understand?"

Caren nodded. "Ten minutes, hurry back."

She locked the doors and watched as he disappeared into the building. Caren hadn't looked at the time when he left. How long had he been gone? She just didn't know, then noticed the countdown on the clock in the Escalade, six minutes left.

"Come back, come back."

Caren looked behind the car then back to the warehouse, four minutes left. One-minute left, and the seconds now counted down. She prepared to move into the driver's seat when Declan opened the door with eight seconds left.

"Where did you come from? I didn't even see you approach the car."

"A trick of the mind, this is for us."

Declan handed a large envelope to her and drove away with the lights off. Caren tore open the top of the envelope and emptied the contents into her lap. There were two passports, a driver's license, a set of keys and piece of paper with an address on it. The passport and driver's license were for Lorna Miller. She stared at the perfect photograph of her with short red hair, and green eyes.

"Should I should become accustomed to this?"

"What ye are looking at is temporary."

"Why is that?"

"Caren, we will change names and vehicles frequently. Our safety will depend on the ability to remain unnoticed, blend in with others. I need the paper; it should have the location of our next vehicle pick up."

She sat not believing what he had just said, these things only happened in the movies. He took the paper from her lap and placed the information in the GPS.

"Is it far from here?" She asked.

"If the directions are correct two maybe three hours north."

Caren looked again at the photographs on the passport and license. They were perfect, how was this possible?

"Don't let this bother ye, lass."

"I'm not sure how to handle all of this, I feel like a criminal."

"Caren, your life is in danger, and we're being hunted. We need to do whatever is necessary to stay alive. It's important we get to the next contact point and change vehicles. Ye have questions, ask them, but know I cannot change my past. Our goal is to work together or we're doomed."

"I need the truth."

Declan pulled to the curb and stopped.

"Lass, I will never lie to ye."

●

The road to Maine
December 26th

Caren listened to the music that played on Sirius in the Jeep. The location for the exchange of vehicles had been behind an abandoned gas station in the black of night, approximately a hundred miles north of Albany.

"Declan, weren't you concerned about leaving a seventy-thousand-dollar vehicle in the middle of nowhere?"

"That particular Escalade is actually closer to ninety and no I'm not concerned. It has probably been picked up."

"I'd like to ask those questions."

He took a deep breath.

"Go ahead lass."

She turned the radio down and began to ask questions about his home, family and childhood. When he began to talk of his time with the IRA the mood inside the Jeep became heavy. He promised to be honest about his past, of who he was in Ireland. It had caused an uncomfortable silence between them and Caren questioned her sanity.

He turned into a fast food drive thru and never asked what she would like to eat. They drove a few miles down the road, before he pulled the Jeep into a picnic area and stopped.

"It's a little cold for a picnic isn't it?"

"Ye are the one who wanted to ask questions. I told ye I would not lie about my past."

"Your past is the reason we couldn't go back, because you're running too."

"Aye, and that is why we need to get out of view. I'm not proud of the things I've done, but they cannot be changed."

"My brother must feel you are the type of man to keep me safe or you wouldn't be here."

There was little conversation between them until they entered the city limits of Caribou.

"Declan, I hope the main store in town is open."

"I think we'll be fine." He said and pointed to the cars in the parking lot.

"We haven't been at the house for two years. The pantry will be low on supplies. I made a list for you."

"Can I buy whiskey in here?"

"No, but there is liquor at the house."

"It will be nicely aged," Declan said, then handed his Glock to her.

"You gave me a weapon with no safety," She told him.

"Is it a problem for ye?"

"No."

"Don't get out or let anyone in."

"Is it always going to be like this?"

"For now."

Caren was thankful the windows were darkly tinted and prayed she would not see anyone familiar. An hour later, the back door of the Jeep opened. She could not believe he managed to push two full carts without tipping them over. She leaned over the seat.

"I don't believe my list was that big."

"It wasn't, but I want to be prepared in case we're here longer than expected."

"I've been watching all the people coming and going to the market. I may have been wrong about the holidays."

"We will have to do the best and stay out sight. I'll check the area once we're settled."

Caren directed him to the front door of her home.

"Our summer home. Declan, I don't know if I can do this. This holds many memories, pictures…"

Declan reached over and touched her arm.

"I'm here lass; we'll do it together, at your pace."

The cold air and silence surrounded them as they left the Jeep. Their senses were heightened with each crunch of fresh snow beneath their feet that echoed through the trees. Caren walked up to the door and brushed the snow off the bright blue gnome.

"Enora's idea. She loves them."

She twisted the small object revealing a set of keys. Caren held the gnome and felt the pain go deep in her heart.

"Lass, I need the security code."

"0401."

Caren stood behind Declan as they entered and the security code was entered.

"We need heat, not many lights for now."

"Follow me, I don't want to go anywhere alone," she told him.

Declan followed Caren into the hallway where the thermostat was located. She increased the temperature, then they moved room to room to check for changes from the two years previous. She closed the doors to the rooms that held the most precious memories. It was obvious after their check that Declan would know they had money.

"The house was winterized so we need to wait an hour or so before turning on the water."

"You're fortunate, lass."

"This house once belonged to Aaron. He had it built. We spent many happy summers here as a family. One Fourth of July he presented it to us as a gift."

"It's very nice, but I am concerned the authorities will come knowing ye have this."

"Our names aren't on the paperwork or tax rolls,"

"I don't understand, the property is yours."

"Yes, it belongs to us but Aaron suggested we leave it in one of his corporation's name. I'm sure it's for tax purposes."

"Hopefully, that will buy the time we need. Ye said there was other property in Florida."

"In Ft. Lauderdale, a three-bedroom condo, that once belonged to Stephen's grandmother. We inherited it when she passed away last year."

"Did ye transfer papers to your names?"

"We had to due to it being an inheritance."

"I would have preferred sand to snow, but it will be the first location that will be checked," He said.

"This is the better option then. You should park in the garage it will be easier to bring in all those supplies."

"Aye, and cover our tracks."

"Don't bother, a storm is coming, according to the radio."

"That would explain all the added shoppers in the market. I had a difficult time with their accents."

Caren shook her head, walked through the kitchen, and opened the garage door. Declan backed the Jeep inside and they moved the mountain of sacks into the house. She put groceries away allowing the tears to run when she found reminders of her children. Enora's favorite brand of hot chocolate, Kieran's package of gum and Stephen's love of Count Chocula.

"Your home is pretty isolated, but I need to check the area. I'll be gone an hour maybe longer. Do I need to leave the Glock?"

She opened a kitchen drawer, removed a Lady Smith and Wesson .380 and placed it on the counter.

"I'll be fine. The individuals that own homes here are usually summer folks. The few that enjoy winter activities live down the mountain closer to the road."

"I'm taking the opener for the garage," Declan said, then disappeared out the back door.

Caren walked into the family room and turned the fireplace on. The thought of sleeping in any of the bedrooms was not an option. The large linen closet on the second floor held enough items to make the large sectional downstairs an acceptable alternative. She had kept busy and hadn't noticed the house developed a grey hue due to the overcast. The heavy drapes and shades would ensure the illusion the house remained unused and the ability to turn on lights. Caren returned to her favorite part of the house and began to cook.

CHAPTER TEN

Change of Plans

Declan moved quickly from the house up the mountain checking the two homes. It appeared there had been no occupants since summer, but his trip down the mountain proved Caren's statement to be true. Out of the three houses below them, the two closest to the main road were occupied. He hoped this would not become an issue in the days ahead. The second burner phone was pulled from his coat pocket and the contact called.

"Marcus here."

"Is Gordon with you?"

"Yes, you're on speaker," Marcus said.

"We arrived without issue in Maine. Do ye have any information from Boston?"

"The authorities are concerned they haven't found any bone or teeth from the house. The holidays have delayed their progress." Marcus said.

"The house and property here are not in the Johnson's name," Declan said.

"That will give you more time," Gordon said.

"Declan, there is a storm headed that way," Marcus said.

"Aye, we should be good as long as we don't run out of food."

"You only have two phones left," Gordon reminded him.

"I only need one so I can call when it's safe to extract us," he said and ceased the call.

The destruction of the phone was quick and easily disposed of in the mountains of Maine. Declan stood in the shadows of several trees and observed the six young men drinking shots of Jägermeister. He turned away and began his journey back to the house. As the garage door opened, he could smell food, bacon, sausage and bread. He tried to recall what Americans called breakfast bread. At this point he didn't care. His mouth began to salivate and his stomach growled when he knocked on the door from the garage.

"It's me, lass."

The door was unlocked and Declan met the barrel of the 380. He held up his hands.

"Are you hungry?" She asked.

"My body says yes, but I need a drink."

"Irish coffee it is. You don't seem the whipped cream type, so I won't add it."

Declan removed his coat and gloves before he entered the family room. He stopped and observed beds made for them. Caren's footsteps made him turn around.

"I'm sorry I can't..."

"Its fine, lass. I wasn't expecting to be included."

"If you aren't comfortable with this there are several guest rooms upstairs."

"No, I prefer to be on the main floor."

He took one of the cups she held.

"I fixed dinner."

Declan was surprised at the amount of food she had prepared. He sat down and filled his plate, twice.

"I'm used to a family of four."

"Leftovers heat well in the microwave. I promise ye it will not go to waste."

Caren rose and reached for their plates.

"I'll get them lass, but ye can fix me another coffee."

Declan cleared the table, while Caren made more Irish coffees. He followed her into the family room. She took a remote, increased the flames and sat down on the hearth.

"Stephen didn't believe in burning wood."

"It's better, no smoke to be noticed."

"Did you find anyone in the area?"

"Aye, one is full of young men, the other a family of four."

"The house with the partiers is a rental. I would guess they're here to celebrate the New Year. The family of four is Lino and Bella Vitale, from New Jersey. I'm surprised they haven't left with the storm coming."

"I'll make another check tomorrow if you're concerned about them."

"I feel certain they will be gone, but another check won't hurt. If the other houses are empty, they will remain that way until spring or summer."

"Ye said something about weapons. Are there more than the .380?"

"In the study."

She motioned for him to follow.

Declan was not prepared for the study as she called it. He felt as if they had been transported to a library in a major city, such as London or New York. The room held an aura of opulence, rich carpets, heavy drapes and expensive wood decorated the room.

There seemed to be no room between the books that filled the shelves ceiling to floor. An ornate desk had been placed near a huge east window for optimum morning light. The only item out of character was the oversized gun safe.

"I would like to take credit for this room, but it belongs to Aaron. The only condition we had to follow was continued maintenance of this room."

"Why such a large safe? It seems out of place with the decor."

"Stephen never approve of guns, but tolerated them since I've known how to use one since I could walk. Aaron purchased this once we began to spend time here with the children."

"What's in the safe?"

"Three hunting rifles, two .38 Smith and Wesson revolvers, ammunition, cash and personal papers."

Caren opened the safe with a combination.

Declan stood back to allow Caren room to open both doors. A moment later she quickly backed away and stumbled into him.

"Are ye okay, lass?"

"Aaron's been here."

"How do ye know?"

Caren moved forward and removed the white rose made from wood.

"He sends me white roses, for birthdays, anniversaries, mother's... he's been here."

"Is there anything else in there that wasn't the last time? I know it's been a while." Declan said.

Caren removed two boxes with white ribbon around them.

"These weren't here, and a Glock 22 is not my weapon of choice."

Declan took the Glock from her trembling hand and held the boxes as the safe was closed.

"Do ye want me to open these?"

"I need a drink without the coffee this time," she said.

"I'll get the bottle."

He returned with two glasses and filled them with liquid courage. Caren took a drink and released the ribbon on both boxes, the first box was full of money.

"I don't understand, we have money here."

"How much?"

"Stephen and I always kept about twenty thousand in the safe."

Declan was surprised at the amount.

"Why so much?"

"We paid the taxes with cash, repairs here are expensive and most of the locals prefer money to plastic. Please count this for me."

Caren gave him the box.

Declan counted it twice to make sure of the amount.

"Eighty thousand. Where is the money ye normally keep here?"

"It's in a lock box in the master bedroom, top shelf in my closet. I'd appreciate it if you would go."

Declan took a moment and found the master bedroom. The box was easily found and brought back to the study.

"Where is the key?" Declan asked.

"This safe is fingerprint secure."

She told him and moved a hidden plate where she pressed her index finger. Caren removed the money and closed the box.

"Does anyone besides ye have access to this?"

Caren shook her head.

"I hope there's a note with an explanation in this one."

Caren opened the second box and was pleased there was a note and one photograph.

"What does it say?"

Caren read the note and passed it to Declan.

If you're reading this my plan has failed. The money will assist you to locate the man in the photograph. His name is Bevan Benjamin, Aaron.

"Caren, the plan hasn't failed totally."

"Aaron must believe it has or this wouldn't be here."

"I have two cell phones left. Once the weather clears, and I can obtain information on the investigation in Boston, we will leave."

"What about all of this?"

"I would suggest ye place everything back in the safe for now."

Declan could hear the clicks of the dial as Caren followed his suggestion. He walked to the east window and pulled the drape away to the sight of heavy snow descending rapidly.

"That doesn't look good."

"Ye know how to handle weapons. What else can ye do?"

"I earned my red belt in karate."

"How long has it been since ye were in a dojo?"

"Why?"

"If this weather continues, we're going to need something to keep occupied. I would feel better knowing you're capable in a fight."

"It has been years, but I believe it will come back to me."

"Good, we'll start tomorrow."

CHAPTER ELEVEN

Alex faced the morning sun as he walked towards his home. He had enjoyed the fresh scent of pine and crunch of snow beneath his feet. This was the true prescription he needed, not another pill as his psychiatrist had suggested. He stopped and, took another deep breath of fresh clean air to clear the fog and voices that plagued him.

His physical injuries had healed, but a neurological problem developed, one that would eventually cause him to be admitted to a total care facility. As he reached the top of the incline, the vehicle parked outside his home meant the job was completed. He entered the cabin, removed his coat, boots and gloves.

"Good morning, gentlemen. I hope you have good news for me," Alex said.

He walked to the fireplace, added wood and stood in front of the flame.

"We had a problem in Boston," Beck said.

"What type of problem?"

"Part of our plan failed," Lee said.

"Exactly which part failed would that be?"

"The explosion in the home blew outward. A portion of the house remained intact," Beck said.

"Intact for how long?"

"Long enough for someone to kick in the front door and carry a body out of the house," Lee said.

"Another player is involved, someone we hadn't counted on," Beck added.

Alex felt the quiver of his hands increase as he walked into the kitchen and poured a cup of coffee.

"Did either of you recognize this individual?"

"No," Beck answered.

"I'd like an explanation," Alex said.

"The plan for the house and car were set. We did not expect any issues," Lee told him.

"Three of the family members died in the car wreck. We believe the person taken from the house was the mother," Beck added.

"Caren." Alex stated.

"Our location was blocked by neighbors, the thick smoke and the arrival of multiple emergency vehicles," Beck said.

"We were unable to follow them," Lee said.

Alex moved to a small rolltop desk where he picked through a large stack of files marked private. He located a small folder and handed it to Lee.

"I'd suggest you check the two locations in this file."

"This will take time and money." Lee said.

"The stranger will be a problem until we discovery an identity," Beck said.

"This whole incident smells of Bevan Benjamin and the CIA," Alex told them.

"It could be Caydon," Lee said.

"Jesus, Lee!" Beck said.

"Do not blame your incompetence on a dead man! I expect results for which you have been paid. If you will excuse me, I need to rest," Alex said.

Both men rose and began to gather their coats.

"We'll check the information ye gave us," Beck said and left the cabin.

Lee hesitated, turned back to face Alex.

"Do you need something?"

"This could get expensive," Lee said.

"I'm not concerned about the cost, get the job done and check in on a regular basis," Alex said.

Lee nodded and walked out the door.

Alex refilled his coffee, added bourbon and moved to the window that faced the mountain. He watched the two men enter their four-wheel vehicle and drive away. He finished the coffee, then threw the cup across the room angry his body and mind were failing. He must continue to live, not give into the disease that plagued him, and see that the complete destruction of Aaron Caydon's legacy was accomplished.

●

Beck drove down the mountain road worried about the continuation of being involved in this job. He glanced at Lee reading through the file Alex had given them. A sign indicated around the next curve there was a scenic lookout. He pulled in the empty lot and stopped the Four Runner.

"What are ye doing, Beck?"

He never answered, but exited the vehicle and walked to the stone wall where he steadied himself. A door closed and he could hear Lee's footsteps approaching.

"It's a bit cold for sightseeing."

"Ye know why I stopped. This is not what we signed up for Lee. I didn't want to say anything at the cabin."

"About Declan?"

Beck unzipped his jacket and unbuttoned his shirt. He ran his hand along scars running across his body shoulder to belt line.

"Bloody hell!"

"A gift from Declan. The bastard carved me up like a Christmas turkey. I spent two weeks in the hospital, four units of blood and six months in an Irish jail."

"I remember ye being out of commission, but had no idea it was due to Declan. What caused him to turn on ye?"

"I've never been sentimental on any job, but Declan seemed to have grown a conscience. We were sent to do our duty and as I began to set the charges at the school, he attacked me. The bastard left me bleeding, and notified the authorities."

"You're lucky to be alive. Declan's the best blade man I know."

"Aye, I have the scars to prove it."

"Can we get back in the car before my balls freeze?"

They walked back and, waited for the seats and vehicle to warm the chill away.

"Lee, who do ye think hired him?"

"Maybe Alex is right. The government could be involved."

"I don't think so. If the government knew this woman was Aaron Caydon's sister they would've been involved long before now," Lee said.

"Ye don't believe Aaron is dead do ye?"

"No, I don't think he can be killed."

"Ballocks!" Beck said, and pulled away from the lot.

"I've been thinking about Declan being involved in this situation."

"Where are ye going with this, Lee?"

"Declan's been in hiding. Why would he take a chance of being killed?"

"My guess, is money."

"Money and safe passage out of Ireland."

"He'd need to trust someone, to chance it," Beck said, and began to laugh.

"What do ye know, Beck?"

"The only person who could sway Declan out of his hole is Ferrell Mallone."

"I thought he was dead," Lee said.

"Old bastard will probably outlive us. Ye know he made a deal with Aaron Caydon for power and money in the early years?"

"Where'd ye hear such lies?"

"Not lies! My daidi (dad) told me on his deathbed. Ye know my daidi and Ferrell's history." Beck said.

"Aye, I do. Brothers in the cause."

"Ferrell promised in life or death to give payment when Aaron called."

"Jesus and Mary, ye believe Declan is fulfilling a blood debt." Lee said.

Beck shrugged his shoulders.

"I know our job has become more difficult with Declan involved.

What's in the folder?"

"The family has a condo in Florida," Lee said and smiled.

"Alex said there were two places."

"A house in Maine, but it belongs to a firm or corporation."

"Where in Florida?" Beck asked.

"Ft. Lauderdale."

"I choose sun, sand and margaritas over snow and ice," Beck said.

Lee turned his cell phone on. "I'll make reservations for Sunday. I hate the damn cold, too."

CHAPTER TWELVE

Ft. Lauderdale, Florida
January 7, 2013

B eck and Lee enjoyed a warm January afternoon in Ft. Lauderdale. They drank margaritas and watched the seagulls pick at the small crabs at the water's edge on the beach. They walked up to one of the benches that lined A1A and relaxed next to the calm blue waters of the ocean.

Beck pulled a cream-colored panama hat off and wiped the sweat away.

"I'm never going to leave here, Lee."

"I have to admit this is an improvement over Wyoming."

"We need to find something we can tell Alex."

"I don't think he'll agree to another week of surveillance without results."

Beck raised his plastic cup. "Here's to the discovery of information that will allow more time in paradise."

●

Johnson Condo

The town car that they waited in went unnoticed with the others along the endless row of condos. They had observed several cleaning crews enter at least four homes, stay an appropriate time then leave. Ft. Lauderdale was busy as the influx of snowbirds had begun the migration from the northern states to spend the winter. Lights were turned off and doors locked early in this community. The two men entered the specific condo cautiously checking for a security system.

"Don't ye think it's odd they have no security system?"

"Beck, have ye seen anything worth stealing besides the microwave in the kitchen?"

"The musty smell makes me think it's been a while since anyone has been in here."

Lee exited the second bedroom. "I've got nothing,"

Beck began to look at the knick-knacks, and silk flowers all around the house.

"This place looks and smells like my grandmother lives here."

Lee held up a photograph of a white-haired lady standing on the beach in shorts and a drink in her hand.

"I know your grandmother, and she's nothing like this."

"Now we go north, Ballocks, I hate the cold," Beck said.

"Do ye know anyone that would be willing to help us deal with Declan?"

"Christ! I don't want to deal with him."

Lee picked up a candy dish, opened it, and took out a twenty-dollar bill.

"Drink money later for us. Beck, did ye know of the reward for Declan's death has been increased?"

"Aye, and have ye seen anyone dumb enough to go after him?"

"We could hire someone to help us kill him," Lee suggested.

"If we hire extra help it means less money for us when the job is finished. We need to work smarter."

"I'll report to Alex and make the reservations to Maine."

"Lee, make sure ye get a four-wheel drive rental, we'll probably need it," Beck said.

"Did ye bring winter clothes?"

"Yes, but I was praying they wouldn't be needed."

Lee picked up a book from the coffee table and two twenties fell out.

"Cheer up, we'll have one more day to drink in the sun."

"Did the old woman not believe in a bank?" Beck asked.

Lee shrugged his shoulders. "Sixty will get us started on a good buzz for tomorrow."

●

Moose, Wyoming

Alex paced the main room of his cabin home listening to steel drums, island music and women laughing as Lee reported on their work vacation in Ft. Lauderdale. He hadn't believed Caren and her savior would go to the most obvious location.

"Lee, the vacation is over! Get to Maine."

"I checked the weather conditions in Caribou. There have been back to back storms across the area. The chance they were able to leave is unlikely."

"The people in those areas are accustomed to difficult weather. Speculation on your part will allow them to escape, again."

"Alex, we need a little support."

"I'll make the deposit, get the job done!"

Alex shook from anger, which would result in a migraine, another irritant and side effect from his injury. He rubbed the back of his neck, and swallowed the required twenty medications to keep him in an upright position. Never had he believed his life and career would end in such a pitiful way.

He needed to get away from the cabin, go for a walk, things would be better if he could breathe the fresh air. He stood and reached for his coat, but stumbled and fell. The front door opened and a familiar face entered the room.

"Alex, are you hurt?"

"Good to see you, Richard. I'm a little weak and unsteady today. I need to get out of here and go walk."

Richard assisted Alex up from the floor.

"Alex, I don't think you should go alone."

"Have you got some time for a friend?"

"I believe the toilet in cabin two can wait, while I go with you."

"Richard, do you remember what you told me that first day I hired you to help me with this place?"

"I said you were a damned fool to think this place could be fixed."

Alex had to admit the old motor court was in a deplorable condition when it was purchased, but after a six pack of hard cider he agreed to Richard's suggestion. The worst units would be demolished and removed, and he would do his best to salvage anything still standing. The three cabins that stood today was all that could be saved. Alex's physical issues began to interfere with his ability to complete daily activities. Richard's assistance came as a friend and without pity.

"Can you help me with my coat?"

The two men left the main cabin, walked down the stairs and headed towards a familiar path.

"Alex, let's not go too far."

"It's good to be outside."

Alex listened to a familiar song that began to play on his phone.

"Do you want to get that Alex?"

"No, it can go to voice mail. I'm not in the mood for family sentiment today."

CHAPTER THIRTEEN

Caribou, Maine
January 16th

eclan felt uneasy this morning during his daily training with Caren. They had converted the large family room into an acceptable practice area. A spinning hook kick was delivered on point by his opponent which caused a hard landing and stars to cross his vision. He refused Caren's offer to assist him and remained on the floor until his head cleared. He had received a painful reminder of why she had earned a red belt.

"How long did ye say it'd been since ye were in a dojo?"

"You're off today. What's wrong?" she asked.

"Distracted."

"You tell me the obvious. I can tell something else is bothering you. I would prefer not to play twenty questions."

"We should consider leaving, things don't feel right."

"We should pack and leave, now," Caren said.

"We need to remove all the handguns, leave the rifles."

"I would prefer not to leave any weapons here for someone else to take and use," Caren told him.

"Once we're out of the state I'll make contact and have us extracted."

"What about Bevan Benjamin?"

"Caren, in a couple of days you'll be with your brother, and Bevan Benjamin won't be needed."

•

Caren opened the safe so Declan could remove the weapons and ammunition. She took the letter and photograph back to the master bedroom and placed it in the duffle with her own clothes, these were important and regardless of what Decan thought she would keep them.

She walked out of the shower wrapped in a towel and, closed her eyes as the memories of a husband and children flooded the room. Sunday mornings with both children in their bed, and laughter as Stephen read them comics. The tender nights between husband and wife flooded her soul. She picked up the family photograph on the bedside table taken two years ago and placed it over her heart. She cried in grief and anger as the life and memory she now held must remain. A soft knock to the door acknowledged what had to be.

"We need to hurry, lass."

Caren wiped away the tears. "Give me ten minutes."

"I'll be outside the door."

She dressed quickly and picked up the duffle.

"Declan, I'm ready. Do we have everything?"

"Everything we agreed on including the whiskey."

She felt a heaviness as they reached the end of the hallway, and took his arm.

"Someone is here."

Declan handed Caren his Glock 22 and one of the disposable cell phones.

"Don't lose the phone. If I go down don't try to help me."

Caren nodded and prepared for a fight, as they entered the main room. The sound of the front door and large glass window imploding knocked them to the floor. Caren opened her eyes to the destruction of the cell phone and Declan attempting to find his weapon. It was difficult to move or to hear with the ringing and muffled sounds. She wanted to move, but could only watch as a stranger wrapped his arm around Declan's neck.

"Hello old friend."

"Beck, I though ye would have learned your lesson the last time we met," Declan said.

Beck tightened his grip. "We're here for her, but your death will add nicely to my pockets."

Caren knew Declan had a few seconds before he would be unconscious and the man would collect the contract on them both. The struggle ended as Declan broke the hold, turned and shoved a knife into the man's abdomen then dropped to his knees severing the femoral artery. Tears slipped from Caren's eyes as Declan fell unconscious to the floor, attacked by a second intruder.

●

Lee holstered his weapon, stood over Declan for a moment and kicked him to be sure he was unconscious. He glanced towards Caren who remained on the floor as he moved towards Beck. He failed to notice as she slowly pushed backwards, and crawled into her son's bedroom. He shook his head at his friend who was dying in front of him.

"Ye stupid bastard! Why didn't ye wait? We had them."

Lee knelt down.

Beck coughed, spit blood and smiled. "Aye, enjoy the money and have one for me."

"The saints protect ye."

Beck grabbed Lee's arm and pointed towards Declan.

"Kill him! Kill him, Lee, before he wakes up."

Lee watched his partner take a final breath. He reached for his weapon but never removed it. The ping of a metal bat hit the back of his head and stopped him. The last thing he would remember was the body of his dead partner.

"Take that, asshole."

●

Caren took her son's metal baseball bat and hit him again, then moved to Declan's location. She was not a nurse, but as a mother, she had been called upon to triage injuries to avoid unnecessary trips to the emergency room. Declan had a pulse and a large bump on the back of his head. She was concerned he had a concussion and might not wake in time for them to leave.

Caren looked at the two intruders, and ran to the garage for a roll of duct tape to secure the one still alive. These men were responsible for the death and destruction of all she loved. She found the Glock and considered killing the second man, when Declan's voice stopped her.

"Caren."

She knelt down next to him, and could tell he was having a difficult time remaining awake.

"Declan, wake up we have to leave. Can you move?"

"Can ye help me?"

Declan immediately vomited as he raised up on his knees. She ran to the kitchen and brought back a cold towel to wipe his face. He looked around the room and pointed to the man that was duct taped.

"Did ye kill him?"

"I intended to pull the trigger and end his miserable life, but you interrupted me."

"Don't leave anything that can be traced to us. Did ye find the other phone?

"Only pieces."

"Help me up, lass."

They made it to the back door that lead into the garage when Caren stopped. She walked back to the family room, picked up their duffels and Kieran's metal bat. Declan vomited again before Caren placed him in the back seat of the Jeep. She took the keys from him and prepared to leave.

"Hopefully the bastard will freeze to death before anyone finds him."

"Take the back roads, stay off the main highway."

Caren's hands shook as the garage door opened. She placed the Jeep in reverse, her right hand held the Glock and the left on the wheel.

"Please God, we could really use a little help right now."

The door opened, she pressed the accelerator to the floor and was surprised no one waited for them. Caren checked the rearview mirror only once as she drove away. A chilled ran down her back as a figure entered the garage.

●

Aftermath

He entered the house thru the garage to view the death and destruction of another plan gone askew. The explosion appeared to have been successful with the damage confined inside. He wasn't concerned about the chance of interference from the local law enforcement with the overturned equipment he had left at the bottom of the road. It would take time to move it, but he didn't wish to stay longer than needed in this place.

A pale body rested in a large amount of congealed blood, the odor of iron and urine mixed with the vomit completed the wreckage he had inherited. The second individual was duck taped, unconscious, possibly dead, next to the fireplace. He had questioned his employer of the need to follow men he knew and thought capable.

"They're fuck ups!"

"I know them and have worked with them in the past. Ye could not ask for better. Alex, I'm not a babysitter."

"In my past, I was told to always have a backup plan. I didn't listen and paid the price. You are my backup."

"It's your money."

Alex was correct, they were fuck ups. He needed to decide if anything could be salvaged from this mess and determine if Lee was another casualty. The movement next to the fireplace was an interesting development. It appeared his initial assessment had been wrong. He knelt, placed Lee's face in his hand, and ripped the duct tape off, which caused an immediate reaction.

"I thought ye two were better than this. Ye let a woman and that traitor kick your asses."

"Donovan O'Shea. Are ye here to finish me?"

"I should, ye stupid bastard, and save the headache with Alex, but I don't have permission."

He removed the rest of Lee's bonds and helped him to stand. They walked over to Beck.

"I assume he's responsible for this screw up," Donovan said.

"He never could wait, always had to jump in front of the train."

"What did ye two bring to burn this to the ground?"

"An incendiary device. Beck left it in the vehicle ten minutes from here."

Lee stumbled towards the door and dropped the keys twice.

Donovan held up his hand.

"I'll go. See if they left anything that might tell us where they're headed."

Lee handed the keys to him and waited, then faced his dead friend again.

"Ye bloody fool!"

His eyes drifted to the blood that had dried on his hands, and reached behind his head tenderly touching the large knot. Lee proceeded down the hallway until he found the bathroom and, washed the blood off his hands and face. A bottle of Tylenol was found in a small cabinet over the sink. He ignored the recommended dosage printed on the side of the bottle and swallowed enough pills to possibly ease the pain. He walked back to the kitchen filled a bowl with corn flakes and smelled the milk before using it. He continued to eat never acknowledging Donovan's return.

"Anything useful?"

Donovan walked into the kitchen and knew Lee had done nothing.

"Tylenol and corn flakes."

Lee pointed to the box.

Donovan set the device and a backpack in the center of the main room. He had not taken time to observe the items that were misplaced around the area.

"Lee, I brought the rest of your supplies. Have ye inspected this room?"

"No."

"Get off your ass, and come in here."

"Jesus, Christ! I see Beck, furniture, pillows, blankets, they were sleeping in here."

"Look again!"

"Donovan, I don't see anything, why are ye busting my balls?"

"Declan didn't waste his time. They were training. Are ye blind?"

"She's not a threat."

"Who put that knot on your head? and wrapped your skinny ass up like a Christmas package? Declan or the lass?"

"I don't know."

"Ye do know, it would be wise not to underestimate her. How much time do we have on this?"

"Beck didn't allow for the bad conditions, thirty maybe forty minutes."

"What was your plan? Set the bomb and just hope ye made it off the mountain?"

"It's Beck's design, and he's the only person that can adjust the timer."

Donovan closed his eyes and wished Lee had died instead of Beck at this moment.

"What can ye do to fix this?"

"I can make another device to give us added time, they'll go off simultaneously."

"If you've finished with your meal, get to work."

Donovan fought the idea to kill Lee, but he wasn't going to explain this mess to Alex. He walked through the house to check as had been requested and ignored but was unable to discover anything out of the ordinary. The family photographs, summer and winter clothing, even the lockbox didn't interest him until he entered the study. This simple job took on an entirely different view. He called out to Lee.

"Lee, bring your ass in here."

"What do ye want now, Donovan?"

"Was this safe open?"

"I didn't know this was in the house."

"Why would they need a safe this size?"

"It probably belonged to Aaron Caydon."

"Holy Mary, what the hell does Aaron Caydon have to do with any of this?"

Donovan crossed himself.

"I guess Alex didn't fill ye in on the entire story here."

"No, I guess he didn't. Why don't ye tell me?"

"This woman is Caren Johnson, Aaron Caydon's sister. Alex has some vendetta and wanted the entire family killed."

"The little bastard! I don't want anything to do with Aaron Caydon."

"Beck believed Aaron was dead."

"What do ye believe, Lee?"

"I don't believe the devil can be killed. Alex swears the man gone," Lee answered.

"Who confirmed it? Did anyone see his body? There is no proof Aaron Caydon is dead, no grave, no bloody fool bragging about the kill. All any of us have heard is bloody rumors." Donovan ranted.

"Then you're not going to like the story I'm going to tell ye about Declan."

"Truth or lies?"

"Depends on who ye believe. Beck's father confessed on his death-bed, that Ferrell Mallone made a blood oath with Aaron Caydon. He believed the marker has been called due."

"Jesus Christ!"

"I'm finished in the main room. We just need to set the timer and leave," Lee said.

"Do it. We've a long trip ahead of us."

"Are ye taking me back to Alex?"

"This is your mess to explain. I'd be careful what ye say to him."

"What's your plan, Donovan?"

"Alex and I need to renegotiate my contract. Aaron Caydon and Declan Mallone are cut from the same bolt of cloth. I'll need more men and money to complete this vendetta of his, if I decide to stay."

CHAPTER FOURTEEN

Caren had driven ten plus hours cursing the weather and roads, praying they had escaped. A small sign indicated a bed and breakfast was just ahead on Highway 100. The home seemed to welcome her as the Jeep was parked in front of the three-story home. She felt relieved as the older couple that owned the business had plenty of rooms available. Caren had the couple enamored at her story of love lost now rekindled, ending today with courthouse nuptials and a need for privacy.

"I'm so embarrassed to ask, but my husband had a little too much whiskey at our celebratory lunch."

Caren completed the registration form.

"No, need to worry he isn't the first groom we've helped to their room."

"Thank you Mrs…"

"Moore, but call me Ruby."

Caren was pleased their room had a sitting area with a small love seat. Jesse had no problem assisting Declan to the second floor.

"Thank you so very much."

The older man smiled and left the room.

She worried Declan had a concussion that needed medical intervention, as he continued to come in and out of consciousness. Caren was tired and a much-needed nap would make it possible to observe him during the night.

The second morning she discovered a private area, near the tree line where she took a moment to grieve. When she returned to the house Declan appeared at the window of their room. Caren checked the hallway and knocked lightly before entering.

"Welcome back to the living."

"My head is killing me."

"If you will sit down, I can get a better look."

He took a seat in the rocker by the window.

"How long have we been here?"

"The swelling is so much better. The answer to your question is Michael and Michelle O'Connell, newlyweds, stopped here two days ago."

Declan raised a brow.

"Newlyweds. Will I need to know the details of our wedding?"

"No. A simple lie, cash upfront for the room and a large tip."

"Do we have a time limit on our honeymoon?"

"I paid for a week. If we need to stay longer, I don't believe it will be a problem to extend.

"I'm foggy on what happened after ye put me in the Jeep."

There was a light knock on their door.

"Mrs. O'Connell?"

Caren held her hand up to Declan.

"Yes, Ruby."

"You missed breakfast dear. I brought some tea and scones for both of you."

Caren opened the door allowing the tall lady to enter the room. Ruby was dressed in jeans and a baby blue sweater that complimented her short grey hair and hazel eyes.

"Thank you, Ruby. It was such a lovely morning, the time slipped away from me. This is my husband, Michael."

"A pleasure to meet ye."

"Oh! An accent. Scottish?"

"Irish."

"I hope we'll see more of you now that you seem to feel better. Those stomach issues can be bad," Ruby said

Caren smiled at Declan.

"He's feeling much better. Thank you for the scones," Caren said.

"It isnt a problem, enjoy."

She smiled and left their room.

"She wasn't what I had expected."

"Mr. and Mrs. Moore are retired teachers who wanted to stay busy. They have owned the B&B for four years."

"Why did Michael have stomach issues?"

"It appears you had too much libations at our wedding reception."

"Where did the names come from?"

She watched Declan as he poured tea into cups for them.

"I found an envelope taped under the driver seat with new identifications and money when I stopped for gas that first day. The one for me had a different last name. When I checked us in, I had to improvise."

"Was there any additional information in the envelope?"

Declan handed Caren a cup of tea.

"I'm glad we didn't exchange vehicles."

He picked up a scone. "Why?"

"The letter indicated there are four additional packets hidden inside the door panels of the Jeep."

Caren was relieved to see him eat.

"I see there was a wig and contacts in the envelope. Blonde is not your color."

"I'm getting used to it."

"Lass, what happened at the house?"

"I opened the garage door, floored the accelerator, and left. Ten hours later we ended up here."

"Cell phones?"

"They're both gone. I heard you call one of those men by name."

"Beck Flanagan and Lee Sheehan, killers for hire and explosive experts. They usually work together for large sums of money."

"What about the third man?"

"Third man?"

"It was probably my imagination. I thought I saw someone enter the garage as we pulled away."

"Can ye describe him?"

"Declan, I can't be sure I actually saw anything."

"Tell me what ye saw. I've never known them to work with a partner, but it is possible."

Caren took a position on the edge of the bed, and closed her eyes.

"A tall individual, long overcoat, cap, no facial hair, black military type boots."

"For someone ye didn't see that was a very detailed description."

Caren opened the small drawer on the bedside stand and handed a local newspaper to him.

"We are front page news here in Vermont,"

She waited as Declan read.

"One body found, means Lee had some assistance escaping, so good memory under a stressful situation, lass."

"Caribou is a small town; the authorities will ask for outside assistance."

"The two explosions will eventually be connected. How often is the paper delivered here?"

"Ruby said every couple of days. They have a computer available for guests."

"Is there any chance another storm is headed there?" he asked.

"I didn't check, why?"

"It would help us."

"Delay the investigation and search of the property," Caren said.

"Aye."

"I'll check the computer this afternoon."

"We can't stay here forever, lass."

"Declan are you sure Ft. Lauderdale is not an option?"

"I would imagine Beck and Lee have already been there, and the authorities will not be far behind them."

"Declan, maybe we…"

"I need to clear my thoughts."

Declan bent over in the chair and held his head.

"Do you feel like a walk?" she asked.

Declan stood and looked out the window.

"I believe that might be helpful."

"I'd suggest the path by the barn."

"Is that where ye went this morning?"

"It's quiet and peaceful."

Caren smiled as he picked up another scone, a jacket, and left the room. She walked to the window to make sure he didn't stumble or fall. They were going to need help and she believed there was someone who could do that. She placed the duffle on the bed, unzipped and displaced clothing until she located the photograph. The younger image of her brother and Bevan Benjamin brought a smile, and hope. She noticed the background where they stood. The memory of strong coffee and sweet taste of powdered sugar, made her salivate.

"Café Du Monde in New Orleans."

•

Declan walked past the barn, into the trees where he stopped and filled his lungs with the fresh smells of a Vermont day. The smoke from the B&B, fresh snow, and a hint of pine all reminded him there were places of peace.

His last conversation with Marcus would haunt him forever, *"What could possibly go wrong in a small neighborhood in America?"* He now lived the very problem of what he thought impossible. They were on their own, chased by old enemies from home, hired by an individual who wanted Caren dead. This person had a long reach and information not easily obtained.

"Mr. O'Connell."

Declan had not heard the footsteps and was startled. He turned around and stepped back. The older man had a trimmed beard, pale blue eyes and was dressed for the weather.

"Michael please, Mr. Moore."

"Sorry, I didn't mean to come up on you, and it's Jesse."

He shook Declan's hand.

"Jesse, what can I do for ye today?"

"It's good to see you up and moving son. Ruby and I were beginning to think we needed to get you to the hospital."

"Aye, too much of the good whiskey and bad food. I feel much better thanks to my wife."

"If you feel up to it. Ruby and I would like for you two to join us for dinner tonight."

"We'd be honored to share a meal with ye and your lovely wife," Declan answered.

"Wonderful, we'll see you around six, enjoy your walk."

Declan watched as Jesse disappeared through the trees. He bent his head and closed his eyes.

"Jesus, Joseph and Mary."

•

Caren knew they had no option except to find Bevan Benjamin and ask for help. She walked into the kitchen and made another pot of tea to take back to their room. Ruby's anise cookies and scones could not be ignored. She added them to her tray and smiled as Declan opened the back door.

"The photograph Aaron left was taken in New Orleans. I think we should…"

Caren stopped when he took her arm.

"We have a problem."

"Did you see something or someone on your walk? Did you get sick out there?"

"No, lass nothing like that."

Caren was concerned at the panic in his voice.

"Tell me what's wrong?"

"Jesse invited us for dinner at six this evening."

Caren picked up the tray filled with goodies and headed back to their room.

"I don't see the problem."

They walked into the room.

"The problem is Michael and Michelle O'Connell, our history, and lives before we married. I do not normally assume a persona with a new name."

He removed his coat and gloves and pointed to his left hand.

"I'll pull a memory and build a life story for us. All you need to do is sit there, smile and, agree with me."

"This could be a disaster."

"If you learn anything, tonight it will be that the women do most of the talking. The men sit and drink."

"What do ye mean pull a memory?"

Caren waited for a moment not sure he would understand.

"I have the type of mind that allows me to remember every day of my life since I was about five years old. I can tell you dates, times, details of clothing, weather, books I've read."

"Ye have an eidetic memory."

"Yes."

"Ye remembered everything when we sparred? That is cheating. Why didn't ye complete the training, receive your black belt, and progress?"

"My incomplete training ceased due to babies and a married life. In my early college years, I destroyed grade curves and caused a number of students to withdraw from classes. I believed my memory to be a blessing, until the day you saved me. I see my son's first steps, my daughter's prom dress, Stephen's face on our wedding day."

Tears ran down both cheeks of her face.

"Caren, please stop. We'll graciously decline the invitation. I don't want to cause ye more pain."

Caren wiped the tears away with the back of her hand.

"Declan, this is something we need to do."

"Alright lass, we'll go. What were ye saying about New Orleans?"

Caren handed him the photograph.

"This was taken at Café Du Monde."

"Ye want to go to New Orleans?"

"I believe there might be information for us there."

"Ye want to find Bevan Benjamin."

"We have no cell phones, no way to locate Aaron, but we do have a clue. I don't believe we have a choice."

"I want to get through this evening first, then we'll talk about where to begin the search for Bevan."

"What about the Jeep?"

"I'll find a place where I can remove the rest of the packages. We'll need to change vehicles frequently, keep to back roads and small towns."

"Internet connections could be an issue in smaller towns."

"We'll find café's or coffee houses, use the library. We need to travel light keep only what can be carried. I would like to exchange the rifles for handguns."

Caren nodded.

"They're not going to stop, are they?"

"No, lass, and I'm sorry for the situation I've placed ye in, but I'll not leave your side until we find Aaron."

Caren could smell food cooking.

"Smells like roast beef, I guess we should prepare for dinner with Ruby and Jesse."

Declan smiled. "Ye lead and I'll follow."

"Strange, that's the same thought I had about you."

●

Declan had been through many a life-threatening situation in Ireland. The simple act of having a meal frightened him above all he'd experienced as a soldier. He managed to keep his hands from trembling or drop anything during dinner. As the evening progressed, he became amazed at the details Caren was able to describe when asked. He was curious if these memories were from her married life, or just a fabrication.

"Michael, do you feel up to a quick trip out to the barn with me?" Jesse asked.

"I'd be happy to help ye. Let me get my coat." Declan answered.

"Jesse, don't ask our guest to work," Ruby scolded her husband.

"It'll be fine. Michael worked on a farm as a boy," Caren told them.

"Aye, it has been a while," Declan said.

"We just need to give the horses some feed," Jesse assured him.

Declan kissed Caren on the head before leaving the house. The cold night air caused him to turn his collar up. He prayed Jesse wouldn't ask anything detailed questions. The two men entered the barn, where Jesse turned on several overhead lights.

"Sorry to take you away from your bride. I find men never get much said when women lead the conversations," Jesse said.

Declan laughed. "I guess I'll be getting used to it."

"The feed is over here. I'll try not to keep you too long."

An hour later, the two men returned to a quiet and empty scene.

"It seems the women finished their conversation," Jesse said.

"Good night," Declan said.

He entered their room and discovered Caren waiting for him.

"You did fine tonight," Caren told him.

"Only because ye did all the talking."

"I believe we've convinced them. It will make the rest of our time here easier," she said.

Declan walked over and turned out the lamp next to the bed.

"Good night, lass."

CHAPTER FIFTEEN

Moose, Wyoming
January 28th

Donovan walked towards the main cabin in response to Alex's text demanding his presence. No amount of whiskey added to his coffee would take the chill, or lighten the threat of added snow here in the mountains. He believed the older style units and this location might have belonged to Alex's family, though he rarely mentioned them. The only reference to his history was the hatred for Aaron Caydon or anyone associated with him. He heard a door close and observed Alex descend the steps of the main residence.

"Walk with me."

Donovan hated the cold, but followed him towards a worn path.

"Alex, what happened in Maine wasn't Lee's fault. Beck was to blame and paid the price."

"Someone needs to be responsible."

Donovan shivered with each crunch of snow.

"Is Lee still breathing?"

"For now."

"If ye intend to continue, I will need another explosives expert to replace Beck."

"She still lives, the FBI and Homeland Security have made a connection between Boston and Maine. You should have killed Lee and explained the mess yourself."

"The fiasco in Maine was not my responsibility to explain," Donovan told him.

"What else?"

"Lee informed me that the woman ye want dead is Aaron Caydon's sister. That little bit of information would have been appreciated."

"I don't see the point of this conversation," Alex said.

Donovan stopped and waited for Alex to turn around.

"The point as ye call it, is I enjoy living, drinking and the pleasures of a lass. It matters not the money if I don't live to spend it."

"The man is dead and buried. What part do you not understand, Donovan?"

"Aye, I've heard the stories, but do ye have proof?"

"I've no proof here."

"What makes ye believe the man was killed?"

"Donovan, I have money to spend if you're interested. Aaron Caydon is no longer a threat to anyone."

Donovan knew this little bastard withheld information.

"If ye don't kill Lee, I'll need him, and a full crew."

"Hire them and get the job finished."

"Declan Mallone is with her," Donovan said.

"Should I know or care who that is?"

"Ex IRA, survived the blast in Maine, and killed Beck with a knife."

Alex laughed. "It sounds like I should have hired him. I assume you two have a history?"

"A traitor to the cause, large reward for his death back home."

"It appears you'll be collecting a double payday then."

"That would be my plan. It would be nice to know who hired him. I find it odd that you hired from outside the States and now Declan appears.

"Christ Donovan! It's just a coincidence, nothing more."

"We need to peak interest in them, to get a direction."

"Place a large reward for information on their location, proof required for payment. Donovan, I want physical proof, understand."

"We should be cautious or too much of a reward might cause someone to go rogue and kill them."

"Then it will be your job to see that doesn't happen. It should be clear the consequences if anyone attempts it. Kill this Declan, but bring Caren back here."

"Why the change in plan?"

"Not your concern. Bring her back here alive and unharmed."

Alex restarted his walk.

"Where's Lee?"

Alex smiled. "The third cabin. The door is unlocked."

"If ye don't mind, I'm going to head back. I hate the cold."

"Donovan," Alex called to him.

"Do ye need something?"

"The next person that screws up, I expect you to kill them," Alex said, and disappeared down the path.

Donovan walked back to the small cabins, opened the door where he discovered Lee naked on the floor, and tied to the bed. Donovan shook his head and wasn't positive if the money was worth the annoyance. The cold inside the cabin made him shiver as he knelt to release Lee.

"Don't worry, I'm not going to kill ye."

Lee pulled the blanket off the bed and wrapped it around his body.

"That crazy bastard left me here to freeze."

"If he wanted ye dead, I wouldn't be here. Ye have another chance to make things right."

"What did he say?"

"Not enough to convince me Caydon is dead, but I'm willing to take his money."

"Have ye got anything warm to drink, food?"

"Aye, get your naked ass up and come on."

Donovan had left the heat turned up in his cabin and left food in the oven.

"Thank ye, coffee or hot tea?" Lee asked.

Donovan poured him a cup of coffee.

"We have plans to make and people to hire."

Lee nodded as he stuffed a biscuit and bacon in his mouth.

"I guess he placed ye in charge?"

"I assume after Maine that will not be an issue for ye." Donovan answered.

"As long as I get paid, I don't give a damn."

"He wants the woman brought back here."

Lee choke on his coffee. "What in Christ's name was his reason?"

"He didn't say. I need a crew."

"Beck has a brother," Lee mumbled, and shoved another biscuit in his mouth.

"No, I'll not take that road, find someone who doesn't have a connection with Declan."

"Ye know that will not be an easy task. I may be able to locate someone here in the States."

"We're going to need a tracker," Donovan said.

"There's only one person that comes to mind."

"Craig Gallagher."

"Ye two are friends, aren't ye?" Lee asked.

"Aye, close as brothers," Donovan said and smiled.

"Ye should be the one to contact him. Jamie Fitzgerald might be available and willing to take a chance on dying. I'll call him. Donovan, where are my clothes? I need a hot shower and something besides this blanket."

Donovan threw Lee a set of keys.

"They're in the back of the car. I wouldn't let him burn them."

Donovan closed the door as Lee ran across the snow to get his bag and into cabin three. He poured a cup of coffee, added a healthy amount of Jameson and turned on his cell phone. Craig was a friend who never failed to come when he called. He didn't want to lie to his friend, so certain information would be omitted, for now.

"Donovan, ye must be in a bind, brother."

"Craig, I've good money to pay, what else do ye need?"

"I need a ticket out of Dublin," Craig answered.

"Can ye leave Friday?" Donovan asked.

"Aye."

"I'll send the information."

"I expect a bottle to be waiting. Donovan, none of that cheap shit."

"Jameson and Tullamore good enough for ye?"

"Aye, it'll be a good start," Craig answered.

Donovan ceased the call as Lee entered.

"Ye look and smell better."

"I called Fitzgerald. He wasn't interested if Mallone or Caydon was involved."

"Ye couldn't convince him Caydon was dead?" Donovan asked.

"Spirit or flesh the man left his mark."

"His response will probably be what you'll hear from anyone back home."

"What about Gallagher?" Lee asked, and pour a cup of coffee.

"I'm working on flights for all of us."

"Donovan, we need to leave this place as soon as we can."

"I agree, we need a central location to work from and I want to get away from Alex."

"I need to replenish my supplies; a larger city would be preferable," Lee said.

"Is Dallas big enough?"

"Aye, I have friends there that will be able to help me."

"I'll not go with ye so if you're arrested no one will come to help. Lee, I won't be able to keep him from killing ye next time."

"I'll make some calls before we arrive. Is there any way we can leave now?"

"Ye don't want to spend another night in these wonderful cabins?" Donovan asked and laughed.

"I'm begging ye. I'd rather sleep in the car."

Donovan threw the keys to Lee.

"Go get your bag. We'll be driving to Billings, and find a place until our flight out the thirtieth."

"What about Craig?"

"His flight to Dallas will be on the first."

"A new city where Declan or Aaron are not well known might prove advantageous." Lee said, and walked towards the door.

"Lee."

He stopped and turned back to face Donovan. "What?"

"Remember what I said. No more fuck ups."

CHAPTER SIXTEEN

Craig Gallagher opened his eyes and looked at the lights of Dallas as the plane began to descend into the airport. This state was three times the size of the United Kingdom, which was difficult for him to imagine. His first-class seat and lovely lass that attended the cabin had been pleasurable. Donovan's call had been a blessing. Family health issues had arisen, and his financial assistance would be required.

"Sir, may I serve you another drink before we land?" the attendant asked.

"Jameson," Craig responded.

She walked away and returned with his drink.

"Thank ye, lass," he said.

She smiled. "Is this your first trip to Dallas?"

"Aye, I hear it is an amazing place."

"Dallas is my home. I'd be happy to show the city."

"Lass, I regret to say, another time."

Once the plane stopped at the gate, he stretched, opened the overhead bin and took out his bag. Craig smiled as he passed the lovely attendant and she placed a napkin in his hand with her phone number. He was ushered towards customs where he was quickly processed through and sent towards the baggage area. He searched the area as it filled with passengers, for Donovan.

"Craig!"

"Mo chara." (My friend.) Craig said and embraced Donovan said. Craig felt a hand grab his long hair and flip it.

"Are there no barbers, or razors in Dublin?" Donovan chided.

"Mind your business. I grew it for the lasses and, don't need your approval."

Donovan laughed. They had been mistaken for one another over the years. The same physical build, black hair and blue eyes caused many a lass to surrender to their charms.

"Do ye have another bag?"

"No, I travel light these days," Craig said, and held up a medium sized duffle bag.

"Are ye hungry?"

"Aye, but I'm more interested as why ye sent for me. Who else is here?"

"Lee Sheehan."

"Is his buddy, Beck, with him?" Craig asked.

"Beck is dead, killed by Declan Mallone."

"Ye didn't tell me Declan was involved."

"I didn't tell ye the person we are searching for is Aaron Caydon's sister either."

Craig stopped. He grabbed Donovan's arm turning him around so they were face to face.

"Bloody Hell! Do ye have a death wish? If I wasn't so tired, I'd kick your ass and get back on the plane."

"Will ye let me explain the situation? If ye still feel the same I'll send your ass back. Craig, I need your help. Lee can barely work his cell phone."

Lee pulled up in the arrival lane, and both men entered the Escalade.

"Lee."

"Craig, good to see ye."

"Donovan told me about Beck, sorry to hear it."

"Bastard never could wait. It cost him."

"Craig, the hotel has twenty-four hour room service, and I stocked the bar with full bottles," Donovan said.

The ride to the hotel was in silence. When they arrived at the suite Craig dropped his bag, walked to the bar, and grabbed the Jameson. He poured a glass and pointed to the table and chairs.

"Donovan, give me some idea of why ye need me."

"A simple job Lee and Beck started has turned into an FBI and Homeland Security case. I've been offered enough money to correct and finish the contract."

"Jesus, brought down the big ones, didn't ye?"

"Beck thought he could take Declan alone," Lee said.

"Why aren't ye dead?"

"He met the fat end of a metal bat," Donovan said.

"The lass?"

"I don't remember," Lee answered.

"Yes, the lass knocked him out, secured him with a large amount of duct tape and left him to freeze. The main room of the house had the appearance of a sparring ring. Declan may have been training her," Donovan said.

"She can probably handle a weapon being Caydon's sister. What makes ye believe they haven't left the States?"

"We found two destroyed cell phones at the house in Maine," Lee said.

"Burner phones?"

Donovan nodded.

"They lost their ability to be extracted. Ye need a tracker," Craig said.

"There isnt anyone better," Lee said.

Craig grabbed the menu and made a fast decision.

"Anyone else want to order?"

"Add a burger for me," Lee said.

"I'll take the club with fries," Donovan added.

Craig dialed room service and placed their order.

"Who is Alex?"

Donovan began to answer when Craig held a hand up, so he poured a drink and waited.

"They are usually fast here with the food," Lee said.

"Thirty minutes isn't fast," Craig said.

"Alex pays all the bills."

"This Alex must have a bottomless pocket. Suites like this are not cheap. Do ye know if Declan or the lass have any money? They won't be using cards unless their stolen or forgeries."

"Unknown, but there was a large safe in the study of the house," Donovan said.

The knock on the door ceased their conversation.

"I'll take care of it," Lee said.

Craig picked up his bag and, motioned for Donovan to follow him in one of the bedrooms as the waiter entered with a cart and set the table.

"Donovan, this is a major cluster. I have no love of Declan, but Aaron Caydon dead or alive is still a problem. He had many loyal to him beyond death."

"Alex swears the man is dead. They're on the run with no one to help them. I need a tracker. I'll not involve ye in any of the killing. I swear."

"He's gone," Lee called out.

"Tracking, that's it. I want the option to leave at any time with full pay."

Donovan held out his hand. "Aye, I give ye my word."

They shook on the agreement and walked out to join Lee at the table.

"I'd like to hire at least two more to join us," Donovan said.

"I don't want to have to lie about Declan or Caydon, it's not good for business," Craig said.

"I may have found someone," Lee said.

"Craig, I can offer a year's worth of money anyone could make in Ireland."

"It will not matter what ye offer if they don't live to spend it. I'll make some calls but don't expect anyone to come. How much time does Declan have on us?" Craig asked.

"About two weeks," Donovan replied.

"I'm going to eat and sleep. We'll start fresh in the morning," Craig said.

"What are ye going to need?"

"My computer and paper maps of the States," Craig said.

"How much time will ye need?" Donovan asked.

"I don't know. Let me pull the crystal ball out of my bag and ask it," Craig said.

Lee chuckled. "That's funny."

"Donovan, ye called me in cold. Declan has a two week head start, and ye expect me to give an intelligent answer."

"Sorry, eat your food and we'll start tomorrow?" Donovan said.

"I'm beginning to wish I had gone home with the lass on the plane."

"Depending on what ye tell me tomorrow, she may have an opportunity to be treated to a taste of Ireland." Donovan said.

●

February 4th

Donovan walked out into the main room of the suite where he found Craig at the couch with his maps spread out over the large table in the main room. The knock on the door kept him from joining his friend for definitive information.

"That will be room service. I took the liberty of ordering for everyone."

"Where is Lee?"

"When I left our room, he was still sleeping off the bottle, but I heard the shower just before your door opened."

Donovan signed the ticket and tipped the waiter after he set the table. Lee appeared his eyes red and only a towel wrapped around his waist.

"Ye will not be eating with us like that. Go put some pants on," Donovan said.

They watched as he disappeared, then returned with a pair of sweatpants and a white t shirt.

"Is it good enough for ye?"

"I prefer not to be looking at your balls while I eat," Donovan said.

"I may have an idea where they are headed," Craig announced.

"A positive destination or generalized area? I'd prefer to give Alex a more detailed report to keep him off our asses," Donovan said.

Craig motioned for them to follow him. They listened as he began to explain his theory their escape.

"I don't believe they went into Canada, but are headed southwest."

"There was a condo in Florida where Beck and Lee spent a week working on a tan," Donovan said.

"Nothing in the place, some photographs of an old lady," Lee added.

They wouldn't go there after what took place in Maine," Craig said.

"Declan will find a way to get information on what the authorities are connecting. They will not stay in one area for more than a week for now." Donovan added.

"My suggestion is to place large bounties for information on them," Craig said.

"Alex made the same suggestion, but I'm not convinced," Donovan said.

"Ye have an issue with it?"

"He's worried about someone not following the instructions," Lee answered.

"If it were any bastard besides Declan we're chasing, I might agree. Ye need to place large bounties for information. Donovan, I know your next question. I can't give ye a definite timeline," Craig said.

"Then that will be what I tell Alex. He can accept it or find another crew."

"Should we move to another city?"

Craig picked up the maps.

"We should remain in Dallas for the next four to six weeks."

Donovan walked away from them and into his bedroom to make a call. He returned ten minutes later.

"What did he say?"

"He wasn't pleased, but will call tomorrow with an address where we can wait," Donovan said.

"I didn't think he would leave us here that long, damn," Lee responded.

"Craig, ye still cook?"

"Aye, just like me mum."

Chapter Seventeen

In the beginning there was speculation that Caren was still alive. The stories began to change and reporters began to embellish, possible terrorist activities, Russian spy kills family and lover. Beck's body had not been identified other than male. Week by week the stories were finally no longer front-page news, interest waned due to the slow progress of the investigation. They knew with FBI involvement, the chances of jurisdiction arguments could and would cause delays. The notoriety of being the agency to break the case and make an arrest overrode common sense to share information with other entities. Caren listened to the voice of the GPS as it directed her to the extended stay. They had changed drivers around two in the morning so Declan could rest. She smiled as he folded his long body in the back seat of the Toyota extended cab truck. She had begun to see the colors of spring that reminded life would be renewed.

This was their seventh week to be on the road after they had left Vermont. They traveled the back roads, stopped at small Mom and Pop motels, even a few campgrounds that had cabins. They took advantage of any location with areas for training, school gyms with a small donation for the janitor, and YMCA's. Declan surprised her one night with an after-hour practice in a small dojo. Caren looked at her watch as she turned the motor off, it was too early to check into the hotel.

She leaned back and closed her eyes. The memory of their last days at the bed and breakfast returned. They were filled with computer searches on Bevan Benjamin and Aaron. The generalized information on Bevan made it difficult to find an address or phone number. Their inability to find information on Aaron, concerned and worried her. The sound of Declan's voice brought Caren back into the present.

Declan raised his head over the back seat.

"Where are we?"

"If the GPS did its job, Clarksville, Tennessee."

"What time is it?"

"Nine-thirty, too early to check in. I could use some breakfast."

Caren put a knit cap over her head.

Declan looked around and found one of the usual places they stopped.

"Waffle House it is."

Caren exited and walked around to see him stretch then shiver.

"Not quite summer is it?"

She handed him a jacket.

They walked across the parking lot and she waited for him to open the door. Orders were placed and much-needed coffee filled their cups. Declan rubbed his face and thanked the waitress. They had agreed to take a chance and remain in Clarksville a couple of weeks. They needed a break from the road, and it was time to exchange vehicles. She had been impressed with Declan's ability to deal under the table, so to speak, on the vehicles.

"Caren, ye look tired."

"We look like zombies."

The waitress returned with their meal and refilled their coffee cups.

"I don't believe we'll need two weeks here."

Caren leaned across the table.

"Have you looked in a mirror lately? We both need a haircut, and I would kill for a spa day."

"I don't need to remind ye to use out-of-the-way shops."

Caren gave him a hard glare and both brows rose.

"I am not going to even respond to that."

"What time can we check in?"

"I think two, but it's not high season here. I might be able to bat my eyelashes and get us an early check in."

"I'll locate a local gun range and gym. It's been too long since we practiced. I'll give us a few days."

"My tired body thanks you. All I want is a hot shower and bed."

Declan handed Caren fifty dollars. "Could ye pay the bill?"

"I'll meet you outside," she said.

A few moments later Declan exited the door in a hurry. He took Caren's arm almost running them back to the truck.

"What is wrong with you?"

"We may have a problem, I think…" He began, but was cut off.

"Jesus H. Christ! We've not had any problems since Vermont. What makes you think there is an issue now? I refuse to crawl back in the truck because you have a feeling."

"Lass, it isn't a feeling."

"I don't give a damn what it is. I'm not leaving! Do you understand me!"

Declan stepped back. "Okay, lass. Just promise ye will be cautious."

"Fine!"

●

Declan remained at the main door of the extended stay as Caren begged the clerk to let them check into their rooms. The young man was hesitant but gave the keys once a fifty crossed the desk for his trouble. He would have preferred adjoining rooms but had to settle for them across the hall.

He smiled as Caren place the Do Not Disturb sign on her door. He dropped his bags on the bed, found the local phone book, located a gun range and gym. Declan thought about the incident after they left restaurant. He should have explained why they couldn't remain and needed to travel on. The number to O'Connor's pub was dialed. Declan had to know if he had made a mistake.

"O'Connor's."

"Good day to ye. I've been told there's a band at the pub."

"Yes, on the weekend." she answered.

"Are they local?"

"The one playing here now is from Ireland, the Fitzgerald's. They're quite good."

"Would they be from Dublin?"

"No, Belfast," she replied.

"I'll come by to see them," Declan said and disconnected.

He closed his eyes. The brothers of Jamie Fitzgerald here, in the same town. What would be the odds? The youngest brother of the Fitzgerald's would be Lee's first choice to replace Beck. Declan didn't believe anyone back home would accept a job against him. He thought of possible options, attempt to force Caren to leave and take a chance of losing his balls or pray he didn't run into the brothers. He drew back the curtains from his window that faced the Waffle House and hoped the decision to remain would not be a mistake.

CHAPTER EIGHTEEN

randon Fitzgerald arrived early at O'Connor's to have dinner and visit with his favorite waitress. He acknowledged the regulars that sat drinking their beer as his eyes adjusted to the darkness of the pub. Clarksville had turned out to be a nice little town for the band and their side enterprise. They played in the bar on the weekend and bought guns during the week to be shipped back home. He pulled the bar stool out at the end of the bar.

"My sweet lass, Sheena."

"Where are your brothers?"

"They had laundry to finish before heading here."

"Do you want the special? Guinness beef stew with cheddar herb dumplings?"

"Sounds good and a large Guinness."

His phone began to play one of their songs, which indicated his brother Jamie was calling.

"Where are ye fools?" Jamie asked.

"Clarksville Tennessee, sweet little gig so far."

Brandon smiled as he took the beer from Sheena.

"I have some information that could lead to a large amount of money if you're interested."

"Of course, I'm interested, as long as it doesn't involve too much work."

"All ye need to do is call a number with information."

Brandon raised his beer

"Information on who?"

"Declan Mallone."

Brandon choked on his beer.

"Christ!"

Sheena started towards him, but Brandon waved her off.

"Lee Sheehan contacted me about a job in the States. He promised more money that I could ever spend. I was packing my bags inside my head when he mentioned Declan and said Aaron Caydon was involved."

"Mother of God, tell me ye told the man to go fuck himself?" Jamie laughed.

"Our mum did not raise fools. I'd love the money, but doubt there is any chance I would live to spend it."

"How the devil are those two involved with each other?"

"He didn't say once I refused, but I told him my brothers were in the States. The offer stands, good money for information if ye see Declan, with proof of course."

"Who's backing Lee?"

"Donovan O'Shea."

"Jamie, we have two more weeks at the pub and one more acquisition. I don't believe Declan would come here for a holiday."

"The bastard is not on holiday. Lee did tell me he's on the run with a lass."

"If I run into them, who do I call for my reward?"

"I'll send the number, and Brandon stay clear. Declan killed Beck."

"Donovan is short an explosives expert. That's why he called ye."

"He'll have to find someone that doesn't know Declan or Caydon."

"I'll be in touch."

He smiled as Sheena brought his dinner, and leaned over so he could admire her assets. The conversation with his brother was quickly forgotten for soft skin and large breasts.

CHAPTER NINETEEN

Caren returned to her room after spending the entire morning at the small spa located at the edge of town. She felt as if her body had been reborn and gladly paid the four hundred dollar ticket, adding a huge tip. The two weeks in Clarksville had quickly passed with work-outs in the gym and several trips to a gun range, hence the last day appointment.

The duffle on the bed had been refilled with clothes bought at several high-end, secondhand boutiques. She laughed at that title, but had found some nice, barely worn clothes. The underwear on the bed from Walmart needed to be laundered, along with a week's worth of workout clothing. The door opened, and Declan entered her room without knocking.

"One day you'll do that and not like what you see."

Caren continued to remove the sales tags from the bras and panties.

"Sorry, lass, I want to leave between midnight and one."

"Why?"

"I'd like to not be caught in the Monday morning traffic in a large city."

She noticed his hair was cut, face shaven, and she didn't recognize the clothes he wore.

"You look nice, Declan."

"I do?"

Caren shook her head.

"Were you able to trade the truck?"

"Aye, found an unhappy woman with her soon to be ex-husband."

"Please tell me this one is clean," she said.

"Yes, lass, I found it to be very clean and comfortable."

"I'm making one last run to the laundry. You might as well add what you have that's worth keeping. I don't want to see anything with holes or worn."

"I thought…"

"You thought what, Declan? I might let you destroy what I just paid four hundred dollars for. Not a chance. I had a difficult time explaining all the bruises. It's a good thing I took the card from the gym or the police would be here."

Declan surrendered and held his hands up.

"Caren, may I take ye to dinner?"

"You aren't worried about being recognized in public?"

Declan lowered his head.

"I apologize for overreacting."

"Are you serious about a meal out?" she asked him.

"Aye, lass I am."

She stopped and closed her eyes.

"I'd kill for something other than fast food and microwave meals."

"Do ye have any requests?"

"The lady at the spa mentioned an Irish pub with a band from Belfast."

Declan hesitated a moment. "That might be fun."

"It does sound like fun, but probably crowded and loud. I think the small Italian restaurant across town and a glass of Chianti would be a better choice," she said.

"Italian it is."

Caren walked across the hall and took the plastic bag of Declan's clothes with her to the laundry on the first level of the hotel. She backed in to the room where two men stood folding clothes. They acknowledged as she entered. She had not seen many people in there over the two weeks. She leaned her head back and cursed. The money for the machines had been left in the room.

"Dammit!"

"What's wrong lass?"

She couldn't speak for a moment as all of Declan's warnings flashed before her with those three simple words.

"I'm sorry. I left my change in the room."

"It's fine, we've extra. How much do ye need?"

She checked the front pocket and found a five-dollar bill.

"Do you have five in change?"

Caren waited as he counted out the quarters. They were neatly stacked on the lid of the washer.

"Thank you. You saved me an extra trip."

"No problem, lass."

The two men left the laundromat. She turned and, grabbed the sides of the washer to maintain an upright position. Caren thought Declan had overreacted when they first arrived. This simple encounter proved the seriousness of their situation. She couldn't decide whether to tell him or wait until they were safely away. She would have to become more cautious, listen, and be aware of their surroundings. The door opened, and she jumped around to see Declan.

"Are ye okay, lass?"

"Yes, you startled me, and I didn't bring a gun."

He gave her a stern look and placed his weapon under the clothes in the basket.

"I made a reservation at the restaurant for eight."

"Eight will be fine, and thank you for checking on me."

"Aye, lass, do ye want me to stay?"

Caren thought for a moment, worried that Declan might know the two men. If they returned complications could arise.

"No, there are only two loads, it won't take long."

After he left, Caren ran the loads on quick cycles and dried only the items that couldn't be hung in the room. She returned and pulled a nice sweater and pair of slacks out for the evening. The much-needed nap would be appreciated later when they left in the early hours. At seven, there was a knock on the door before he entered. The man before her was dressed in slacks, a dress shirt, and jacket. She returned the Glock and picked up a small purse.

"Do ye have a weapon in the wee purse?"

"Yes."

"Ye look nice, lass."

Caren hadn't thought about her appearance since she now lived in wigs and contacts. She walked back into the bathroom and faced the image. The short brown wig and deep blue contacts, minus the dark heavy makeup, allowed a familiar reflection. She caught the tear before it left her eye and returned.

"Sorry, I forgot my lipstick."

They left the building, and Declan opened the door to a black Lexus SUV.

"Clean and comfortable."

She smiled and entered the vehicle taking a moment to scan the area. Tonight, Caren would to be the one to watch around the corners and alleyways.

CHAPTER TWENTY

O'Connor's Pub

The pub was packed for their last performance and the announcement of an extra hour added to their set. Sheena brought them their first round on the house as the three began to set up. Brandon's relationship with the waitress had progressed over the last two weeks. He had spent more time in her bed than his own at the hotel. He would expect a grand send off after the pub closed tonight.

"Ye haven't been around the hotel much the last couple of weeks," Patrick told him.

"Why should I hang around the two of ye when I can be enjoying myself with that," Brandon said nodded his head towards Sheena.

"The last acquisition has been packed and on a ship to home."

"Good now we can spend a month playing, drinking and pleasing the lasses before we go back."

Brandon grabbed his crotch.

"Shall we see if these bastards will overfill the jar tonight?" Patrick asked.

Brandon picked up his instrument.

"Let's empty their pockets."

The night seemed to progress quickly. The tip jar was filled and emptied three times before "Last Call" was announced by the owner of the pub. Men shook their hands and women kissed their faces as the staff pushed them out the door. It had been a prosperous night for them and the pub. Brandon watched the manager pull money from the register to pay them.

"You are welcome back here anytime," he said.

"We've enjoyed it," Brandon said.

He took the money and shook hands with him.

"Good luck on your next one."

Patrick walked up to his brother.

"Will ye be spending the night in your own bed?"

"Aye, and do not be bothering me. I'll find ye both in the morning."

"Jimmie and I will tear down the set. Have fun with your lady."

Brandon finished his drink and walked to the front door where Sheena waited. He put his hand in the middle of her back.

"Are ye ready, sweet Sheena?"

"I hope you haven't had too much to drink. I have plans for you tonight."

"I know what you're thinking, lass, and there isn't enough drink to stop me from keeping ye happy."

The drive to the extended stay was quickly made as Sheena's hands were exploring his body. They were headed to the outside back door when she pulled him into her body before he could get the key out. Brandon unbuttoned her blouse and reached inside.

"Brandon, stop, someone will see us."

"I do not care, lass. I need ye."

He shoved her hand down the front of his pants.

The sound of voices caused Sheena to open her eyes.

"Stop, there are people out here."

"Where?"

She lifted his head and pointed around the corner. Brandon lost any interest he'd had in Sheena when he recognized Declan. They were getting into a car at the side door. Their conversation was low, but he made note of what Declan said to the lass he was with. He moved back around the corner.

"Jesus, Mary and Joseph. We've been staying in the same fucking hotel."

"Do you know them?"

Sheena buttoned her blouse.

"Aye, and I just won the bloody lottery."

He opened the camera app on his cell phone took several photographs of Declan, and the woman. He wasn't able to get the number on the back of the vehicle without being seen. They walked around the building as the vehicle drove away.

"That's an expensive SUV," Sheena told him.

"Do ye know what it was?"

"I think it was either a Lexus or Mercedes."

Brandon smiled, then located the text message from Jamie. The two-week-old number was entered. A moment later the ringing stopped.

"I need to speak with Donovan O'Shea."

CHAPTER TWENTY-ONE

Dallas, Texas
Condo in Deep Ellum

Donovan finished his Jameson and thought about the last eight weeks. The cell phone he purchased had ceased to ring in over two weeks. In the beginning, there was hope as call after call indicated Declan's location was known. The individuals would release information once money had been received. He had received permission from Alex to increase the bounty with an even stronger warning for the leeches. He didn't believe Craig was wrong, but time continued to slip away as his friend spent more time with the woman from the plane, than here working.

He took a deep breath and started towards his bedroom when the cell began to buzz. Donovan returned to the table and answered the phone.

"I need to speak with Donovan O'Shea."

"O'Shea here."

"Brandon Fitzgerald, are ye still interested in Declan Mallone?"

"Fitzgerald, Jamie Fitzgerald's brother?"

"Aye, I am."

"What do ye have?"

"Does the offer of money still stand for Declan Mallone's location?"

"Aye, but only if the information can be proved."

"I'm in Clarksville, Tennessee with my brothers. We've been playing at a little pub here for a few weeks. Declan and a small woman left here maybe ten minutes ago in a Lexus or Mercedes SUV."

Donovan looked at his watch.

"What have ye got other than your word it was him?"

"Hang on to your dick," Brandon told him.

Donovan's cell dinged and he enlarged the photographs.

"Did ye get a number on the vehicle or see his direction?"

"You're lucky I got the picture. I want no dealings with him or that devil Caydon. I did hear the word Memphis, maybe New Orleans, just before they left the hotel."

"Color of the vehicle?"

"Take your choice man its dark out here in this parking lot. Just a minute, lass. I'm conducting important business."

"Brandon, it's cold out here," A female voice said.

Donovan shook his head.

"Ye said they were at a hotel."

"Aye, they were at the same place we've been staying. What was the chance?"

"They'd not been seen until now?" Donovan asked.

"Aye. Stop touching me until we get inside, lass."

"I can hear ye have other business to attend. Where do ye want the money sent?"

Donovan took down the account number Brandon gave him.

"When can I expect payment?"

"Eight hours and you'll see the money."

"Nice doing business with ye, and tell Lee good luck finding anyone to replace Beck."

Donovan walked across and knocked on Craig's' door.

"Craig! Wake up."

Lee opened his door and looked at Donovan.

"He's not here."

"Out with the woman?"

Lee nodded and walked out of his room.

"What has happened?" Lee asked.

The front door opened. Craig held up his phone.

"Are ye texting me?"

"Aye, they've been seen," Donovan answered.

"Where?"

"They left Clarksville, Tennessee less than thirty minutes ago. They are possibly headed south towards Memphis or New Orleans."

Craig walked over to the table and opened a map.

"Do ye trust me, Donovan?"

"Tell me."

Craig took his finger and placed it on the map.

"New Orleans."

"Lee, ye need to call that American," Donovan instructed.

"Brody."

"Tell Brody to be here in thirty minutes," Donovan said.

"I hope he's ready to go to work," Lee said.

"I hope he lives long enough to spend the money," Donovan said.

"Donovan, once Declan is dead, I'm gone. I want no part of what will happen to Caydon's sister, or take a chance to be seen by her," Craig said.

Donovan nodded.

"Same account for your money?"

"No, I need to have this money placed in another account. Once I'm gone from the States, I'll text ye the account number," Craig answered.

Lee turned to Craig.

"Beck would be laughing his ass off if he could see the three of us," Lee said.

"Why? Because we believe the devil is still alive?" Craig said.

"Aye," Lee answered.

"Craig, check the area between Memphis and New Orleans."

"What are ye thinking?" Craig asked.

"If we can cut them off before they reach the city, it would mean fewer civilian casualties," Donovan said.

"It would be nice to not worry about the locals," Craig said.

"Brody will be here within the hour. I can be ready in twenty," Lee said.

"We need to leave once he arrives. Craig, are ye packed?"

"I have a few things to put in my bag. Declan has three possible routes into New Orleans, none of them will allow us to catch them outside the city."

Donovan joined Craig, and looked at the map.

"I don't understand why this is so damn difficult."

"Ye know why. He's always been a lucky bastard," Craig said.

"This means we must go into New Orleans and wait," Donovan said.

"Do we have contacts in New Orleans?" Lee asked.

"I know a few in the French Quarter. What we need are eyes on the streets," Donovan said.

"I hear the beignets are worth the trip," Craig said, and walked towards his room.

"What about your stewardess?" Donovan asked.

Craig smiled. "She has a flight out this morning. We said our farewells."

Donovan followed suit and prepared to leave. He looked up as Lee stuck his head in the bedroom.

"Brody is in the lobby."

"Heads up," Donovan said, and threw the keys to him.

"Is Craig ready?" Lee asked.

"I'm here."

"Lee take my bag. Ye and Craig pull the car around to the front of the building."

"What are ye going to do?" Craig asked.

"I have to make a call."

Donovan walked through the condo to check for anything that could be traced to them. Due to the time, he made the decision to leave Alex a text.

"We're on the move to New Orleans."

CHAPTER TWENTY-TWO

Slidell, Louisiana
April 27th

Caren walked out of the trailer just before dawn with a cup of coffee. She stopped at the concrete picnic table and tried to find a clean place to sit. Two weeks after leaving Clarksville, they changed directions and ended up in Huntsville, Alabama, where Declan traded the Mercedes for a truck with a trailer hitch.

A few days later, he left the local hotel they were living in and returned with a travel trailer. She wasn't sure what had brought on all the changes, but after the incident in the laundry room, she didn't ask.

They had spent their days in small camping areas and continued to search for information on Bevan Benjamin. Caren closed her eyes and, listened to the night birds. The sweet memory of Stephen as he wrapped strong loving arms around her and their plans for a final family vacation.

"Caren, we need to make a trip to Maine, it's been two years."

"No, it can't possibly have been that long has it?"

"Yes. I received a notice on the taxes. You know there is always maintenance to been done."

"I'll call the service in May and have it ready for us. I hope Kieran will be able to go."

"It will be nice to have one last family vacation, before our children grow up and fly away," Stephen said.

"Why are ye up so early?"

She wiped the tears from her face and turned towards Declan.

"I needed a little time to make a couple of decisions."

"What type of decisions?"

"Whether I am going to leave you here tied to a tree or lock you in that damn small trailer," she said.

He opened the screen door and walked out.

"I know it's been tight these past two weeks."

Caren stood up.

"Tight is putting it mildly!"

"If ye will wait…"

Declan was cut off.

"Wait, for what? The grass to grow, the flowers to bloom, no! We are no closer to finding Bevan than when I found his picture in Maine. I believe there is information for us in New Orleans. I need a regular bed, bath, and some gumbo!"

She moved closer to him with each statement.

"Let me go into New Orleans first…"

"No!"

Declan looked around to see if anyone heard her. He held up his hands.

"I refuse to sit here and wait for you. What was all the training for if you can't trust me to watch your back? No, we go together!"

"Okay, lass, okay. We'll leave the trailer, take the truck, and go in for a couple of days, no longer."

"Good. I'll pack, and we can go in an hour."

"Don't ye want breakfast?"

"I'll have beignets and coffee at Café Du Monde."

●

New Orleans, Louisiana
Bed & Breakfast

Caren waited outside her room as Declan entered and checked every possible place a human could be hidden. She was excited to be away from the trailer and close to Jackson Square. She dropped the duffle, threw herself on the bed, and sunk into the plush duvet. She turned over in the bed and discovered fresh coffee, juice and beignets on the table. This was his apology for this morning at the camp, and she understood why it had taken so long for him to check them into their rooms. She sat up to thank him but the door was closed and he was gone.

She removed a few items from her duffle and hung them in the closet. A few moments later, water began to fill the large claw-footed bathtub. Caren found the jazz station on the television, and placed a complimentary lavender bath fizz bomb in the tub. A beignet in one hand and coffee in the other she lowered herself into the hot water. As her eyes closed a voice called out to a young girl. A strong memory of years past came forward as if it were yesterday.

"Caren, Caren! I said do not touch anything in here," Aaron said.

"Okay, Aaron. Who is that?"

She pointed to a large painting of a woman.

"That little miss, is a very great lady. Her name, Marie Laveau," A deep male voice answered.

"Who are you?" Caren asked.

The man smiled, looked at Aaron and began to laugh. He reached down and lifted Caren into his arms.

"I am Etienne. The keeper of this shrine and seller of many wonderful things."

Aaron took Caren from him.

"Did you receive the answer you needed?"

"Yes, sir."

Aaron took both of Etienne's hands.

"It has been too long." Etienne said.

"Can we talk?"

"Of course, I always have time for you. The ladies will watch and give her something sweet to drink," Etienne said, and motioned to a woman behind the counter.

A lady took Caren's hand. "Come little one."

Caren remembered the tall man's beads; long braided hair and the large cigar with smoke that encircled and moved with him. She turned towards her brother and heard the man ask.

"My friend, what can Etienne do for Papa Legba?"

Caren opened her eyes.

"Maire Laveau."

She exited the tub and felt renewed as the softest towel in the world dried her body. She opened the door, picked up the Glock, and walked naked into the main room, where Declan stood. The music and memory had distracted her from hearing his reentry. Startled, she raised the Glock.

"I told you this was going to happen, didn't I?"

He turned away from her.

"Lass, I'm sorry."

She proceeded to the bed and put her underwear on.

"Does your girlfriend put up with this shit? Just barge into her apartment or house anytime you want?"

"Girlfriend?"

"I figured you had a girlfriend since you seem to know how to buy women's clothing."

"No, I don't have a girlfriend. The reason I knew how to buy clothes for ye is because I have four sisters."

Caren was surprised at his comment.

"Oh."

"I have no girlfriend for fear of retaliation against me."

"You can turn around, not that it matters."

Caren walked back into the bathroom.

"I left to protect them," he said.

She wanted to ask about his family, but was concerned about what he might say.

"I need to dry my hair, then pair up a wig and contacts."

"Caren, are we going somewhere?"

"First to find some gumbo, then to Marie Laveau's Voodoo shop."

"Why?"

Caren came out of the bathroom with a shoulder-length red wig and light green contacts. She pulled the wig into a ponytail and ran it through the back of a baseball cap.

"You should know why. New Orleans has the best gumbo in the world."

"No, why are we going to a Voodoo shop?" he asked.

"Aaron took me to Marie Laveau's when I was a child. He told a man named Etienne he needed to speak to him."

"Any idea of what their conversation was about?"

"He called Aaron, Papa Legba, and no, I was a child so not privileged to adult conversations."

She grabbed a small backpack, and slid the Glock inside. She was amused his face was still red.

"I assume we're walking," Declan said.

"It's the best way to see New Orleans."

Chapter Twenty-three

Bourbon Orleans Hotel

Donovan stood on the balcony off the main room of the suite. The lack of information each day made him doubt his friend and regret the decision to come to New Orleans. He would give his contacts a few more days to search the French Quarter and Jackson Square. He had no desire to explain another failure to Alex. Donovan picked up the silver coffee pot, filled his cup half full, then added Jameson to complete his drink.

"A little early for Jameson isn't it?" Craig asked.

"It's Jameson or Bailey's."

Donovan pointed to the bottles.

"Bailey's for me."

Craig poured a small amount in his cup.

"We'll need to leave if they don't show up in the next couple of days. Were ye wrong on this, Craig?"

"I'm not wrong, Donovan. They will come here."

"It doesn't take four weeks to drive here."

"It's possible Fitzgerald was seen. Ye know Declan always had a second sense about things. It kept us alive in some of the worst situations back home."

"I remember. The bastard saved my life on more than one occasion."

Craig refilled his cup with coffee and Bailey's.

"Give it a few more days."

"I increased the amount of money for information, again."

Craig stood next to Donovan, drank his coffee, and observed the individuals on the street below.

"A woman can hide, clothes, wigs, glasses, but Declan will not easily be disguised. Someone will see him. Where's Lee and Brody?"

"Café du Monde. Where they've gone every day to wait."

•

Café du Monde

Lee and Brody took a back table away from the street. They listened to the sound of Jazz being played to entertain the tourists that stood in line at the café. Their early arrival assured the location needed and continuous orders for coffee and beignets.

Brody shoved another beignet in his mouth.

"They're not coming. It's been too long."

"Possibly, but Declan doesn't follow the norm."

He handed Brody a napkin.

"I have no complaint. It's been easy money for me."

"Brody, do ye see that?"

Lee pointed to a woman dressed in black.

"Lee, the people here dress like they're always going to a funeral. It gives me the creeps."

"Ye bloody fool. She's walking towards our table."

A woman dressed in a thick heavy black-laced dress, shawl and umbrella stopped at the table. She raised a veil with open fingered lace gloves, painted nails that matched the woman's blood red lips. A pale face and dark Smokey eyes looked down on the two men. She reached in a pocket and removed a piece of paper.

"I understand, you are searching for two special individuals," she said.

"Aye."

Lee reached out to take the paper. The note was withdrawn from his reach.

"In New Orleans nothing is free," she said.

Lee placed a small envelope on the table.

"Ye best not be lying, lass."

She dropped the paper on the table.

"I would hurry. They will not be there forever," she said.

Lees' legs shook as the woman replaced her veil, opened the

umbrella and walked away from the table. He turned towards Brody who's face had no color. The first line contained numbers to an account, the second advised of a location where Declan and Caren were being observed.

"What does it say?" Brody asked.

"Gumbo Shop, cook watching them."

"Let's go."

Brody stood up, but was pulled back into his chair by Lee.

"Ye bloody fool, sit down. Do ye wish to die? I need to call Donovan."

"What is the problem? It is one man."

Lee held his hand in Brody's face.

"They've been seen at a place called the Gumbo Shop. We're heading that way."

"Remember what happened to Beck," Donovan said.

"If they leave, we'll follow them," Lee said.

"I'm on the way," Donovan told him.

"I want ye to sit your ass in the chair and listen closely. Declan Mallone is the best IRA soldier ever trained. He has more kills than any three men, gutted my last partner with a knife, and has a second sense that kept a lot of us alive back home."

"You're killing one of your own?"

"I'd kill my own family for the amount of money this job is paying. My advice is to follow orders and don't be brave," Lee warned.

Lee pulled out his cell to find directions to the Gumbo Shop.

CHAPTER TWENTY-FOUR

Gumbo Shop

Caren closed her eyes, removed the spoon from her mouth and savored the taste of all that New Orleans offered in one simple bowl of gumbo. The food exploded in her mouth and brought back wonderful memories of years ago. She could see Declan's bowl had remained untouched. He couldn't even relax long enough to enjoy the bowl of heaven that was just a few inches in front of him.

"Declan, I will kill you if that bowl of gumbo is wasted."

"Sorry, lass."

He picked up a spoon and began to eat.

"There is no better gumbo in the world."

"Lass, we've been noticed."

She looked around the restaurant.

"By whom?"

"The cook."

"If you noticed the cook has been out on the floor to talk with several of the customers."

"Yes, but he didn't stop here to speak with us."

"No, what of it?"

"He passed our table, walked back where he could see us, and made a call."

"You're sure?"

"There was an oddly-dressed woman in here about twenty minutes ago. Ye made a comment about her clothes."

"I remember. You couldn't see her face due to the thick veil."

"The cook gave her a piece of paper and she left."

Caren sat back in her chair.

"Twenty minutes, you said."

"Yes, maybe a little more."

She took two more bites of her gumbo.

"We need to leave. Declan, I don't want anyone in here hurt."

"Nor I, lass."

Declan left a fifty on the table and they walked away from the restaurant. Marie Laveau's shop was two or three blocks away. As Caren entered the front door, the sounds and scents were the same as the time she last walked the wooden floors. She turned to see Declan had remain at the doorway. He jumped as she touched his arm.

"Declan, why are you so uncomfortable?"

"The city, these buildings, hold a long, strange history. It's difficult to understand beliefs I have no knowledge or understanding."

"Declan, I need you to come with me."

She waited for a moment and walked up to the counter where a female cashier waited for the next customer.

"Excuse me, is the owner here?" Caren asked.

"Who is asking?" the cashier asked.

"Papa Legba."

The woman's face changed from question to concern. She pressed a button under the counter.

"Please, wait here," the woman's voice trembled.

A tall well-built black man with long dreadlocks, multi-colored tunic, and loose-fitting pants, walked from the back and motioned for them to follow him. Caren couldn't believe what she had seen. This was the same man from her childhood.

She turned and motioned for Declan to follow. They entered an office filled with incense, relics and an altar inside a closet. The man closed the doors, walked to a large table, picked up a lit cigar and placed something in his pocket. He motioned for them to stand before him. Caren opened her mouth to speak.

"Hold your thought," he said.

Caren stopped and waited as he blew smoke on them, spoke words she didn't understand over them. She had missed the bracelets of colored beads and multiple necklaces he wore with charms.

"Please sit. I am..."

"Etienne, I remember you."

"You were the child with Papa."

"How is it possible you have not changed in all these years?"

Etienne looked down on Caren.

"Why are you here asking for Papa Legba?"

"We need to find information on her brother," Declan answered.

He walked behind the table, sat down, and took a long drag on the cigar. Etienne let the smoke slowly seep from his smiling lips. He motioned for them to sit.

"You are no longer the child that was here, but there is much to learn. Your legacy is not for me to tell. Papa should not lie to those he loves; it brings the darkness."

"I must find Aaron. Can you help us?" Caren asked.

"You must visit Marie Laveau, Saint Louis Cemetery One, at three. The answers you seek will be found there," he said.

Caren acknowledged, stood, and left the office ahead of Declan.

"Tall man," Etienne called.

Declan turned back to face him.

"Danger surrounds you. Blood and death are coming," Etienne said.

He threw a set of beads to Declan, who caught them with one hand. He allowed them to drop their full length. He took a moment and stretched his hand back as Etienne approached.

"I have no need of these."

Etienne laughed as Declan slowly exited the office. As the door began to close, he smiled once more.

"Nothing can help you, tall man, they are for the woman."

Declan found Caren in the main section of the store.

"I think we need to find a back door, lass."

The woman Caren hand first spoke with motioned for them to follow. She opened the back door for them to leave. As they passed, the woman took her hands and spoke softly.

"The people searching for you have offered a large sum of money for information on where you can be found."

"Thank you," Caren said.

"Tell your brother, Lavanna sent you to safety."

"I will," Caren said.

Declan watched to make sure the door was closed as they left Marie Laveau's.

●

Bed and Breakfast

Declan kept to the back streets and alleyways on the trip back to the bed and breakfast. He couldn't shake the words Etienne had said to him in the shop, which worried him about tonight and the trip to the cemetery. He was concerned their location in Slidell was compromised. Declan walked across the hallway to Caren's room and knocked before he entered. She peered from the corner of the heavy drapes, and didn't acknowledge him.

"Lass, I need to go back and move the trailer."

"Did you leave something there that can be connected to us?"

"One set of dirty clothes."

"Leave them, didn't you set up some type of camera system?"

"Aye, I did."

"Check it."

"I need to get my computer."

He returned and could hear her in the bathroom. The image of the campsite began to take focus.

"Lass, ye might want to come and see this."

"Did someone break in?"

Declan pointed to the computer screen as she walked up to the table. The trailer was completely engulfed in flames. People were gathered around it. She heard someone say to call 9-1-1. They continued to watch until the fire department arrived and extinguished the flames. The small trailer had been reduced to blackened metal and ash. Declan began to pan the camera around the area.

"Are you searching for something?"

"Someone, I might recognize from home. The amount of money being offered will bring out all the maggots."

"Declan, who's paying these people?"

"I don't know, lass. The person in charge appears to have unlimited funds and is intelligent enough to not dirty their hands."

Caren walked back to the window again and moved the curtain.

"It's a long time until three in the morning."

Declan had picked up a map of the city when they checked in. He opened it and began to trace the distance.

"I think it would be best for us to travel on foot tonight. It appears to be maybe twenty minutes from here."

"Walking the streets of New Orleans at what two thirty in the morning is not exactly safe. We won't be the only ones with guns."

"The night favors me, it always has."

"I don't see how anything will assist us. You aren't exactly small."

"I'll use what is available to keep us safe."

He placed his knives on the table next to the computer.

Caren walked over to the telephone and picked it up.

"Room service?"

Declan took the receiver out of her hand.

"No, lass, tell me what ye would like, and I'll go get it."

"Do you believe it's safe for either of us to leave here until dark?" she asked.

"Room service it is."

CHAPTER TWENTY-FIVE

Marie Laveau's

Donovan followed the directions on his phone to the corner of St. Peter and Bourbon Street. The large number of tourists made it difficult for him to locate Lee or Brody. He made the decision to lean against and hold his position until someone found him. If they were in the shop, he knew innocent casualties would not be avoidable. He jerked when Lee touched his shoulder.

"What the hell are ye doing. I could've killed your ass."

"I've been calling your name for ten minutes," Lee told him.

"Where is Brody?"

"Across the street."

Lee pointed to where he stood and, Brody waved.

"Jesus, where did ye get this idiot?" Donovan asked.

"Where is Craig? We could use another pair of eyes."

"Ye know where he is. I promised no part of anything other than the tracking. How long have they been inside?"

"Maybe twenty minutes. Caren is wearing a red wig, and baseball cap."

Donovan motioned for Brody to come to their location.

"Lee, check for a back-door exit. If ye see them, follow that's all."

"What are ye going to do?"

"Brody and I are going through the front door."

●

Donovan disliked these types of shops. It was full of tourists wasting money on cheaply made items that would eventually end up in the trash. There seemed to only be one person working and she was at the register. They walked around pretending to be interested in the items that filled the shelves. When the last customer exited, Donovan nodded to Brody who closed the door and locked it.

"You cannot do that," she told him.

Donovan walked to the counter and placed his weapon in front of her.

"This will not take long. I need some information?"

She backed away slightly.

"Information?"

"We've lost some of our friends. It's very important that we find them."

"There have been many people in here since the shop opened," she said.

Donovan took a breath. He did not want to kill this woman.

"What is your name?"

"Lavanna."

Her voice trembled.

"Lavanna, the friends we are attempting to locate would be easy to recognize. The man is very tall and speaks as I do. The woman is small with red hair and a baseball cap."

"I have not seen them," Lavanna replied.

Donovan knew she was lying.

"A shame. We had hoped not to search the entire French Quarter today. I'll take these," Donovan said.

He handed Lavanna a coffin shaped tin of breath mints.

Lavanna's hands shook as she rang up the sale.

"Four twenty-five."

Donovan handed her a hundred-dollar bill.

"Keep the change."

He removed the weapon, took his purchase, and turned to walk away.

"I might have seen them." Lavanna said.

Donovan smiled and returned to the counter.

"I would be more than pleased to accept any information ye might have on them."

He took a large roll of money from his coat and placed it in front of her.

"You won't come back?"

"We are just concerned for our friends."

Lavanna took a moment to write something on a piece of paper. She held it up and waited.

As he pushed the money towards her, the paper was placed on the counter. He placed the information in his pocket and nodded for Brody to open the doors.

"You should know death follows them," Lavanna said.

Donovan stopped and twisted his head slightly so she could hear him.

"I am death."

Donovan stopped outside the door as tourists entered the shop. He could see a tall man had joined Lavanna at the register. He positioned out of view in order to hear their exchange, curious the man had not appeared before their exit.

"You sell your soul for the money he gave you," Etienne said.

She back away and held the money in Etienne's face.

"This will allow me to hide from the devil," Lavanna told him.

The man turned away from Lavanna and began to laugh.

"No one hides from the devil. You will see, you will pay."

Lee exited the alley and walked towards him.

"They must have left before we arrived."

"Ye and Brody check the area and come back in an hour to the hotel."

●

Bourbon Orleans Hotel

Donovan walked back to the hotel pleased with the information he had paid a high price for and laughed at the irony it involved a cemetery. He would never understand why the bastard hadn't just followed orders, that's what soldiers did, when it involved the betterment of the group. Instead of being admired and wealthy, Declan was hunted, damned to death. He opened the door and stumbled over Craig's bag.

"Craig! Are ye going somewhere?"

"Aye, home. My mum's ill and asking for me. My sister said it's bad."

"Go, call when you're free."

Craig picked up his bag and shook Donovan's hand.

"I hope you'll not need me."

Donovan held up the note from Lavanna.

"If this leads me to Declan ye will not be needed."

"I left information where to send my pay."

"I'll send it today," Donovan said.

Craig's cell phone rang.

"My taxi is here."

"Slán," (Good-bye) Donovan said.

"Slán," Craig said.

Donovan hated to see Craig leave but he wasn't a soldier. He poured a drink and walked out on the balcony. It would be hours before dark, and he needed the time to familiarize himself with the cemetery. Donovan mapped the location of Marie Laveau's tomb on his cell phone.

"Where is Craig headed?" Lee asked.

"Home, family emergency," Donovan answered.

Lee and Brody joined Donovan on the balcony.

"We're going to be short tonight," Brody stated.

Donovan looked at Lee in disbelief.

"We could have a problem," Lee said.

"What type of problem?"

"Two men stopped us in Jackson Square with information," Brody said.

"Declan and Caren were staying in a KOA campground in a small trailer in Slidell," Lee told him.

"A trailer? That answers why they didn't come here straight away. What's the problem?"

"It's been destroyed," Brody said.

"How?"

"Fire, nothing left but a melted frame, purposely set," Lee told him.

"Declan?" Brody asked.

"No, not his style. It appears someone cannot follow the rules," Donovan said.

"It doesn't appear to be local," Brody answered.

"You're sure it was set?"

"Aye," Lee answered.

Donovan stood for a moment and finished his drink.

"The locals swear it wasn't them?" Donovan asked.

"Yes," Brody answered.

"This could be someone from home. The bounty on him is high," Lee said.

"I'll make some calls. I would prefer not to be killing any of my brothers from home," Donovan said.

"Declan left a bloody trail of men after his mum died." Lee said.

Brody couldn't hold back any longer.

"What does his mother have to do with any of this?"

Donovan raised his head, and stopped the call to Ireland. He walked over to Brody.

"I'll speak of this once and no more. Lee, have ye told him anything about Declan?"

"No details." Lee answered.

"Declan deserted his team on an operation that could have meant changes for our cause. The job failed, men and women died, it caused bad blood and a contract placed on him. Family is sacred for most of us, but someone set a bomb in his mum's car."

"Who in God's name would do something like that?" Brody asked.

"No one ever came forward. It's believed the person involved, was connected to the members of his team that perished," Lee said.

"Declan began to take his revenge one body at a time. He left little to identify, and all died in misery. Do ye understand now why no one goes alone after him?"

"It explains why there aren't more of you," Brody said.

"If things go well tonight, we won't need to worry about more men."

CHAPTER TWENTY-SIX

The three men had traversed the wall to enter the locked cemetery and made their way to the mausoleum of Marie Laveau where Donovan had taken his position. He took a drink from a silver flask and shared a small amount with the dead, then marked three X's on the tomb. He had discovered no information or package for Caren at this location. The only items of interest were gifts to the Voodoo Queen, who had no use of them.

He had sent Lee and Brody to check the perimeter ten to twelve graves on each side of his location. There was no way to enter the cemetery than over the walls. He heard heavy footsteps approaching his position.

"Jesus Christ! Lee, can ye possibly make any more noise? I heard ye coming four graves away."

"Have ye seen Brody?"

"Not since ye left here," Donovan answered.

"This blood fog is as thick as home."

Donovan handed Lee the flask.

"Aye, have a drink."

"There's Brody."

Lee pointed to a figure that ran towards them.

"Why in the virgin's name is he running?" Donovan asked.

Brody fell face-down at their feet. They helped him stand, and placed his pale body against the stone wall of the tomb. His hands shook, his speech was garbled and incoherent.

"What's wrong with ye?" Lee asked.

Brody's voice quivered.

"Ghosts, I saw the dead walking this cemetery."

Donovan closed his eyes.

"Ballocks!"

"Christ you're too old to believe such nonsense," Lee told him.

"It's true, I saw them."

Donovan walked over and grabbed Brody by the jacket.

"We've a job to do, man up or leave," Donovan said.

Brody broke away from Donovan's grasp and pushed him away.

"I'm out of here. You deal with the dead," Brody said.

They stood stunned, as Brody ran towards the wall, topped it and disappeared. Donovan leaned against the mausoleum.

"Did ye see anything, Lee?"

"No."

Donovan checked the time. They were in the worst situation anyone could be against Declan.

"I'll not go against Declan in this fog without extra help," Lee said.

"Agreed, this weather is just the type of cover that will allow him to kill us and never be seen in the process. Lee, are ye sure there isn't someone out there?"

"I saw nothing."

"I think he may have seen Declan and Caren. This cursed fog changed their shapes and caused him to perceive them as ghosts."

Lee stepped back.

"That's a stretch even for me."

Donovan took out his weapon.

"We'll make a quick check, then leave this place. I do not believe in ghosts."

"I would prefer ye not get too far from me," Lee said.

They walked a row apart and checked each through-way between the mausoleums. Donovan slowed his pace, twisted back to the sound of footsteps and a sharp whistle. He quickened his steps as he approached Lee's location.

"Brody may have seen this."

Donovan advanced to the gated crypt where the impaled body of Lavanna hung. The money he had paid for the information was gripped in bloody hands and the rest lay around the grave.

"A ghost didn't do this."

"Declan?" Lee asked.

Donovan turned to Lee.

"No."

"We're not alone."

"Someone is shadowing us," Donovan said.

"It's time for us to leave this place," Lee said.

The two men moved towards the wall where they had entered earlier. Lee went over first. He called from the far side of the wall.

"Come on man. What are ye waiting for?"

Donovan walked back ready to jump when laughter was heard over the cemetery. He turned and backed into the cold concrete, weapon ready for what approached. The laughter continued, and then, the echo ceased. He could not see anyone but felt a presence. There was someone, or something breathing in his face.

"You not as bad as you think. The devil, he walks here tonight, he comes for you."

"Who are you!?"

His body shook uncontrollably. He had never been unnerved in his entire career as a soldier, but this voice was pure evil.

"Leave this place, before you die," the male voice said.

Donovan moved quickly over the wall, but the man's laughter followed them until the cemetery was no longer in their view.

CHAPTER TWENTY-SEVEN

Declan observed the clouds as they floated across the sky and gave the moon an odd appearance. He hoped they would continue covering the light to make their trip less arduous, to be among those who walked the dark streets. Voodoo, witches, charms, incense, and the heaviness of tragedy left by hurricanes hid in every corner of this city. He would be glad to leave New Orleans and its history behind.

The hair on Declan's neck raised, an indicator this could not end well. He could hear Caren in the bathroom, her duffle packed and ready next to his on the bed.

"I discovered information on the cemetery."

"They only have guided tours, the gates locked at three, yesterday afternoon."

"Ye don't have a key, do ye?"

He heard Caren laugh, but knew she worried about the danger they could face. He could feel the beads Etienne had thrown at him being moved bead to bead like a rosary in his right hand. He jumped when Caren touched his arm.

"I didn't think anything could scare you."

"It's this town. We should forget about the cemetery and leave."

"Leave without the information that might help us. I don't feel Etienne will would send us into danger. We don't have an option." she said.

Declan looked at the beads in his hand.

"I know, lass."

"I admit a trip to the cemetery during the devil's hour isn't on my bucket list."

Declan crossed himself.

"Lass, stay close to me, but if…"

"If you go down, leave."

Caren finished his sentence.

He took the beads and placed them around her neck.

"These are for ye, a gift from Etienne."

Caren touched the beads, and placed them inside her shirt.

"We need to go."

They slowly faded into the darkness of the streets. A mist began to form and become thicker as their journey continued. Declan was aware of the homeless that roamed the city during the light, but it was a different evil that wait for them. His chosen path was to avoid the possibility of those encounters. The streets were empty, no individuals stood in the doors or alleyways to send them on their way. It appeared all obstacles to their destination had been cleared.

●

Saint Louis Cemetery One

Caren stood before the gates of this old cemetery and observed the toll the passing years had taken upon the walls. She placed hands upon the cracked and peeling bastions. The question of whether they would withstand another storm of any magnitude was questionable. She reached and gently pushed the gates in hopes they would open.

"I guess we're climbing," she said.

She felt Declan's hand move her closer to the gate. The mist increased, and obscured them from the sight of anyone who passed the cemetery. She began to hear light footsteps on gravel. The figure of a woman, dress in a white blouse, long skirt and tignon slowly took form on the inside of the cemetery.

"Declan, do you see her?"

"Aye, careful now, lass."

The woman approached the locked gates and took a moment to observe them through the metal bars.

"Do you come at this hour to see Marie Laveau?" she asked.

"We have been sent, with respect," Caren answered, and handed the woman a gift of money and jewelry.

"You may enter this place," she told them.

The woman took something from her pocket and placed it on the gate. As she backed away the gates opened and allowed them entry. Caren reached and took Declan's hand, as the mist became suffocating and limited their vision to a few feet. She felt Declan drop her hand and step forward to prevent the woman from touching her.

"It's fine, Declan."

The woman raised her head.

"Tall man, I am not your enemy."

He allowed the woman to place her hand on Caren's chest where the beads lay.

"You have been deceived, but all has been equaled in this place."

"I do not understand."

"Marie has visitors, so you must go another way to receive what is yours. Follow this path past ten graves, three to the left and in the doorway. The answer awaits."

They glanced towards their destination and turned back to thank the woman, but she had gone.

"I believe we should go."

"Where is she?" he asked.

Caren leaned into to him.

"Now, Declan."

She pulled him away from the gate.

●

Declan had always been the one to deal in death, but he felt it from every mausoleum doorway they passed. He knew who the unexpected visitors were, and he felt Etienne would not betray them, which left Lavanna. He understood the lure of money, and security it offered, a trait Donovan was proud to exploit. He should have concluded this would be a possibility, though the warning they received seemed sincere on her part. He continued to wait for an attack as they arrived at the location given to them.

"This is it."

"Hurry, lass."

"It's here."

She picked up the box and joined Declan. They turned to walk back to the gates when the woman appeared in the fog and pointed behind them.

"The gates cannot be reopened. You must go another direction."

They could hear the laughter of a male voice.

"Declan," Caren called out.

"This way, tall man," she said.

They turned to see her motion for them to follow two rows away. He reached for Caren's hand and moved them rapidly between the graves.

"Where is she?"

"There."

Caren pointed towards the far wall where the woman now stood.

"Mary, protect us. How did she get there so fast?"

"Declan, stop asking questions when there are no answers."

They approached the wall and found a brick staircase to help them over the top. Declan sent her first, to watch for anyone that might be coming for them. He topped the wall and could see the woman as she walked away. A death chill ran over him as she turned and faced him. Her words were spoken in his ear.

"The devil walked here tonight, but you are in his favor. Do not forget your promise to the woman."

Declan closed his eyes, dropped to the pavement, where he found Caren standing next to their pickup. His hands trembled as he pulled the keys from his pants pocket, opened the door, and found their bags were in the back seat of the cab. Neither of them whispered a word as Declan drove out of New Orleans and into the morning sunrise.

CHAPTER TWENTY-EIGHT

Donovan never returned to Wyoming after the night in New Orleans. He and Lee caught a flight home to Dublin two days later. The experience had shaken them and caused him to question his sanity. He had been trained for a tangible enemy, not fog and voices.

He continued to regret his association with this job and would enjoy the opportunity to tell Alex to kiss his ass. The unlimited flow of money, and opportunity to collect the bounty on Declan from home, was too much to give away to someone else.

He rubbed his head and neck as the conversation and explanation of their failure to Alex replayed in his memory.

"*Ghosts, fog, voices. What type of fool do you take me for, you bastard! Declan played you, and now, they're gone.*"

"*Two men cannot take Declan. I've come home to hire more men, or ye can do this yourself.*"

"*Do what you need, but get your ass back here and finish what you've been paid to do.*"

"*It will take time.*"

"*I'll be gone the month of July. If you return early you know where the key is located.*"

"*I'll do what I can.*"

"*Donovan, be back here by the end of summer or you will be the one hunted.*"

"*One other issue. The men I need will not come cheap.*"

Donovan's phone buzzed. This was an indication money had been transferred to his "work" account.

"Donovan, on your quest for replacements, acquire men who aren't afraid of their shadows, ghosts or this Declan. I have a suggestion."

"I'm listening."

"Hire women instead."

Donovan looked at his cell phone.

"Prick."

He had sent Lee west to Galway to search for reinforcements. He had been told to "Fuck off" too many times as of late. Lee opened his front door and entered.

"Did ye find anyone, Lee?"

"No, the word is out on Declan and the resurrection of Aaron Caydon."

"Alex has given us until the end of summer to hire a team and return to the States."

"I have another place I can go."

"Where?"

"Limerick, there might be a couple of contacts willing to go if the price is high enough."

"Lee, ye need to move quickly. We don't have a lot of time and multiple arrangements will need to be made."

"What about their pay?"

"Double whatever they demand," Donovan said.

"Double?"

"Yes."

Lee took a beer from the fridge and opened it.

"Ye can drink that on the way to Limerick."

"I'll be back a few days."

Donovan knew the offer of that amount of money would eventually get him a team, though most would never live long enough to collect their pay. His cell phone buzzed.

"Craig, it's good to hear from ye. How's your mum?"

"She made it through the worst, resting well at my sister's. What's this I hear about ye looking for another crew?"

"Can ye have a pint with me this evening?"

"Aye, I'd like to know what happened after I left ye."

"I could use your help. I'll double what ye were paid in New Orleans."

"Double ye say? with the same options as before?" Craig asked.

"Whatever ye want."

"What time at the pub?"

"Come around seven. I need to see if I can find some favors to call in before ye get there."

"Good luck with that, Donovan. All the men I know have already heard the stories."

He would have to buy a lot of beer and whiskey tonight if he intended to call in favors. He thought about the suggestion women be hired. Though Donovan preferred a male team, there were two he would accept. If Lee failed, he'd make those calls.

CHAPTER TWENTY-NINE

Panama City Beach, Florida
Marina
July 4th

Caren walked along the shoreline of the beach and stopped to face east for another beautiful sunrise. The short trip from New Orleans to Panama City had been made in total silence. The first two weeks they lived in small hotels, then moved to cabins in KOA or Good Sam campgrounds. Declan never spoke to her of their experience in the cemetery.

She found solace in the early morning trips to the beach. It allowed time away to grieve privately and continue to move forward and find Aaron. She allowed the sun to shine upon her face before locating the small turquoise scooter. The scooter made the twenty-minute ride from the beach back to the houseboat fun. Caren never believed she would be able to say that word again, or laugh, but Declan had made it possible with a simple mode of transportation. She parked the scooter next to his and entered the main cabin.

"I've found a private gun range for us to practice," Declan said, as she entered.

Caren removed the baseball cap.

"Good morning to you, too," she said.

He attempted to stand up.

"A public range is not a good idea here."

The living quarters were small which caused an adjustment and patience when moving about the boat. The ability for the boat to be mobile and away from the sounds of drunk loud tourist, made the limited space bearable.

"If you are wanting coffee, I'll get it. What's your concern about the public range?" Caren asked.

"There is a chance we may face a closer inspection of our identifications being from out of state."

"You think the owner of a private range would gladly accept our financial gratitude for the use of his facility."

"Yes, exactly."

Declan jumped as several firecrackers exploded close to their location.

"You know this is only going to get worse as the night goes on since its Independence Day."

"I may take us out on the bay tonight."

Caren took a place across the table from him in the breakfast nook. The box from New Orleans had been placed on the table.

"The view of the cities fireworks display will be nice, but we're not going to get away from all the celebrations. Should I be concerned about our finances?"

Declan shook his head.

"We have enough money to buy this place and live here forever."

"Forever is a long time in cramped quarters."

He pushed the box across the table.

"Ye should open it."

She reached and began to remove the paper. A large cigar box marked Havana was open, and Caren emptied the items it held on the table.

"Oh, more money for you to count."

He reached and moved the money to the side.

"I'll count it later."

"New identifications to add to the ones we still haven't used. Any idea about this?"

"Lass, why are ye asking me?"

"Sorry, I'm trying to make sense of all this."

She took out what appeared to be a greeting card, opened the envelope, and removed what look like a gift card.

"What does it say?"

Caren handed the item to him and, left the table. She returned with the laptop.

"Long-Bowe B&B. Where is Waynesboro Georgia?"

"Waynesboro is about six or seven hours north of our present location. The bed and breakfast is on the outskirts of town," she said.

"Check for availability," Declan told her.

"You do remember it's summer and probably one of their busiest times."

"Check anyway," he said.

She ran a finger down the screen.

"Booked, booked. The first opening would be September 8th. How long can we stay here?"

"I didn't sign a contract, the man said as long as I paid the rent it was ours."

"We've been in this city and on the boat longer than any location. It's a little out of character for you."

"Aye, the situation in New Orleans left me questioning things, but it doesn't mean I haven't worried about being discovered."

"How much longer will it be safe for us to remain here?"

"My thought with the houseboat and scooters were to blend into the community as summer tourists. I've been checking the stories on Boston and Maine to see if we have any concerns," he said.

"Are there?" she asked.

"The stories have diminished, but it doesn't mean the cases are not being investigated, we need to be cautious."

"What's really bothering you, Declan?"

"The individual after ye will not give up. The next time he will have a full crew and with a leader who is organized."

"Crew? What do you mean by crew?" she asked.

He leaned back into the cramped seat.

"They will need enough individuals that will be able to control or kill me in order to take ye."

The memory of Maine and Boston left her silent. If two individuals were responsible for causing that type of destruction, what would a full crew of men be possible of inflicting on them or innocent bystanders?

"I know you're out checking the area, have you noticed anyone asking questions or seem out of place?" Caren asked.

"No, but if there is any doubt, I'll move the boat to a different location."

"Will the owner agree to that?"

"I spoke to him on the sturdiness of the houseboat being out on water. He assured me it would do fine away from the marina if I wished to take her out," Declan assured her.

"What if we need to move to another location?"

"I'll call and request permission to leave for a quieter marina," he said.

Caren picked up the gift card. The white letters had turned yellow. She made a reservation for two weeks starting the eighth of September, and was surprised the old number was accepted. A confirmation code appeared and was written on a piece of the brown paper from the box.

"I don't believe the scooters will be appropriate for the trip to Georgia."

"Aye, it's barely a fit for me as it is. I'll find something when it's time for us to leave."

Declan closed his eyes as another round of firecrackers began to pop.

"I think your idea to move out into the bay would be a nice choice anytime you want to go."

"Aye, now would be that time. Could ye release us from the dock, lass?"

She started out the door, when Declan threw the baseball cap and hit her head. She picked it up.

"I'm only going to be out there a few minutes, no one will see me," she said.

He shook his head and pointed to the cap. She shoved it down over her ears and began to remove the lines as the motor on the boat began to hum. Caren knocked on the side to let him know they were free to go, but froze as someone called her name.

"Caren! Caren Johnson is that you?" the female voice called.

She didn't need to look at the woman to know who had recognized her. Caren walked on board and ignored the woman that continued to call out. She waited until they were away from the marina before speaking to Declan.

"We may want to spend a few days out here, actually we should probably find another spot to park."

"Who saw ye?"

"My neighbor from Boston. They were gone last year, out of the country when everything took place."

"We'll wait a few days then dock in another location. I'll make a call from the new marina to the owner."

"Do you think she'll call the authorities?" Caren asked.

"Lass, what would ye do?"

"I don't understand how she recognized me."

"It might be the shirt you're wearing."

Caren held the shirt out then walked away. She returned ten minutes later with two shirts that had been cut in pieces in a plastic bag. The shirt that identified her had been purchased at a church festival, from the woman who had called out on the dock. This incident proved she could no longer hold to the past, their lives depended on the ability to remain unnoticed.

"Could you dispose of these when we dock?"

"Aye, sorry lass."

"It's my fault, I took them from the house in Maine not thinking of the church emblem on them. Who would've believed she'd be in Panama City?"

"Ye don't have anything else?"

"No, what's in the bag is all that can tie me to Boston."

"People make mistakes, but ours could have permanent consequences."

"A lesson learned."

"Let it go, Caren. Tomorrow will be another day and we'll face it together."

CHAPTER THIRTY

Moose, Wyoming
July 29th

Alex never enjoyed forced family gatherings as a child and detested them now that his body had begun to fail him. This would be his final year for family reunions with planned activities, dogs and screaming children. He would no longer be the pitiful disabled member of the family.

His balance failed which made him grab the bench and fall into the seat. He dug through the carryon bag and found his medication. He was thankful for the small amount of water left from his flight which prevented a dry intake and delayed response of the pills. He closed his eyes and could feel the tension building towards a migraine.

"Sir, do you need assistance?"

Alex thought of being rude but raised his eyes to a Hispanic girl of approximately eighteen. He looked at her airport badge.

"Vivian, I believe I need a wheelchair if you don't mind."

"I saw you almost fall, sir. Are you going to be okay?"

"Yes, yes, thank you," Alex said.

"I'll call for a wheelchair," she said.

Alex hated these embarrassing moments, but his body continued to fail.

"Where can I take you?" Vivian asked.

"Arrivals, I have a car and someone waiting."

She proceeded into the baggage area.

"I have a driver waiting for me."

Richard walked over to the wheelchair.

"Can I help you to the car?" Vivian asked.

"No, Richard will assist me. Thank you."

She placed her hand on his shoulder, then walked away.

"Your luggage is already in the car. I was becoming concerned," Richard said.

"I'm ready to go home."

The trip from the airport began in silence. Richard glanced in the rearview mirror.

"I repaired the roof on cabin three and filled your pantry yesterday."

"I'm expecting company very soon," Alex said.

"How soon?" Ricard asked.

"It's a little early but they will be coming before the end of summer."

"How many are you expecting?"

"Six, eight, maybe more."

"Why so many, Alex?"

"It appears the project needs additional help."

"You've had some issues, I agree."

"Richard, you're being nice."

"I'd like to make a suggestion."

"Please," Alex said.

"If this plan flounders, find a way to finish it alone."

Alex lowered his head, grasped his hands in an attempt to stop the shaking.

"Richard, tomorrow a delivery of double bunks will be arriving, please replace the full-size beds in all the cabins."

"What do you want me to do with the full-size beds?"

"I've made arrangements with the company to take them away."

"Who is this?" Richard asked.

Alex looked over the seat to the sight of Donovan and another man with luggage outside his home.

"He's early."

●

The Return

Donovan wasn't sure if Alex would be back this soon, but he took a chance. Access to one of the cabins would not have been an issue but he didn't wish to be found trespassing by the maintenance man. He wasn't averse to sleeping in the car but preferred a bed. The sight of Alex's car made the decision for him.

"Craig, don't say anything to him."

"All I want is some food and a bed."

They watched as Richard helped Alex out of the car, obtained his luggage and headed towards them.

"Welcome back, with this early arrival I assume you are ahead of schedule," Alex said.

"I have people that will be here in a few days," Donovan said.

The men made their way up the stairs and into the main cabin.

"I'll be here early to get started on the cabins," Richard said.

"See you tomorrow," Alex said.

Donovan watched as Richard walked out to his vehicle and left.

"I had to promise a lot of money to the people coming."

"I would imagine most of them will not live to collect their wages," Alex said.

"They're soldiers, and death is part of any operation like this one."

Alex walked over to a key rack and pulled a set to cabin one. He then threw the keys to Donovan.

"Richard will be replacing the beds with bunks, four per cabin. If you need more than that, someone will have to sleep on the floor. If you don't mind, I've had a long day and need to rest."

The two men walked out and took their bags to the first cabin. Donovan opened the door then backed away.

"Ye might want to give it a minute to cool down in there, Craig."

"I'll get the cooler from the car. I need a beer after that little conversation," Craig said.

The two men moved their chairs into what little shade they could find.

"I can see ye have questions, Craig."

"Are ye going to tell me he is truly in charge of this job?"

"Aye, the man with all the money."

Donovan's cell began to buzz.

"Is that Lee?"

"Aye. Let me put him on speaker. Lee, go ahead."

"I've done the best I could, but including Brigid, we only have nine."

"Six with the three of us?" Donovan asked.

"Aye."

"Jesus, everyone has heard," Craig said.

"The rumors are spreading faster than a dry summer fire in the States," Lee said.

"Lee, I want all of ye here on the third."

"It'll be close," Lee said.

Donovan ceased the call and looked at Craig.

"You're lucky ye have that many to come. Is that the same rumor ye told me?" Craig asked.

"Aye, most won't go against Declan. That old drunken fool, Ferrell Mallone has been talking to anyone who will listen. He's swearing on the holy book the devil released Caydon from hell to come back and reign havoc down upon everyone."

Donovan threw both his hands up in the air.

"Old fool! I never believe Caydon was killed but where did he go?" Craig asked.

"I don't know, but Alex swears he's dead. The man has information up there that could answer that question."

"I know what you're thinking, Donovan."

"The man will have to go for his medical tests eventually. I'll take advantage of that time," Donovan said.

"Who is Brigid?"

"Brigid Murphy, trained by Beck, but has a better temperament and follows orders."

"Good to know there will not be another Beck to deal with. Donovan, whether the room is hot or cold I'm going to bed," Craig said.

"I'll be in soon."

Donovan finished his beer, then took a walk around the cabins and back to lock the car. He could hear a loud conversation between Alex and a female from an open window. He moved closer and smiled when the word mother was spoken.

CHAPTER THIRTY-ONE

aren closed her eyes, leaned against the round column, and listened to the birds sing most of the morning. The room she had been given in the old Georgia home had a feather bed. It enveloped her like a mother's arms around her children.

She thought back to Florida and the relocation of the houseboat to Smuggler's Cove due to the incident in Panama City. Declan had made several trips off the boat to check the area for anyone that might be searching for their location. Once he felt comfortable, she was allowed to leave the boat.

One morning, a few days later, she had taken a different path to the local store and passed a small A-framed church. She stopped and listened to the light bells that rang. They seemed to be calling to her. The next moment, she opened the doors, walked slowly to the front of the church, and knelt down to pray. She raised her eyes to the multi-colored stained glass cross, with the image of Christ nailed to it. Caren moved from the alter to a pew, closed her eyes and let the tears fall. When she opened them, a woman wearing the collar of a priest stood before her.

"Good-morning. May I join you?"

"Yes, please."

The woman took a place on the same pew, and pulled a tissue from her pocket. Caren leaned into the priest and cried.

"What may I do to help you, child?" she asked.

"I don't wish to burden you," Caren said.

The woman took Caren's face and raised it to meet hers.

"Why do you think I wear this collar?"

Caren nodded. Over the next hour she spoke of her loss, emptiness and need to find her brother. When she finished, Caren blew her nose and took a deep breath.

"Thank you. I've needed to do this for some time," Caren said.

"You might benefit from the weekly meeting we have for survivors. There is no cost, and no one will ask questions."

Caren nodded and obtained the day and time. A few weeks passed. One morning, she turned before entering the church and called to Declan.

"It might do you good to come inside."

He walked around the church.

"It's too late for me, lass."

"Only if you permit it."

"If this gives ye peace, then peace it be."

She watched as he disappeared, but knew he was never far.

The mistake in Panama City had been a blessing in disguise. She was sad to leave, but she must have answers. The squeak of the screen caused Caren to turn and smile when he joined her on the steps. He pointed across the driveway to the fields being harvested.

"It's an early harvest this year."

"How would you know that?"

"The innkeeper, Derrick, told me. Their only guests, Gloria and Nevin have been invited to join them, for lunch," Declan said

"Declan, who chooses these names?" she said and made a face.

"Why are ye asking me?"

"Were you aware they have only been here two years?"

"Who told ye?"

"The lady of the house loves to talk. Daisy said, they'd been here two years. The management and upkeep became a burden for her husband's parents."

"According to Derrick, this property was purchased years before the Civil War. The Bowen family still owns it."

"Isn't their name Long?" she asked.

"The Bowens and Longs became connected through marriage, but the Bowens own the land. I discovered a well-kept family cemetery."

Caren held up her hands.

"No more cemeteries!"

"Aye, one was enough."

They turned around as the screen door opened.

"Lunch is ready," Daisy said.

"We've been summoned," Caren said.

Declan extended a hand to Caren.

"Lass, I'm not happy that ye have not worn a disguise since we've been here."

"I need a break to be myself. There's no one here. I'll wear a cap if someone comes, or put on a pair of blue contacts. Please just this once."

"Just this one time."

They walked into the kitchen where Daisy had set the corner bench table for them. The bright sunflower cushions on the chairs and bench matched the curtains and added to the charm of this bed and breakfast. The yellow suncatcher in the window made Caren blink as she moved across the bench. She listened as the wooden floors creaked with every step made on them. The memories this home and kitchen must hold caused a smile to form.

"It's so lovely here. Thank you for asking us to lunch." Caren said.

"I have always loved this part of the kitchen from the first time Derrick brought me home to meet his family," Daisy told them.

"Gloria said ye have been here for two years."

"We were spending more time here than home in Savannah. Mom and Dad were getting older and needed help," Derrick said.

"Derrick was given an option for an early retirement. I suggested he take it and we moved here. I have never regretted that decision," Daisy said, then leaned over and kissed her husband.

"We say grace at our meals, if you are not opposed," Derrick said.

Caren reached out, took Declan's hand and then Daisy's.

"Not at all."

"We thank you for the blessing of this day. Lord, we ask that you place your hands on our guests, Gloria and Nevin. Amen. Dig in Neven, there's plenty," Derrick said.

"How are your rooms?" Daisy asked.

"Outstanding," Caren answered.

"Very comfortable," Declan answered.

"Daisy, the card we presented was a gift. Would there be any chance to know who purchased it and how long ago?" Caren asked.

"Those records are probably gone with the outdated computer my father owned. The main drive shorted out and caught fire," Derrick said.

"I know we've never used paper or cards," Daisy said.

"My parents stopped hand-written gift cards four or five years ago."

"Are ye telling us this was purchased possibly five years ago?"

"I would say a minimum of five, possibly longer. Of course, we are happy to honor it," Daisy said.

"Odd the person didn't sign it," Derrick said.

"Aye, we thought the same."

"We have guest books for people to comment on their stay," Daisy told them.

"How far back do they go?"

"Mom started them ten or fifteen years ago."

"Would it be possibly to see the ones from 2001 thru 2005? It's possible our family enjoyed a night or two with your parents and purchased the card," Caren said.

"I'll get them for you after lunch," Daisy said.

A few hours after lunch, Caren and Declan sat in the wooden swing on the large porch, drank sweet tea, and waited for the books Daisy promised. She had been thankful there would be only five to read for that time period. The screen door swung open, and Declan jumped up to help the woman that held a large tray.

"Thank you, Nevin."

"This is quite a load, ye should have called for me for help."

"Goodness what did you bring us?" Caren asked.

"Sweet cakes, some chocolate chip cookies right out of the oven and the guest books you asked to see," Daisy answered.

"I've an errand to run. Good luck on your search."

Daisy waved and walked to the B&B Jeep.

"I can't believe that Jeep is drivable, it's must be twelve or thirteen years old," Declan said.

Caren laughed and took one of the books from the tray.

"Lass, what do ye expect to find in these books? Your brother would not have used his real name."

Caren's initial disbelief that Aaron was anything but a businessman and loving brother had begun to abate.

"I may recognize his writing."

"I'll be of no help to ye then. I'd like to go for a walk if ye feel safe?"

Caren pulled back the edge of a small quilt next to her and displayed the Glock.

"I think the only danger is the squirrels stealing the cookies," she said.

She watched Declan disappear down the road towards the large house used for family gatherings. Caren began with 2005 and read page after page of lovely, sincere words of the warmth and friendship found at the B&B. She had completed 2002 when Daisy returned.

"Any luck?"

Caren shook her head.

"Maybe the person ordered the card online."

"No, the gift card you used was purchased here," Daisy said.

"I've one more to check."

Caren held up the last guest book.

"If you do find a name I'll see if there are any paper files to check."

Caren opened the last guest book dated 2001. She closed her eyes when she reached July. She was beginning to think she was wrong. She started to read the entries for July fifteenth. There was a lengthy compliment in Aaron's signature prose. His favorite song by Three Dog Night. She had found him.

"Daisy."

Caren called as she entered the house.

"Did you find something, Gloria?"

"Do you know this man?"

Daisy took the book and looked at the signature.

"Can't say that I do."

"Any chance for paper files with his information? I believe he may have bought the gift card," Caren said.

"Is he a family member?"

"He's a good friend of our family."

"Derrick's in the office he may be able to help us."

Caren was relieved, as she was led into a neat and orderly room.

"What a nice little office," Caren said.

"I never could abide disorganization."

"Derrick could you help Gloria? She may have found the person who purchased the card."

"I'll try. What year?"

"It's from 2001," Caren answered.

Derrick rubbed his forehead.

"Gloria, those files were all destroyed. I'm sorry."

"May I have a copy of this page?" she asked, and handed him the book.

"Of, course."

Derrick swiveled in the chair to the small printer and made two copies.

"Thank you."

"I wish I could do more," Derrick said.

Caren walked out into the hallway and found Declan. He held the quilt she'd left on the swing.

"Sorry," she whispered and took the quilt which still held the Glock in the folds.

"Have ye looked at these pictures?"

"No, why?"

"We need to ask about this photograph."

Declan pointed to a photograph of four women dressed in World War II uniforms.

"What's so important about this one?"

"The smallest woman of this group, her name is Nancy Small-Benjamin."

●

Caren hadn't rested well this evening, and the clock's continuous flip of the minutes and hours was an irritant. The passage in the guest book had left only questions. How could Aaron know she would end up here some thirteen years later? Would the photograph on the wall lead them to Bevan's location? Caren walked downstairs to make coffee, but Declan had arrived first.

"I see you haven't slept either."

"Lass, I need to see the comment Aaron left in the guest book."

Caren pulled a copy from the pocket of her robe and handed it to him. He took a few minutes to read it and frowned.

"What's wrong?"

"This sounds like a song."

She laughed.

"*Out in the Country*, was released in 1990, by a band called Three Dog Night. Aaron loved the song and believed it spoke of world conditions to come. The guest book comment is the refrain from the song."

"Bud Johnson, is an alias."

"The name means nothing to me. It's the song."

"Oh! Good morning. You two are up early," Daisy said.

"I hope ye don't mind that I made coffee?"

"Please, make yourself at home. Did you discover who sent the card?"

Daisy took a flavored creamer from the fridge and held it up to them.

"No, thank ye."

Caren shook her head.

"I spoke with Mother last night. She said, the card was bought years ago as a gift. It was put away and forgotten, she discovered it a few months ago and thought I might enjoy using it," Caren explained.

"Bud Johnson?" Daisy asked.

"A friend of my father's from childhood."

"Well, glad you discovered the answer."

"Daisy, ye have an extensive family history hanging on the walls.

I have a question about one of them. May I retrieve it?"

"Of course."

Daisy smiled as he left the kitchen.

"He's quite the charmer," Caren said.

"Gloria, I love your cousin's wonderful accent."

Declan brought the photograph into the kitchen, and gently placed it on the table.

"Who are these women in the photograph?" he asked.

Daisy smiled and shook her head.

"The women in this picture were nurses who joined the military when Pearl Harbor was bombed. They were all from Georgia and over time became known as the "Georgia Peaches." The first woman is Dawn Goodson, next Pam Lyles, Susan Bowen and Nancy Small. This land was once a huge tobacco farm before the Civil War owned by the Bowen Family. They owned several sections of land. Over time, the acreage was sold. All that remains is the bed and breakfast, the Big House, and family cemetery."

"I noticed that Nancy Small has Benjamin added to her name," Declan said.

Derrick entered kitchen.

"Sweetheart could you tell them about Nancy?" Daisy asked.

Derrick poured a cup of coffee and joined them at the table.

"The story is going to be abbreviated as some information has been lost over the years," Derrick said.

"We'd be appreciative of anything ye wish to share with us," Declan said.

Doctor William Benjamin was in love with Susan Bowen. She did not have the same feelings for him. Bill was called back into service after the war began. Nancy Small's father, a physician, watched over his practice here in Waynesboro. Bill and Nancy met briefly, but it left a spark in her heart, with hope they would meet again. Susan Bowen was killed overseas, Nancy became ill, and Bill contracted malaria. The train that brought Susan home is where Bill and Nancy rekindled their friendship. They married a few months later.

"Do ye know where Bill and Nancy moved after the war?"

"Moved? Bill senior was the community physician here for years and Nancy was his nurse. Their oldest child, Bill junior, became a physician filling his father's position. Junior passed away two years ago. It was shortly after we arrived. His wife, Donna, is who I went to see yesterday."

"What an interesting history," Caren said.

"Aye, more than I expected. Did they have a large family?"

"The Benjamins have been here since World War II, involved in the community and have given much to Waynesboro. Bill and Donna had three children, Bevan, Barton and Belinda. There are six grandchildren and eight great-grandchildren," Derrick said.

"I would imagine they all live here or close to help their mother," Caren stated.

"I wished that were true, but their children all moved away. It seems the country life didn't appeal. Bevan works for the CIA, lives in Virginia, and Barton is an attorney in Miami," Daisy said.

"What of the lass, Belinda?"

"She loved being a wife and mother for her three children. When the children left home, Belinda obtained an English degree and has written a successful series of children's books. She and Landon live outside of Denver," Daisy answered.

"I'll replace this."

Declan took the photograph back to the hallway.

"Nevin's always been a history buff. I appreciate you taking time to tell us a small part of the Bowen history," Caren said.

"It was a very small part. You should stop over at the family cemetery. I think you'll find it interesting," Daisy said.

"Daisy, is there a farmer's market available in the area?"

"Yes, not far from here and one of the largest in this area. You and Nevin should go and enjoy the day. I usually go but need to open the Big House for a wedding this weekend. Would you two be so kind as to pick up some things for me if you go?"

"Daisy, don't bother our guests. I'll go tomorrow for you," Derrick said.

Declan returned to the kitchen.

"Derrick, it'll be our pleasure," Caren said.

"Wonderful. It's going to be busy for us the next few days. Gloria stop by Donna's booth and say hello. She sells holistic salves, oils and herbs," Daisy told them.

"It sounds like a nice way to spend the day."

CHAPTER THIRTY-TWO

Donovan gave instructions to his team for the day's exercise in the mountains. He turned when the lights of Richard's pickup arrived. The man waited like the servant he was, for Alex to descend the steps. This meant there would be no interruptions today which would allow some peace. Donovan had pushed everyone since their arrival with every scenario they might encounter including the sudden midnight runs into the mountains. The ones not used to such training returned injured, but not incapacitated. In a few hours he would take full advantage of Alex's absence.

Lee walked up to Donovan's location.

"Where is he going?" Lee asked.

"Doctor appointments, tests. He'll be gone all day," Donovan answered, and smiled.

"Any chance he'll be gone overnight?"

Donovan turned back to Lee and observed the team had not left for the daily assignment.

"Lee, why is the team still here?"

"We could use a night in town, release some steam before we leave."

"I guess none of them had the balls to ask me a few moments ago," Donovan said.

"I volunteered," Lee said.

Donovan whistled and motioned for everyone to come back.

"I understand ye think a night on the town is in order. Who believes that Declan Mallone is drinking beer and relaxing?"

Donovan waited.

"We've been working our asses off. Jesus Christ, it's just one night," Brigid said.

Donovan turned to Lee.

"I see the only one of ye with any balls is a woman. Your asses have been worked off for a good reason. Ask Beck. Oh wait, ye can't! If any of ye feel a night in town will extend your life expectancy for even a day, go ahead."

"We've training to do," Lee told them.

Donovan continued to stand until they disappeared down the path.

"I could hear ye inside," Craig said, as he walked up to Donovan.

"This is not a bloody party. They can celebrate when we're finished, if any of them are still alive. I need your help."

Donovan walked towards the main cabin.

"Do ye think this is a good idea?" Craig asked.

"I know the bastard has information on Caydon. The files in the house are originals not copies," Donovan answered.

"If we get caught..."

"He'll be gone most of the day. I need a couple of hours. If I don't find anything, we'll leave," Donovan said.

"Two hours. Promise me Donovan."

"Aye, no longer."

They walked up to the front door and Donovan managed the lock without difficulty. He quickly began to check files for any information on Aaron Caydon, but at the end of two hours, had discovered nothing. They carefully replaced every item, and locked the door.

●

3:30 pm

Donovan and Craig sat outside cabin three when the cell began to buzz. He let it go to voicemail. The sound of a car coming up the drive made both men stand.

"He's back early."

Donovan listened to the voicemail Lee had left.

"Problem?"

"Lee said one of the team fell and needs stitches. Will ye call. Tell them to head back and pull the kit out. I'm being summoned."

They watched as Alex motioned for them.

"I'll handle it for ye, go see what the master needs."

Donovan made his way to Alex's location.

"You're back early."

"I cancelled the session with the idiot psychologist today. I do not need anyone probing or digging into my mind. I'd like to speak with you and Craig. Give me thirty minutes."

"One of the team is injured and needs some stitches," Donovan said.

"Will a trip into town be required?" Alex asked.

"No, we'll be able to handle it."

"Good to know."

"Do ye need some assistance?" Donovan asked.

"Richard will help me; your team is headed this way."

Donovan turned around to check his team. The injured man was still walking, so he knew it couldn't be too severe.

"Will an hour be acceptable?" Donovan asked.

"Of course, see to your people."

He met Craig in cabin one, where the wound was assessed, stitched, and antibiotics given to help prevent infection.

"We'll go back out in the morning," Lee said.

"Hold up, ye may get that night off. Craig and I have a meeting in the main cabin."

They walked up the stairs and could see Alex had changed out of the suit into sweats. He was studying maps on the table as Donovan knocked.

"Come in, gentlemen."

They joined him at the table.

"How is your team member?"

"He's had worse," Donovan answered.

"It appears you have good control of your team. Is there an issue with you heading out say within the next forty-eight hours?"

"Craig, what do ye think?"

"We could leave now if needed," Craig answered.

"It's time to put them to their task, check back with me tomorrow around noon. If you two will excuse me it's been a long day. Good night gentlemen. Donovan, lock the door as you leave."

Alex never looked back as he left the room.

They stopped at the bottom of the stairs. Craig looked at his friend.

"What the devil was that about, Donovan?"

"Games, secrets, always making me guess. It's been this way since I came onboard."

"Why haven't ye killed him?"

"Money," Donovan answered.

●

September 14th
Noon

Donovan prepared for another cryptic conversation with Alex as Craig knocked on the bathroom door. He hoped it would be more informative than last night's fun and games.

"Ye need to see this, Donovan."

He opened the door and followed Craig to the screen door. They watched as three vehicles pulled into the parking area. One individual ran up the stairs with an iPad and keys.

"What is this?" Donovan asked.

"I would say we will have more than bullshit to discuss today."

"Are ye ready, Craig?"

"Aye."

They left the cabin together and could see Alex on the porch.

"Any idea?"

"Craig, have ye ever noticed how he enjoys looking down on us?"

"Aye, like a lord of the manor," Craig answered.

As they approached the steps, Alex turned and walked inside.

"I can't put up with this much longer, Donovan."

"I believe our salvation is at hand."

They didn't bother to knock and entered. Both men were shocked to see Alex's posture straight and balanced. His hands no longer shook.

"I have information. They've been seen," he told them.

"Where?" Craig asked.

They walked over to the table where Alex pointed to the circle he'd marked.

"Waynesboro, Georgia," Donovan said.

"Where did this information come from?" Craig asked.

Alex didn't answer the question and waited for Donovan to place the location in his phone's GPS.

"They were seen at a farmer's market this morning," Alex said.

Donovan raised his head.

"Ye have some proof it was them?"

Alex turned on his phone and presented a photograph to Craig.

"That wasn't very intelligent to go out in public without some type of disguise."

"Her unusual eyes caught the attention of several people," Alex said.

"Declan probably wasn't far away," Donovan said.

Alex motioned for Craig to swipe to the next photograph.

"Ye would be correct," Craig said.

"The town doesn't appear to be large," Donovan said.

"They are probably in a small hotel, bed and breakfast, or rental house," Craig said.

"They may be staying in another travel trailer," Donovan said.

"I'm going to save you some time. They are presently guests of the Long-Bowe Bed and Breakfast since the eighth," Alex said.

"How much driving time, Donovan?"

"Thirty plus hours."

"Jesus, Mary," Craig said.

"If you should miss them, I would suggest a northern direction towards the D.C. area," Alex said.

Craig glanced from the map towards Donovan.

"I see three options once they leave Waynesboro," Craig said.

"If they go north it will possibly be through this mountain area."

Donovan traced the road.

"The Shenandoah National Park; a place where people disappear easily," Alex said.

"Our arrival will not go unnoticed in a smaller town. We will need to send two in for a quick recon," Donovan said.

"I'll need regular updates."

Alex walked over and opened his hand. Donovan took the two sets of keys.

"Any other information you'd like to share before we leave?" Donovan asked.

"No, I think you have enough," Alex said.

He walked to the door and opened it for them to leave.

Craig hit the bottom step first, entered their cabin, and began to pack.

"How much time are ye giving everyone, Donovan?"

"I want to be gone within the hour."

"The team may not be close, it could take them an hour to return," Craig said.

"Then they'll be some fatigued bastards."

Donovan walked out of the cabin, and texted Lee to have the team double time back. As Craig walked out, the door keys to the extended cab pickup were thrown to him. His phone buzzed with a response.

"Where are they?" Craig asked.

"Lee said close, fifteen minutes."

"Donovan, ye know that little bastard is not telling us everything he knows."

"Again, ye mean."

"Ye noticed he avoided my question."

Donovan nodded his head and could hear the team. He whistled and motioned for them to meet him.

"It's time to leave. I will give ye forty minutes to pack, and definitely shower. Be fast now."

The team quickly disbursed to their quarters.

"Do ye know anything about him?"

"Alex answers the questions he wants and ignores the rest. I'll tell ye one last time the only thing I give a damn about is his money in my pocket. As long as he is willing to spend it, I am happy to take it from him."

"I took time to look through a few of the files in the house, and ye are right they're originals. Did ye notice he wasn't stumbling or shaking today?"

It appears his appointments yesterday had positive results. It could be new medicine or an experimental treatment. I was worried he was going to demand to go with us," Donovan said.

"I just want to finish this job, collect my money and go home," Craig said.

"Donovan, there are a couple still packing, but we're ready," Lee said.

"Craig muster everyone up. I need to get my bag."

Donovan ran inside, grabbed his bag and met his team.

"Listen up! All the bags in the SUV, and five of ye in it. All equipment except sidearms in the truck, and now, for the bad news. We have a thirty plus hour drive. This means we drive in shifts, eat in the vehicles, stop only for petrol and the toilet."

There were a number of profanities. Craig walked up next to Donovan.

"Get it off your chest now, nothing will change the situation. Lee and Brigid are with us, six hour driving shifts. We will stop down the road to fill the coolers, make it count," Craig said.

They watched as the team split, loaded up equipment and bags as ordered.

"I'll take the first shift, there are a number of arrangements to be made over the next hours," Donovan said.

"Lee, Brigid and I can work on those."

Donovan glanced at the side mirror and shivered.

"What's the problem?"

"Glad to leave this place and him."

Craig turned back to see Alex wave as they drove away.

"Egotistical bastard."

CHAPTER THIRTY-THREE

Declan walked the property line of the Long-Bowe just before dawn. He had been uneasy since their trip to the farmers market on Saturday. Caren had not used a disguise the entire time they had been at the bed and breakfast. He had not been agreeable with this decision, but relented since the location of the bed and breakfast had been isolated. This failure caused a number of side glances, due to her unusual eye color. Every cell phone had a camera in them which meant they had probably been photographed at least once.

When they mentioned Daisy had sent them, Donna Benjamin was delighted to speak of Bevan and all her children. He worried now for Derrick and Daisy, they needed to leave to avoid any confrontation. Declan walked through the trees and stopped, as Caren walked towards him with coffee.

"Did you find anything?"

"No."

"You believe someone is here."

"Aye, lass, I do."

Caren looked up at him.

"Then we should make our apologies for leaving early, pay the bill, and go today. Declan, I do not want these people placed in danger."

"Are ye packed?"

Declan turned and looked back to the woods.

"I packed yesterday, when I noticed you leaving before dawn."

"Do we have all the information for Virginia?"

"I couldn't directly ask Donna for her son's address. She did give me the name of the city," Caren answered.

"I hope we will not have to knock on every door," Declan said.

"I'll see what Daisy can tell us this morning without it being too obvious."

Declan finished his coffee.

"We should go back."

"It's been nice, I truly wish we could stay longer."

"Lass, if what I feel has arrived, everyone here is in danger."

"Would you like to tell me about your second sense?"

Declan leaned against the tree. He knew this discussion was eventually going to take place.

"How long have ye known?"

"I first suspected in Maine, but in New Orleans there was no longer a question for me."

"I made people believe it was due to my training; something I developed to protect other soldiers."

"It's like my eidetic memory. These come from our family," she told him.

"My mum, she was a seer. Our whole family line, I am the only man to ever receive the gift."

"What about your sisters?"

"They've never admitted it. My time as a soldier enhanced and brought it to fruition. My mum was murdered, and it haunts me that she didn't see. I blame myself."

"I don't understand?"

"I feel if she hadn't been worried about me, she'd have seen the bomb. Since her death, my gift has enhanced times four. I know ye have questions about the scars on my back, it comes from my involvement with past associations."

"I am so sorry to have intruded, Declan. It was not my intent."

"It was time, lass."

They returned to the house and entered the kitchen where Daisy was busy with breakfast.

"Daisy let me help you," Caren said.

Declan listened to their conversation. He was impressed with the way Caren could obtain information from people.

"When we were at the market, Donna told us, that Bevan lives in Reston, Virginia."

"Yes, he does, and has a lovely family." Daisy said.

"Is Reston a large town?"

"It's larger than Waynesboro. I remember Donna saying they wanted to live away from D.C."

"I understand. It's important to protect your family," Caren said, then took a moment to clear her throat.

"I understand they live in a nice neighborhood. Donna laughed and told me there was a boundary dispute close to their property between Herndon and Reston."

"Daisy, we are unfortunately going to leave today," Declan said.

"Oh, is there a problem with your rooms?"

"No, nothing like that, everything has been perfect. Gloria and I need to be at another B&B tomorrow. This is completely my fault."

"Nevin misjudged the travel time. We will be happy to pay for any extra charges," Caren said.

"No, that will not be necessary. Please leave a note in the guest book before you go. I love to read what our guests think."

"I'll be pleased to leave something special for ye."

An hour after breakfast, Declan stood in the main room and finished the entry in the guest book. He left a message for anyone that might intend to harm this family.

"Ready?" she asked.

"Yes. We need to leave."

"You didn't change out vehicles this time?"

"I don't believe it will make a difference if we've been compromised. The truck is solid, something we may need on the road," Declan answered.

They walked out to the black Ram pickup where Derrick and Daisy waited.

"Thank you for a nice visit." Caren said.

"Gloria, it's been a pleasure to have you both."

Daisy gifted the left-over morning muffins to them.

"Nevin, come back anytime."

Derrick shook his hand.

"Aye, I will."

"Where are you two headed?" Daisy asked.

"West, towards the coast," Caren said.

They drove away from the B&B with the knowledge should anyone inquire about their presence false information would be given.

●

The morning chores at the Long-Bowe proceeded as they always did when guests left. Daisy cleaned, changed linens, placed fresh flowers in each room and prepared for the next guest. She walked into Derrick's office with a sandwich and observed a smile that seemed to grow as Daisy approached the desk.

"Why are you smiling?"

"We've had a good year so far. If it continues, we'll show a profit," Derrick said and took the sandwich.

Daisy wrapped her arms around Derrick and kissed the top of his head. The sound of motorcycles outside stopped any further conversation. She walked to the window and observed two riders.

"Derrick, you didn't accept another reservation and not tell me, did you?"

Derrick joined her at the window.

"No, they're probably lost."

"I'll go check," Daisy said.

It wasn't unusual for people to stop and ask for directions. The signs that advertised the Long-Bowe often drew individuals to stop and inquire to prices or availability. Daisy walked out on the large porch and waited until both riders removed their helmets.

"Good day to ye," Brigid said.

"Hello, can I help you?" Daisy asked.

"We saw your signs and wanted to stop. Would ye be so kind to show us your home?"

"Please come in, and we have vacancies if you are interested," Daisy said.

"It's one of the reasons we stopped," Brigid said.

Daisy opened the door for them to enter. She was the perfect host and gave the couple the tour and short history of the Long-Bowe.

"Would you like something cold to drink or something to eat?"

Brigid looked at her partner. He nodded.

"Aye, thank ye."

"We have guest books if you'd like to read what our visitors have to say about their stay at the Long-Bowe."

"Where would those be located?" Brigid asked.

"In the next room, I'll bring your drinks in there," Daisy said.

She motioned for her partner to follow into the parlor where the guest book was proudly displayed. Brigid acknowledged Daisy when she joined them with refreshments.

"Who is Nevin and Gloria?"

"A lovely couple, cousins actually, taking a cross country trip. The man has the same accent as you. They left early this morning heading west."

The two unexpected visitors finished their drinks and left the Long-Bowe. Derrick walked out on the porch as they rode away.

"Are they coming back?"

"I don't believe they will," she answered.

"What did they say?"

"The woman didn't say too much, she seemed to be more interested in who had been staying with us."

CHAPTER THIRTY-FOUR

Glade Spring, Virginia

Declan knew the truck didn't need petrol, but it was better for it to be full. He needed time to think what would be ahead of them. If this was his plan, he would set a detour to force them off the main highway for control and privacy. A small group would continue to force them forward into an ambush. He looked up as Caren walked around the truck with two bottles of water.

"Would you like to inform me why we've been stopping every half hour?" She handed him a bottle.

"I think ye know why."

"It would be nice to have…"

Caren stopped mid-sentence to the sound of screeching tires.

They turned to see two motorcycles slide across the street, after being struck by a logging truck. She dropped the water and ran towards the wreckage before Declan could stop her. One body was pinned beneath massive trees that had broken free. The second body had landed in the main drive of the station. She stopped to check for signs of life. The rider's head was twisted, and, her bones protruded through the leather pants. Declan raised the visor on the helmet and backed away.

"We need to go!"

"Declan, she's…"

"She's dead."

He scanned the area to make sure no one had seen them at the body. He took Caren's arm, moved quickly back to the truck, and pulled the map of Virginia out to look at their choices. The sounds of sirens and flashing lights came from all directions.

"The road is going to be a bloody mess for hours."

"You know that woman?"

Declan turned back at the carnage of the wreck, and several individuals had gathered around the body.

"Brigid Murphy, an explosives expert for hire, and someone who would follow orders."

"They were following us."

"Aye."

"I think we need to keep on the main highway," Caren told him.

"If we continue, there will be a detour ahead us," he said.

"Ambush."

"Aye, we'd have to run the blockade."

"Declan, do we have a second choice?"

"Take the detour, fight our way through them."

"Those aren't choices they're just different options with the same outcome, we have to fight," Caren said.

"They have lost two from their team."

They turned back to see several highway patrol and local police pull into the parking lot of the station. One officer turned towards them, Declan took Caren in a protective embrace and buried her face in his chest.

"Did you see anything, sir?" the young officer asked.

"No, my wife is very upset about all of this," Declan responded.

"Stay there."

"We need to go before they decide to speak to us," she said.

"Aye, we need to prepare for what is ahead."

They were rerouted by authorities back to Highway 81. He became anxious the longer they remained on the highway. Declan suddenly took the exit to Highway 77 south, drove a few miles, and then turned down a dirt road. He took the map, opened the door and walked to the back of the truck. A few minutes later Caren appeared next to him.

"Declan, we can't stay here. There's too much traffic on the main road. We're exposed."

"We should've taken the park roads into the mountains."

"Declan, we took what was the best choice."

"Aye, but it wasn't, I feel like a coward running when I prefer to fight. I know we're still outnumbered."

"We need to see where this road goes. Maybe, there's another option."

Declan lowered the tailgate, took the map, and traced a route with his finger.

"If we continue on 77 until we reach 221, the road will head north towards Lynchburg."

"I suggest we drive into Alexandria and find a place to stay for a few days," she said.

"Lass, I'm going to need some time to arrange safe places for us."

"I'll do some research on the information Daisy gave me, and check the county clerk's office."

"No outside trips without a disguise."

"Understood."

"Caren, the men chasing us do not care about civilian casualties. In order to obtain their objective, they will kill everyone in their path."

"I know, I promise."

They returned to the pickup and prepared to leave. Declan looked in the rearview mirror, his thoughts reverted to Boston. If he had just contacted the family sooner, they would be safe, alive. Caren would be with Aaron. He could not change the past, but would make sure she had a future.

CHAPTER THIRTY-FIVE

Clifton Forge, Virginia
Noon

Donovan and Craig walked out of the small diner into the chill of a light wind off the mountain. They walked back to the small motel around the corner where he had procured nearly every room. The owner was happy to accept them for an indefinite time. He had sent the rest of his team to the designated location to wait, and they would go every day until the plan was completed. His cell phone vibrated in his pocket.

"You're on speaker."

"I'm on my way to meet Brigid and her partner. They're on the move," Lee said.

"She made positive identification?" Donovan asked.

"Aye, no doubt. He left a message for anyone checking on him," Lee said.

"Message," Craig said.

"What kind of message?"

"The owners of the bed and breakfast keep a comment book for their guests. Declan left a warning," Lee said.

"Christ! Donovan, he knew we were here."

"What was the warning?"

"He would return one day to celebrate the long life of the B&B and its owners."

"In plain words, the location and owners are to remain untouched," Craig said.

"What about the owners. What did Brigid tell ye?"

"They had no idea of the true identity of their guests," Lee said.

"When did they leave?" Craig asked.

"They left two hours ago in a black Dodge Ram pickup. They told the couple at the bed and breakfast they were headed west."

"No, they are headed this way," Donovan said.

"Are ye sure?" Lee asked.

"Jesus, Lee. Have ye forgotten everything? Ye never give the correct information to anyone that could be asked or interrogated," Donovan said.

"I'll contact the team. Let them know Declan is coming. Anything else?" Craig asked.

"They are to follow the plan, no variance or I'll kill them myself. Lee, when ye catch up to Brigid, the same information goes for everyone. We have a chance here to be successful and, leave here alive, wealthy bastards. Don't get brave and do something stupid."

"Aye," Lee said.

"Where did Brigid say to meet them?"

"Wytheville."

"Keep me informed," Donovan said.

Craig walked back towards Donovan.

"I have been assured they are in position and ready."

"We'll leave here once Lee picks them up. I need to be sure only Declan is killed."

"Have ye called Alex?" Craig asked.

"I think it might be wise to wait," Donovan said.

"In case the plan doesn't succeed."

"I would prefer to give him good news instead of another explanation of failure."

"Aye, I wish ye'd had a few more men," Craig said.

"Money is a powerful weapon to lure men, but it means nothing compared to demons and the rumors a dead man has returned."

●

Wytheville, Virginia

Lee felt positive after his conversation with Donovan and increased his speed towards Wytheville. The team would be in their positions off eighty-one and Den Hill Road. He believed this time the plan would succeed this time. He began to notice the amount of traffic had increased. In another mile it was bumper to bumper. The highway was at a total standstill. He stopped and exited his vehicle, but the sound of a speaker caused him to turn around.

"Sir, you need to return to your vehicle."

The officer was on the shoulder next to his car. Lee walked over to speak with him.

"What's the problem, officer?"

"A major accident with fatalities at the next exit. It will take hours to clear the scene. Traffic is being rerouted," the officer answered.

"I was meeting friends at the next exit. They were driving a black Ram pickup. Could ye check to make sure it wasn't my friends?"

"Just a moment," the officer said, and checked his computer.

Lee hoped the fatalities were them. He could report their death, pick up Brigid and her partner, collect their money, and go home. He almost smiled as the officer turned back to him.

"A black pickup you said?" the officer asked.

"Yes, I pray it isn't them."

Lee felt like the pot of gold was at the next exit.

"Your friends should be safe. This accident involved motorcycles."

"Were there fatalities?" Lee asked.

"Yes. A man and woman."

"I appreciate your time. They're probably caught up in all this traffic. I'll give them a call."

Lee returned to the vehicle, and leaned into the steering wheel. He reached for the cell and pressed Donovan's number.

"Lee, are ye three are on your way?" Donovan asked.

"There has been a complication."

"Someone had better be dead."

"I believe Brigid and her partner have been killed," Lee said.

"Killed how? Declan?"

"No, a traffic accident."

"Have ye seen Declan?" Donovan asked.

"I'm at a standstill in traffic. The only thing I see is the back of about forty trucks and cars," Lee answered.

"Jesus Christ! Find a way to get out and meet me in Blacksburg."

The next hour and a half, Lee inched his way to the second Wytheville exit, then reversed his direction. They had failed again and, lost two team members. Lee began to shake and pulled to the side of the road. The voice filled his mind, the one from the cemetery that night in New Orleans.

"The devil has come for you."

•

Blacksburg, Virginia

Donovan had contacted the team and sent them back to the motel in Clifton Forge. They were given orders to pack and be ready to leave in the morning. He relented and allowed them a night to relax with a harsh warning.

"Any team member that brought interest from law enforcement would be killed."

He had never been involved in a job with such failure. If he believed in curses, this operation would be it. They sat in a back booth where he could watch for Lee in the small coffee shop.

"Donovan, what now?" Craig asked.

"Wait for Lee and back to the motel," Donovan said.

"My time is up here. There's not much more I can do to help ye."

"Aye, the only person that knows anything is Alex."

"Donovan, ye need to push that little bastard harder for information."

"He has held back information from day one of this fiasco. His vendetta is stacking up the wrong bodies."

"Something else is bothering your mind. Don't be lying to me because I'll know," Craig said.

"Declan's second sense isn't due to his training or by accident," Donovan said.

"What are ye trying to say?"

"The training only focused what he already possessed naturally, made it stronger."

"Ye sound like you've had too much Jameson," Craig said.

"Did ye know his mum had the sight?"

"Are ye saying she was a seer?" Craig asked and crossed himself. Donovan nodded.

"Did Declan tell ye?" Craig asked.

"No, that fool Ferrell did, but I never believed in such stuff. I grouped it together with Leprechauns, pots of gold, and banshees."

"What changed your mind?"

"A foggy night in New Orleans."

Donovan waved as Lee entered the shop.

"What are ye going to do about the issue in Wyoming?" Craig asked.

"Confront Alex, and demand answers," Donovan answered.

"What if he doesn't answer ye?"

"I take my pay and try not to kill him. We'll see how well he fairs trying to find another crew to take on Declan and the ghost of Aaron Caydon."

"I think ye should kill him. The bloody bastard knows too much about all of us," Craig said.

Lee stopped the waitress, ordered something, and joined them.

"Who gave ye the information on Brigid?" Donovan asked.

"A Virginia highway officer," Lee said.

"Neither of them had identification," Craig said.

"Their fingerprints will identify them," Donovan said.

"What now?" Lee asked.

"Craig make arrangements to take a flight out of Roanoke. I'll have a car pick ye up at the motel.

"We'll have a pint when ye get back," Craig said.

"Lee, ye work alone from this point forward," Donovan said.

"Bloody fools keep getting killed," Lee said.

Donovan looked at his cell phone.

"Ye are just putting off the inevitable," Craig asked.

Donovan nodded and placed the call to Alex.

"The news is not good."

CHAPTER THIRTY-SIX

Moose, Wyoming
September 29th

The cold north wind caused Alex to steady himself. He waited outside his home for Donovan to dismiss what was left of the team. It appeared Caren's savior was quite the adversary, and he wished again to have hired this Declan first. He would obviously have succeeded, and Alex would be celebrating victory. This failure and Richard's earlier suggestion, had him form a new plan of total control. There would be one last job for Donovan and Lee. He would accept no refusal.

"Donovan! You and Lee come inside."

Alex turned and entered the cabin.

"What the hell does he want?"

"Donovan, I'm ready to go home," Lee said.

"Aye, I cannot imagine what he has to say."

"Just kill him. I don't care about the money.

Donovan checked his weapon.

"I may just do that very thing."

Alex heard them as they kicked the snow off their boots before they entered. He motioned for them to sit down at the table as they entered his home.

"Any issues?" Alex asked, then handed Donovan a full bottle of whiskey.

"A few," Donovan answered.

"What type of issues?"

"A couple felt their pay should be increased due to time wasted," Lee answered.

Alex placed three glasses on the table.

"Should I be concerned?"

Donovan held his hand up.

"They were given options. Leave here alive and very well paid, or not at all."

"I see they opted for the first."

"A few had to be reminded that this job was not to be spoken of once they returned home," Lee said.

"I have one item I wish to discuss with you."

Lee glanced towards Donovan.

"What could we possibly have left to discuss?" Donovan asked.

"One final job."

"Alex, what the hell makes ye believe the two of us would accept another job?"

"We had an entire team that failed," Lee added.

"A direct approach and this," Alex said.

He threw two large envelopes on the table. Both men opened them and began to count the bundles of hundred-dollar bills.

"Ye have my attention," Donovan said.

"Half now, the rest when we return."

Alex walked away as his phone rang. Donovan poured a drink and sat back in his chair.

Lee leaned over the table.

"I don't know about this."

"I want to hear what he has to say."

"Your greed is going to get us killed," Lee said.

"I apologize but arrangements had to be confirmed."

"Ye made arrangements before either of us agreed to your offer," Lee said.

"Do I detect hesitancy?"

"Three dead, four failed operations, and ye are no closer to your goal," Donovan said.

"It was bad luck. That's all," Alex said.

"You've held back information that might have been beneficial. Why?" Donovan asked.

"You have a choice to join me and receive another envelope to match what's on the table or leave with nothing. Do you really want to return to Ireland with the strong possibility a story of your failure will beat you home? I do not believe that will be good for future business."

Lee touched the stack of money.

"Another envelope just like this one?" Lee asked.

"Yes."

"I'm in," Lee said.

Donovan glanced at the stack of hundred-dollar bills.

"This is the last one," Donovan said, then emptied his glass.

Alex took a moment and, filled their glasses to seal the agreement.

"Here's to the last job."

"The last job," they said.

"I have one last arrangement to be made, it could take a couple of days," Alex said.

"What type of arrangement?" Donovan asked.

"A private plane."

"Praise the saints. I couldn't face another cross-country drive," Lee said. Where to this time?"

"Virginia. Sorry gentlemen, but I detest road trips," Alex said.

Lee filled his glass again, and looked at Donovan.

"You're coming?" Donovan asked.

"Yes," Alex said.

"Why?" Lee asked.

"Things should end where they began," Alex answered.

"Jesus, let's go Lee. Text us when it's time to leave," Donovan grabbed the bottle.

"I will do that," Alex said.

CHAPTER THIRTY-SEVEN

Caren filled her coffee cup and walked over to the padded bench in the small breakfast nook of the house. She watched the birds from the bay window as they gathered for their morning feast, only to be scattered by their nemesis, Mr. Squirrel. She took a sip of black coffee, settled into a favorite spot and hoped the dreary morning clouds would dissipate. She placed her cup on the ledge and reached for the information they had gathered over the last few weeks. The highlighted sections of the map were the neighborhoods they had checked with no success. She raised her head as Declan entered the kitchen.

He filled his cup.

"What's the plan for today?"

"The same as yesterday and the day before that. Continue to search until we find him."

"Ye look worried."

"Bevan is our only connection to Aaron."

Caren turned her head back towards the feeder.

"Let me have a look, lass," Declan said, and took the map.

"We have three neighborhoods left. He must live in one of them."

"Unless he has moved," he said.

"We'll know in the next couple of days. Any signs we've been discovered here?"

"I haven't seen anything, but that doesn't mean they aren't here. Can I get ye more coffee?"

"Yes, thanks."

"Today's choice of dress will be business or casual?"

"Business, if you were able to get the identifications we needed," she answered.

"I was successful, but they did not come cheap," Declan said.

Caren took a sip of coffee

"We're not running out of money, are we?"

"Ye remember the box from the cemetery?"

"Yes."

"I still haven't counted the money."

"Today is a holiday for some government agencies. I want to leave by nine in order to catch as many people home as possible."

"I'll shower and get ready," he said.

Caren watched the man who had been her companion and bodyguard for the last ten months. He had carried and comforted her through the worst time imaginable. Declan had made her smile more than once since Boston; an impossible thought due to the tragedy she had endured. She finished another cup of coffee and proceeded down the hall.

"Dammit!"

Caren stopped at the bathroom door.

"Declan are you okay?"

"Yes, lass, I just bumped my head on this bloody small shower again."

Caren smiled.

"Are you bleeding?"

"No!"

"I'm headed to my room."

"I'll be ready in twenty," he said.

Caren had offered him the larger room with the bigger shower, but being a gentleman, he refused. She knew this was the fourth or fifth time he had fought with the showerhead. Twenty minutes later, Caren had dressed and packed her duffle. She walked into the kitchen and dropped it next to Declan's. She turned when Declan entered the kitchen from the garage.

"Is there an issue?" Caren asked.

"I almost shot the neighbor's cat, again."

"Too much Jameson last night?"

"It's possible, but it feels different outside today."

Declan picked up their bags.

She was pleased the clouds had cleared to a brighter day. It was a good omen. He drove them into the next neighborhood on their list to be checked. Fall had come to Reston. Each home they passed was decorated with ghosts, goblins and pumpkins. Caren closed her eyes and attempted to stop the memory of her children.

"Mom, make Kieran stop," Enora screamed.

"She's being a baby," he said, and began to chase her in his Wolf-man mask.

"Stephen, did you buy extra candy for tonight?"

"Caren, Caren!" Declan said.

She opened her eyes.

"Is something wrong?

"Ye grabbed me, lass, did ye see something?"

"Sorry, we can stop here."

She waited as he removed two wallets from his jacket and handed one to her. The face on the identification indicated she was an investigator for Fairfax County Police Department.

"It's time to see if these things are worth the money we paid."

"This is very impressive," she said.

"Lass, are ye ready?"

Caren didn't answer but took the gun from her holster, chambered a round, and replaced it.

"I would appreciate a quick overview of today's story," Declan said.

"We're attempting to locate witnesses in a bank robbery."

The photograph of Bevan and Aaron was pulled from her pocket.

"Lass, he isn't going to look like the photograph."

"It's all I have for a reference."

She placed the photograph back in her pocket and joined him at the first walkway. The holiday would only affect government workers today, and it was apparent most people in the neighborhood had regular jobs. She stopped and waited for Declan to turn around.

"What's wrong?" he asked.

"I think we should have done this after five. Most of these people are at work."

"Caren, we have two houses left. If no one is home we'll return this evening."

"Two more."

The sound of motorcycles startled both of them. Declan stepped in front of Caren in a protective stance. She tugged on his jacket and pointed to the newspapers stacked on the steps of the next house.

"One less to check," she said.

Declan opened the gate to the last residence. They both turned and noticed the same motorcycles pass the crossroad again as they proceeded to the front door of the house.

"Your turn, lass."

"Ready?"

"Go ahead, I'm not comfortable with the motorbikes."

Caren rang the bell and was pleased to hear a dog bark.

"General! Hush."

The voice of a child admonished the dog. A young girl of ten or eleven opened the door.

"Good afternoon, young lady."

"Hello," the young girl said.

The chocolate lab with a gray muzzle stood guard next to the her.

"Are your parents' home?"

Caren presented her badge and identification.

"Dad! there's a lady here with a badge asking to speak to my parents."

The girl called in a child's sing song voice.

The sound of heavy footsteps in a hurried pace approached the front door. A tall man with black and grey hair greeted them.

"Can I help you?"

Caren removed the photograph and closed her eyes.

"Bevan Benjamin?"

"Yes, what is this about?"

Declan had stepped off the stoop, but returned as the door opened.

"We've been searching for you."

She noticed the expression on his face as she presented the identification again.

"Sarah, I need you to take the General out back please," Bevan said.

"But…"

"Now."

His firm but stern fatherly tone was obeyed.

"Yes, sir."

Sarah took the dog and walked away.

"Sir, may we come in?"

"I'm a fairly good judge of people and excellent at false identifications. The one you have just presented is one of the best forgeries I've had the opportunity to inspect. If you intend to enter my home you will properly identify yourself. Who are you?"

"We need to get inside. Tell him, lass."

"My name is Caren Johnson. I'm searching for my brother, Aaron Caydon."

CHAPTER THIRTY-EIGHT

Today was the end and the beginning of a life and world without Aaron Reece Caydon. He thought about all the circumstances that occurred to get to this day. Caydon had caused enough death and heartache over too many decades. His life and lies had left a bloody trail across the world, but now, it was over. Bevan thought about the box that contained the ashes of Caydon lying in the trunk of his car as he drove to the cemetery. This act was self-imposed; a final responsibility to the world in order no others would rise.

As he stood in the bright sunshine of this Texas morning, a clean breath of fresh air swept by Bevan's face. When the backhoe finished, he waited until the caretaker motioned for him to approach the grave. He walked slowly to the opening and placed the ashes of Archidamus Karsten Werner into the grave. It was then filled, and the ground was leveled. The case file and all information on Caydon's genetic makeup had been burned in his fireplace. His personal information had already found its way into the shredder.

Bevan stood for a moment and looked at the lonely graves of the family before him. The only identification that they had ever existed was the dates of birth and death for Karsten and Liesel Werner on a dirty metal plate. It was sad that this simple acknowledgment would have to remain as it stood. He knew somewhere Caydon's daughter existed, but he prayed she would remain unknown, never to be found.

●

The memory and young woman's announcement had kept Bevan speechless for a what felt like an eternity. In ten years, there had been no need to repeat Caydon's name. Why had she searched for him? Who had given his location? Why does she need Caydon? He wanted to tell her Caydon was a sociopathic murderer and was dead. Bevan wished he could shut the door and pretend these people weren't here. He began to realize what their presence might mean and jumped as his wife touched his arm.

"Bevan," Laura said.

"Laura, could you and Sarah go to our bedroom?"

He felt his wife's hands trembling as she released his arm and walked away. He turned back to the strangers at his door.

"I need a moment before I allow either of you into my home," Bevan told them.

"We need to come inside. Someone may have followed us," Declan said.

"You brought them to my front door!"

"Please," Caren said.

"Remain in the entry until I settle my family."

Bevan unlocked the outside door.

They entered, and his home was secured with everyone now inside.

"Thank you," Caren said.

"Do not leave this entry until I return," Bevan said.

He walked to the master bedroom, where his daughter and General were on the bed watching a movie.

"Mommy's in the closet," Sarah said.

Laura exited with a weapon.

"I hope you'll not need that," he said

"Who are these people?"

"I would like for the three of you to leave and not come back until I call you."

"I refuse to go anywhere until you answer my question. Bevan, don't try to lie your way out of this one. Strangers do not appear on our doorsteps for no reason."

Bevan smiled at his defiant wife.

"The woman is Caren Johnson. She's looking for her brother, Aaron Caydon."

"Oh my God, Bevan."

The color drained from her face.

"My concern will always be for your safety, please go. I'll call when they've left the house."

He walked over and held his wife.

"Sarah, please take the general and go to the car."

"Where are we going, Mommy?"

"We're going to take General to the park."

Laura walked back to the closet and pulled two prepacked bags out.

"To-go bags?" Bevan asked.

She nodded.

"I've lived with you long enough to know obstacles can take longer than an afternoon."

The changes in their home and daily lives had been a direct cause due to Aaron Caydon. He watched as his wife took the weapon and placed it in a side holster on her belt. He followed her to the garage, kissed both, and waited until the closure of the garage door assure his family had left. He reentered the closet, opened the gun safe and obtained his service weapon. Bevan placed it in the small of his back and returned to the front entry.

"I'll ask that you leave your weapons on the table. I'll place mine first," Bevan said.

"I can live with that," Declan said.

"Agreed. I'm here for information and your help," Caren said.

"We can speak in here," Bevan said.

They were led into a formal living room.

"Thank you again for allowing us inside," Caren said.

"I would normally do a body search, but I will take your word those were your only weapons," Bevan said.

Caren looked at Declan.

"Give them to him."

Declan reached in the small of his back and removed two knives. He placed them on the coffee table in front of Bevan.

"Thank you."

"I'm Declan Mallone."

He walked over and shook hands with Bevan.

"How long will your wife and child going be gone?" Caren asked.

"Until I'm sure it's safe for them to return. Please sit down. Why have you been searching for me?"

"One reason is because of this."

Caren handed the photograph to him.

"Where did you get this?"

Bevan remembered the day the photo had been taken. He leaned back into his chair. They were celebrating the end of their first successful case working as partners. He couldn't understand how it was possible for her to have this.

"It was left at my summer home in Maine, with a large amount of money. In the last ten months, I have lost my family, my home, and my way of life. The information I have to tell you will take longer than an afternoon."

"Are you associated with the bombing in Maine? What about Boston?"

"Yes, both."

"My office received information weekly on this investigation. The FBI believe you orchestrated the entire situation."

"I can assure you. I did not kill my family."

"What about you, Declan? What's your story?"

"I'm here to protect her."

Bevan thought about Laura's reference to obstacles. He needed to know why Declan was Caren's personal security. There had been only one photograph taken in New Orleans. He had attempted to give it to Aaron, but he refused to take it. The last time Bevan set eyes on it was four years ago. He had kept it locked in the bottom drawer of his desk at the office. He needed to make a call. There was one person who could check on this puzzle, someone who was familiar with Caydon.

"I have an associate that would be helpful. May I call him to come join us?"

"Declan, I see no reason to object."

Declan shrugged his shoulders.

"I'd feel better if our odds were increased."

"Please, make your call," Caren said.

"Bevan, contact your wife and inform her not to return. It's not safe," Declan said.

He stood to leave the room.

"My wife knew they would not be returning when I kissed them goodbye."

He walked down the hallway to his office, shut the door, and picked up the phone on his desk. If he made this call, it could have repercussions, but sometimes a price had to be paid. Bevan pressed the direct line to his office at the CIA.

"What's up, boss?"

Bevan heard the squeak of his chair.

"I thought I might find you there."

"Bevan, this is the last time I do you a favor. The desert training was literally a pain in my ass. I'm still pulling cactus needles from places I'd rather not mention."

"Lane..."

"I sent you my full report, and we need to have a long conversation about my request to go back to field work. I hate all this damn paperwork and whining about reports not being sent on time. You need to saddle up and get back here."

"Lane!"

"What?"

"Do you have any plans?"

"You know it, boss. I have a hot date with my couch, ESPN, and a six pack of Guinness. Why are you asking?"

"I need for you to put ESPN on hold, and get that six pack on your way to my house. I have an issue of importance here, and it will require your assistance."

"Bevan, I don't know what kind of an issue you have at the house, but it will   have to wait. I'm drinking beer, eating pizza with Fred and watch some football, in about an hour."

"This is not something I can put away and fix later. You need to listen to me. This is an ARC problem."

He could hear the chair squeak as Lane changed positions. The next noise was the sound of a drawer open and a candy wrapper being torn open.

"I'm on my way, boss."

"Lane, before you leave. I need you to open the locked bottom drawer on your right."

"You know I don't have a key."

"It's never stopped you before," Bevan told him.

"What do you need, boss?"

"There is a small six by six envelope under the metal box."

"Found it."

"Open it and tell me if there is anything in it,"

"A note that says, 'Thanks for the memory.'"

"Get here as soon as you can," Bevan said.

He picked up the wooden frame that held the photograph of his wife and child. It appeared his office was not secure. Caydon had once entered his home, tied Laura to a chair while she was pregnant and threatened the lives of everyone he loved. Lane's last encounter left him wounded and his partner near death. He smiled as the cell rang.

"Is everything good at the house, Bevan?"

"You were correct in taking the bags. This is going to take more than a few hours."

"I didn't think this would be something the dog park could fix. How did she find us?"

"I'm not sure, but Lane is on his way to help. We will be gone for an undetermined amount of time. Do you have enough in those bags to last you for a week or more?"

"We'll go to Waynesboro and check on your mother. I knew home-schooling would be beneficial one day. If we need anything, I have plastic."

"Call me tonight when you stop."

"We'll be fine."

"Give my love to Sarah."

"Please be careful."

Bevan ended the call and, walked back to where his guests had been left. He discovered Declan at the front window.

"Did you contact your wife?"

"Yes," Bevan answered.

"I hope the individual ye called arrives soon," Declan said.

"An hour maybe less."

"It might be safer if both of you, come with us," Caren said.

"If it's not safe for my wife and child to be here, then I agree."

CHAPTER THIRTY-NINE

Bevan Benjamin's home
Dusk

The urgency in Bevan's voice, and mention of Aaron Caydon, pushed Lane to make a fast trip for a cold six pack and two more PayDays. He had no idea why after ten years there would be any reason to speak that monster's name. Lane had pushed the death and destruction as far away as possible in the recesses of his mind.

He arrived, parked in his usual place in front, and grabbed the beer and candy. When he reached for the handle and found it locked, an alarm sounded in his brain. Lane had a key, so he reached in his pocket. He found it and unlocked the door.

"Boss, what's the deal with the locked door? You called me remember?"

He discovered the assortment of weapons displayed on the entry table.

"Bevan!"

"Are you armed?"

"You know I am. I see yours, but who the hell owns the others? Why are all of them out here?"

"Lane! Leave your weapon on the table and come inside."

He shuffled the six pack of beer and placed his weapon with the others. He walked into the family room and regretted his decision.

"Declan Carrick Mallone, you bastard!"

"Good to see ye too, Lane. I'll take one of those beers."

Lane threw a can towards him.

"I thought you were dead," Lane said.

Declan caught it with one hand.

"Ye wished I was dead."

Declan tapped the top and opened the can.

"Knives?" Lane asked.

"On the table," Bevan answered.

"All of them?"

"Today, I felt two would be enough. If I had known we would be meeting again, I would have brought them all."

"It appears we're going to have a little more to discuss than finding your brother," Bevan said.

"We should go," Caren said.

"Declan can ride with me."

"Lane, this isn't going to be an issue, is it?"

"Not for me," Declan answered and emptied the can.

Bevan became concerned when Declan answered first.

"Lane! Is this going to be a problem?" Bevan asked again.

"No."

He observed Bevan walk to the front closet in the hallway and pull a black duffle out.

"This is going to take more than a day," Bevan said.

"I have one in the car. Let's go, Declan. Time to catch up," Lane said, and made a note where Declan placed the two knives from the coffee table.

The four reached the entry, weapons were reclaimed, and Declan tossed a set of keys to Caren.

"Our car is at the end of the street. Please apologize for me, when you speak again to your wife."

"My wife has become accustomed to adjustments at any given time. It is one of the reasons our daughter is homeschooled."

Lane secured his weapon and was impressed with Caren's handling of the Glock. The security alarm was set and the four of them walked to the end of the block where a black SUV was parked.

"We have a safe house," Declan said.

"Is it far?"

"It's located on the other side of town," Caren answered.

"Caren, give me a moment," Bevan said.

He motioned for Lane to follow him.

"This is not exactly what I expected when you said ARC problem."

"What do you think?"

"You're asking me? Declan Mallone, ex IRA soldier, in the company of a madman's daughter. This is a new one for me. What's the plan?"

"Lane, this is one time I don't have a clue. I'm afraid until we hear what Caren has to say we'll be flying blind."

"Well, I'm hungry. Hope she likes Asian."

Lane and Declan waited until the SUV had left to walk back towards his Jeep. He motioned for Declan to circle Bevan's home. They met in the backyard and checked the alley.

"Did ye see something?"

"It was your demeanor when we left the house."

"Things have been difficult for us."

"Are you hungry?"

They walked back and entered the Jeep.

"I could eat. Ye still eating those shitty PayDays?"

"You still killing children?"

The long silence indicated Lane should have taken the knives.

"I don't do that anymore."

Declan checked the side mirror.

"Since when?"

He repeated the same check on the driver's side.

"Since they killed my mum."

Lane turned in his seat and faced Declan.

"I'm sorry about your mum. She was a good woman, but our sins don't always rest upon the shoulders of those who commit them do they?"

Lane started the Jeep and drove away.

"Aye, but she had nothing to do with my work."

"I assume you are or have avenged her death?"

"A few have paid, but not the one who actually murdered her."

"Declan, what did you do to warrant a family member's death?"

"The one thing soldiers aren't supposed to do."

"You left your team on an operation."

"I couldn't…"

"Hold that thought. Any requests?"

Lane drove into the local Asian drive thru.

"No, we'll be good with whatever ye order."

"Welcome to the Happy Duck, can I take your order?" a male teenage voice asked.

"I need a number three and a number four with extra egg rolls."

"How many extra egg rolls?"

"Eight extra egg rolls and a number six with three extra orders of fried rice," Lane said.

"I'll have your total at the window, pull forward."

Declan shook his head at Lane's order.

"Jesus, ye haven't changed."

"There are four of us eating. I don't want to run out."

He leaned out the driver's window and took three large bags from a teenager.

"I thought that was you, Lane. Thanks for the tip."

Lane drove to the exit and pulled into traffic.

"Declan, what the hell are you doing with Caydon's dau…sister?"

"Daughter?"

"Where are we going?"

"Ye passed the turn three blocks back on the way to the Happy Duck. What do ye mean by daughter?"

Lane made a U-turn at the next light and knew he had made a huge mistake.

"How long have you been on this job?

"I don't play like that, ye answer my question first."

Declan could see the lights of a firetruck coming fast.

"I see them," Lane said.

He pulled to the curb as two Reston City firetrucks passed them.

"We need to hurry," Declan said.

"It must be a bad one to send two."

"This is not a good sign."

Lane stopped two blocks away from the fire that had consumed a residence.

"Your safe house, I assume."

"Caren."

"They're probably on the other side of the trucks."

His cell buzzed with a text.

"Where are they?" Declan asked.

"I need the address of the backup location."

"Lane move your ass. I'll tell ye when we are away from here."

"Does this happen often?"

"Unfortunately, aye."

CHAPTER FORTY

Falls Church, Virginia

The trip to the condo would not take long, and Declan would be happy to get the bags of food out of his lap. He continued to check the side mirror for uninvited guests. He thought about the slip of information Lane had given him. What else did he know that concerned Caren? He realized this job involved details that were purposely deleted.

"Lane, circle the block a couple more times."

When they reached the condo on the fourth round, Lane stopped.

"I hope the food is still hot."

They reached the door and found it slightly open.

"Lane."

"I see it."

They placed the bags down and pulled weapons.

"Put your weapons away. I saw you coming," Bevan said.

"We'd been here sooner if Declan hadn't insisted on the scenic route times four."

Lane picked up the food.

"Were you followed?"

"No, where's Caren?"

"Upstairs in the shower," Bevan answered.

"I understand my charge is Aaron Caydon's daughter," Declan said.

Bevan looked at Lane and closed his eyes.

"I slipped, sorry."

"Sister or daughter, which is it?" Declan asked.

"For the moment she will remain his sister. I need to make a call and obtain some paperwork."

Lane was shocked at Bevan's comment.

"You saved information?"

"Two items I believed might be needed one day," Bevan answered.

"I guess today is that day," Lane said.

"I had prayed this day would not come," Bevan said.

"Declan, I want to know why the hell you're involved in this?"

Bevan held his hand up to stop their conversation when he heard Caren on the stairs.

"Lane, you're not going to believe this," Bevan said.

Both men stepped back as she came into the room.

"You two look like you've seen a ghost," Caren said.

"You have a strong resemblance to another individual," Lane said.

"I've never been told that in my life," she said.

"The lass has had to wear disguises for months."

"Bevan, I would like to eat and start my story tomorrow."

"I do not have a problem with that."

"It appears the events of the past ten months have finally caught up with me."

"Is there an alarm system here?"

"I don't trust them," Declan said.

"Yes, there is an alarm system that can be set internal or external," Caren answered.

"Lane, decide who takes first watch," Bevan said.

"Declan and I will do it together. We need to catch up."

"We have this place for three days," Declan said.

"There is another safe house if we need to leave," Caren said.

"We can make that decision later," Bevan said.

Lane emptied the contents of the bags.

"Damn, the egg rolls are cold."

"The microwave works and you are welcome to use the stove," Caren told him.

"Thank you, kind lady."

The sounds of pots and pans began to fill the kitchen. Lane watched as Caren filled a plate.

"If you will excuse me, I'll eat in my bedroom."

"Can I help, lass?"

"I'll be fine."

Caren placed a bottle of water in her robe pocket.

"Good night," Bevan said.

They watched as she disappeared upstairs then began to fill their plates. Lane and Declan found places on opposite sides of the table. They stopped eating when Bevan walked past them.

"Where are you going, boss?"

Bevan's phone played a song. He placed his plate down.

"Your wife?"

He nodded at Declan and walked away, but returned a moment later.

"Are they in a safe place?" Declan asked.

"Yes, she stopped south of Richmond for the night. They're going to Waynesboro."

"What's wrong, boss?"

"I need to call Bentwood."

"Who is that?"

"An old friend."

"He has the information doesn't he, boss?"

Lane watched as the call to Bentwood was made and left on speaker for all to hear.

"Hello Bevan, I assume the information you sent ten years ago is needed," Bentwood said.

"Yes."

"I'll overnight it."

"Thank you," Bevan said and ended the call.

"Boss, go to bed."

"First, I would like to make a clarification. I do not care about your differences. Put them aside for now. There will be another time and place for you to deal with them. Do I make myself clear?"

"Yes, boss."

"Declan."

"Aye, I will."

Bevan took his food and disappeared upstairs.

•

They finished their meal in silence, cleared, the table and placed leftovers in the fridge. Declan returned to the table and began to place his knives in a row to be sharpened. He watched as Lane took two beers from the fridge.

"I'll make the first check, then we need to talk."

Lane placed a can of beer on the table.

Declan didn't answer as he spit on the stone and began to drag one of the knives across it. He wondered how this situation would eventually play out between them. He smiled when he felt Lane's presence behind him.

"Did ye forget the promise to your boss? Pull up a chair and put your ass in it."

Lane turned a chair around and straddled it.

"I have a few questions."

"I'm sure ye do. You're looking a little out of shape."

"Bevan has been out for a few months. I've been helping in the office."

"Desk job, ye say. I thought you'd packed on a few."

Lane leaned back and patted his abdomen.

"Muscle dude, all muscle. You want to tell me how you got involved in this mess?"

"I received a job offer paying an unbelievable amount of money and the opportunity to disappear from Ireland."

"Who made the first contact?"

"Ferrell."

"I didn't know he was still alive."

"Aye, and he can still outdrink either of us.

"How are your sisters?"

"All married with families. They asked from time to time if I'd heard from ye or knew if ye were doing well in the States."

Declan began to chuckle.

"Are you thinking about the confession you did in my name?"

"Aye, ye did a year's worth of Hail Mary's."

"You never told your family why we went separate ways, did you?"

"I didn't want ye to not be welcomed at our table whether I was there or not."

"Declan, tell me about this job."

"It was a simple job; go in, extract the family and leave. Things didn't go as planned."

"I can see that, or you wouldn't be sitting here. Who hired you?"

"Two men, an older guy. Doc Morres and one about our age named Marcus."

"What about Marcus's last name, and why didn't you ask questions?"

Declan laughed.

"Lane, the amount of money I was offered, why the hell should I?"

"What else?"

"The training…"

Lane interrupted him.

"You're a soldier, why would you need to be trained?"

"I asked the same question, but Marcus informed me I wasn't Caydon's soldier. The bastard ran my ass into the ground for weeks, in some type of advanced type of military training. I'll tell ye this, if all his men were trained like I was, he has an army."

"How were you supposed to contact this Morres, or get Caren where she needed to be?"

"I had four burner phones, used two, and two were destroyed in Maine when the house blew up."

"Who did that?"

"People ye know, Beck Flanagan and Lee Sheehan, but there are others involved. I first thought they might be after me. Ye know there's money for my death, and those two would be happy to collect it. As Beck was trying to kill me, he boasted they were after Caren."

"Anything else?"

"I killed him before I could ask who sent them."

"Caren said something about ten months. That's a long time to be on the run."

"Aye, she'll tell ye more tomorrow. Apparently, there was a backup plan I wasn't part of that involves cryptic clues that led us here. We have more money than we could ever spend."

Lane bent his head over the back of the chair.

"I have something to tell you, but I need your word it will not be repeated to Caren."

"Why?"

"Promise on your mother's soul, Declan."

"Aye, on my mother's soul, I'll not tell her."

"The road you're on is a dead end."

"Are ye lying to me, Lane?"

"Losing your touch?"

Lane pointed at the table.

Declan hadn't felt the knife as it cut his thumb, blood had begun to pool. He walked to the sink and turned on the faucet. Lane handed him a paper towel.

"Are ye telling me the man is truly dead?"

"The last time I saw Aaron Caydon was ten years ago as he bled out on a cold stone floor."

"Did ye kill him?"

"No, sorry to say. I was late to the party."

"Then who got that close?"

"Kyleigh."

"MacNeil?"

"He wasn't the savior she'd been told."

Declan placed both hands on the sink.

"Jesus, Mary and Joseph. Christ! I can't tell the lass her brother/father is dead. I wish ye hadn't told me."

"I don't want you to say anything, Declan. The information that is coming will explain things to her, but I'm curious about the clues and money. Do either of you have an idea of who left them?"

"She believes he left them."

"It's not possible."

"Ye know there are those who do not believe he is dead."

"Apparently the individuals chasing you are not worried about him. This is one time you can believe what I say. Kyleigh emptied a full clip into him center mass."

"When is the last time ye heard from Kyleigh?"

"I haven't seen or had word from her in five years."

"She's dead, Lane."

"Would you like to explain how you know that?"

"Three years ago, she was involved in a gun buy that went bad."

"Dammit, she swore to me that part of her life was over."

"Kyleigh lived on the edge, and took one too many chances."

"It appears you are following the same path."

"The individuals after Caren will do anything, kill anyone, to take her. Lane, we cannot fix what happened in our past."

"No, we cannot."

"I do not want any harm to come to the lass. I'm asking if ye'll have my back until she's safe?"

Declan never moved as Lane stood within inches of his face.

"Until this is situation is finished, I'll have your back as long as I don't find one of your knives in mine."

Declan began to walk away, but Lane grabbed his arm.

"Go ahead get it off your chest."

"Declan, your past leaves a bad taste in my mouth. I don't give a damn what saint you've prayed to, or penitence you've attempted for redemption. If you lie to me, or cross me, I will kill you where you stand."

"Ar uaigh mo mháthar geallaim," (On my mother's grave, I promise.)

Lane never moved.

"Glactar leis." (Accepted.)

"Ye surprise me."

"In what way?"

"I figured you'd given up our language."

"Riamh." (Never.)

CHAPTER FORTY-ONE

Falls Church, Virginia
Condo
October 15th
Noon

As Caren's eyes began to focus on the clock next to the bed, she believed it had stopped during the night. She could see daylight and moved to the window which verified it was truly noon. She had not slept past six-thirty in twenty years, it could be the events of yesterday had given her hope and peace. The smell of food hastened Caren's movements downstairs.

"Good afternoon."

Caren looked at the men at the table.

"Good to see ye slept in," Declan said.

She poured a cup of coffee.

"I'm pleased to see you and Lane didn't kill each other."

"There's food in the oven," Declan said.

"We've come to terms for now," Lane responded.

"Nice to know," Bevan said.

"What is this?"

"Laura calls it, morning breakfast dump."

Caren laughed, as the first bite melted into a wondrous mixture of flavors.

"Well, it's wonderful despite the name. Bevan, the information I have is involved and lengthy. It may be to your advantage to record or video it, I'm not opposed to either."

"We could use our phones," Lane said.

"I will assist you in any way possible to find my brother."

"Declan, who could have markers out on you?"

"This is not about me, they are after Caren," Declan said.

"Are you sure about that?"

"Positive," Declan answered.

"He had a brief opportunity to speak with one of the individuals," Lane said.

"Lee Sheehan and Beck Flanagan explosive experts from home," Declan said.

"They were responsible for my family's death and the destruction of the home in Maine."

"This information was told by?" Bevan asked.

"Beck, just before he died. He said their focus was on Caren," Lane answered.

"It appears you two had quite the conversation last night after I went to bed," Bevan said.

"There was someone else with them," Caren said.

"Who?"

"Not sure. Caren caught a glimpse of someone entering the house when we left," Declan answered.

"You couldn't identify him, Declan?"

"Lee caught me off guard. If it hadn't been for the lass, I wouldn't be here."

"Declan had passed out in the car and didn't see him," she said.

"It would be nice to know who else is involved," Lane said.

"Bevan, it appears my brother was more than just a businessman. What type of work would cause his family to be murdered?"

"He was involved in sensitive assignments during his years in the military," Lane said.

"He made a number of enemies while working for the Company."

"Company? What company are you speaking of?" she asked.

"Due to national security reasons, I am unable to give any details of his time with the CIA," Bevan said.

Caren began to laugh.

"My brother worked for the CIA? This is a joke."

The room became quiet. "Aaron Caydon worked at one time for the CIA as an agent. That is all I am allowed to tell you," Bevan said.

"You're serious. Declan, is he being serious?"

"I believe him, lass."

"It's true, Caren," Lane added.

She didn't understand why Aaron hadn't mentioned his association with the CIA. The national security card was a ploy when the government knew more that they were willing to explain.

"I guess we should begin," she said.

Bevan rose from the table.

"Do you have a journal or diary?"

"No need. The lass can remember every day of her life down to the last detail."

"Eidetic memory," Bevan said.

"A curse if you want my opinion."

"What is your earliest memory?" Lane asked.

"Lane, I have detailed memories back to the age of five."

"We can make notes if needed," Bevan said.

"I'd appreciate if we could do this in the other room," Caren said.

"Lane and I will make a couple of checks outside."

Caren began to clean the kitchen.

"Lass, I will take care of this later."

She joined Bevan in the main room. Declan and Lane left the condo to make a check of the area. She hadn't noticed Lane's appearance in detail until this morning. His stocky build, was a stark contrast to Declan's slimmer build. She had to look twice at his eyes, to make sure they were truly two different colors. One hazel, the other a deep blue.

"You and Declan have been extremely fortunate."

"The man has a wicked second sense, that has saved us more than once since Boston."

The front door was locked when the two returned.

"Things good outside?" Bevan asked.

"We're good," Lane answered.

"Caren, you have our attention."

"In June, 2004, a man delivered a wooden box containing two envelopes. One was a letter from Aaron advising he would be away for an undetermined time. The letter said he had found love and wished me happiness. The second contained a cashier's check for ten million dollars, which we placed in our lock box and never cashed. Eight years later, on December twenty-third, 2012 my life changed forever. My home was bombed, and my family was killed in a car wreck."

"Are you okay?" Bevan asked.

"I need to get something to drink."

She left the room.

"The missing money," Lane said.

"What missing money?" Declan asked.

"Aaron kidnapped the brother of a billionaire ten years ago. A large ransom was paid for the brother's return. I retrieved all, but ten million," Bevan answered.

"He sent it to Caren," Declan said.

"It appears he did," Bevan said.

Caren returned with a bottle of Jameson, and four glasses. She poured a small amount and drank it. She prayed the warmth of the liquor would make the rest of the story easier to tell.

"I hate to drink alone."

"Caren, do you still have that check?"

"Yes."

Bevan looked at Lane.

"Was there a reason you didn't cash it?" Lane asked.

"My husband is…was a hard worker, invested well, and we didn't need the money. He felt such a large sum would cause issues so we left it."

"Can you continue?" Bevan asked.

She nodded.

"I woke up in a motel with a strange man who I thought had kidnapped me…"

The rest of the afternoon Caren told the story of their journey in vivid detail. She stopped occasionally to refill her glass, take a Kleenex to wipe away the tears or go to the restroom. She repeated details when asked and ended the story with their arrival at Bevan's home.

"Gentlemen, I need a break and something to eat."

"I'll fix ye something."

"Caren, I am sorry for your loss. I have a few questions. Did Aaron ever talk about your parents, or his involvement in the military?" Bevan asked.

"Aaron never mentioned his time in the service. Our parents were killed in a car accident, and we were placed with a loving family but never adopted."

"What is your maiden name?"

"Werner."

"I hope there is a copy of your birth certificate in the lock box," Bevan said.

"I had one. It was in my Boston home. Aaron will have the original."

"I'd like to talk about the information in Maine. You believe Aaron left the boxes with information and money."

"I'm positive."

"Is there any possibility someone could have obtained access to the home in Maine?" Lane asked.

"A set of keys were left in a statue outside," she answered.

"Then it is possible someone else could've left the information and money," Bevan stated.

"I agree, anyone could have entered, but only three people had a combination to the safe, Stephen, myself and Aaron."

"You were there two years ago," Bevan said.

"My family was at the cabin two years ago this past summer. The items I found were placed after we left."

"I have to know what makes you positive Aaron left the money and photograph?"

"Bevan, what makes you believe he didn't?"

"Caren, please this is very important." Bevan said.

"Inside the safe was a Glock 22 and a white wooden rose. He sent white roses for all my special occasions. The Glock is not my weapon of choice and was not present in the safe when we left the house."

Caren observed the color drain from Bevan's face. He rose and paced the main room for several minutes.

"Lane, find another location for us."

"What's wrong with the other safe house?" Caren asked.

"Declan!"

"Aye."

He handed Caren a plate of food.

"Declan how close is the next safe house to this location?" Bevan asked.

"Thirty to forty minutes from here."

"Not far enough. Lane, do your parents still have property in Virginia Beach?"

"Yes, but it isn't available, I do have access to a sweet little place in Fredericksburg."

"We need to have access to it starting tomorrow."

Caren stood as Bevan took his coat and walked towards the front door. She took his arm and stopped him.

"Bevan, what do you know about me?"

He looked down at her.

"It's complicated."

"Boss, it will take me a few hours to make the arrangements," Lane said.

"Text me the location. I'll meet you tomorrow evening."

Bevan left them all standing attempting to understand what had happened.

Caren walked over to Lane and took his arm.

"What are you two not telling me?"

"I can't answer that," Lane said.

"Then tell me this, where is he going?"

"To get the answers."

CHAPTER FORTY-TWO

Alex stood at the bottom of the stairs in the cold dark cellar. He turned the flashlight on and searched the floor for any vestige of what had taken place years ago. His frustration grew as the stone floor refused to reveal the place where Caydon had died. The anger built rapidly and his hands shook so violently he dropped the light.

"I should've have been the one who killed the bastard. It was my right!"

"Alex!" Donovan called.

"Down here."

As the upstairs switch was flipped, the overhead light revealed the empty room. The sheer steps caused Donovan to hesitate unsure of his footing.

"Christ, these bloody things are dangerous. Who the hell would do that?"

"This home is over a hundred years old. People used what was available and made it work."

"I bet many broke a leg or two."

Alex ignored him, picked up the flashlight, and continued to search the floor.

"Did you return the motorcycles?" Alex asked.

"Aye, and wiped them down. What are ye trying to locate down here?" Donovan asked.

"Where is Lee?"

"He went to buy supplies. I know what you're searching for," Donovan said.

"I doubt that."

"I couldn't understand why ye brought us all the way out here."

"The fire you two started in Reston is still the top story on all the news stations for one," Alex said.

"You're trying to find the exact spot where Caydon died, aren't ye?"

"What if I am. It's my business."

"Why do ye care since the bastard is dead?" Donovan asked.

"If I told you what this meant to me, it wouldn't be possible for you to ever understand," Alex responded.

"Why don't ye share your reasons? I'd like to know why this vendetta is so personal."

"No."

"Alex, what are we doing out here?"

"Where the bloody hell are ye? I need some help up here," Lee called out.

"Go help Lee and let me be," Alex demanded.

"Aye, but I believe he feels the same as I about things."

Donovan left and slowly made his way upstairs.

"What were ye two doing in the cellar?"

"Alex was hoping to find a drop of Caydon's blood on the floor."

"Bloody hell, is this where he was killed?" Lee asked.

"According to information I have obtained, yes," Alex answered, as he exited the cellar.

"Alex, tell me we're not here to satisfy your sick obsession of Caydon," Donovan said.

"This will all be over by Sunday."

"Ye believe Declan will be stupid enough to walk into a trap," Donovan said.

"Ye are going to get us killed. We've lost enough good people," Lee said.

"Good you say, then why aren't they still alive?"

"Ye bloody bastard!"

Donovan stopped Lee.

"This job has been doomed from the beginning," Donovan said.

"We've been thwarted at every turn," Lee said.

"Ye know there is someone else involved. There has to be."

"Who? The ghost of Aaron Caydon perhaps? I believe it was your inability to have a plan that worked," Alex said.

"What makes ye believe everything is going to work out this time?" Donovan asked.

"I have an offer they cannot refuse."

"What would that be?" Donovan asked.

Alex looked at both of them.

"Do you know what your problem is?"

"No, please tell us," Lee said.

"You have no patience."

"Jesus Christ, I'm sick of your shit answers," Donovan said.

"What do you want us to do?" Lee asked.

"Follow orders," Alex said.

Donovan walked to a wine cupboard and took out two bottles of wine.

"At least the collection here is decent. I want to know how ye were able to rent this place?"

"The same way I've done everything else, money. Why?" Alex asked.

"Who wants to stay in a house where someone died? What about you, Lee?"

"No one knows what happened here," Alex said.

"I don't believe ye," Lee said.

"This house was sterilized," Alex said.

"By who?"

Donovan began to laugh.

"The government, ye ignorant ass."

"What do you know, Alex?" Lee demanded.

He smiled, turned and began to walk away. His hand reached out to steady himself.

"Have a drink, Lee."

"Aye, if my ass is going to have to sit and wait, I might as well get drunk."

Alex turned back towards the pair.

"Donovan, we have something to do tomorrow."

"I'm here to do your bidding."

Donovan raised his glass.

"What do ye plan to do until then?" Lee asked.

"The one thing I have been forced to do for ten years, wait," Alex said.

Lee began to put away the supplies he had brought inside.

"Do ye want a drink?"

"Aye, and fill it to the top of the glass, Donovan. Did ye notice he's having troubles again?"

"I guess it wasn't the miracle he'd hoped it would be."

●

Reston, Virginia

Bevan drove into the garage, watched closely as the door dropped, and locked him inside. He held the envelope from Hawaii and attempted to process the information that Caydon had been in Maine two years ago. He deactivated the alarm, turned on a light, and wished for the familiar sounds of home. The laughter of Sarah, the loving arms of his wife, and wagging tail of the General.

The simple things had become his whole world, which made Caren's loss too close. He could not go back and face her without first answering his own questions. Bevan opened the fridge and removed a bottle of water instead of the cold beer he truly wanted. He moved to the kitchen table, opened the envelope, and allowed the photograph of Vanora to slide into his hands. He placed the worn photograph presented next to it. The cell phone interrupted his thoughts.

"We're set for tomorrow in Fredericksburg."

"Text me the address. I'll meet you there."

"Where are you, boss?"

"At the house. Needed to check on a few things."

"Do you think that's a good idea?"

"I'm not concerned. However, I have some ghosts to clear out before I come back."

"I know the feeling. Take your time. We have the location indefinitely."

"I should be there late tomorrow."

"We'll be there," Lane said.

Caren was a true combination of her parents, with attributes of her mother and the memory of Caydon. He knew the poor copy of the birth certificate and photograph would definitely cause more questions than answers. He wasn't sure she would believe the information and worried it would cause her to distrust him. The buzz on his phone would be the address Lane promised. Bevan frowned at the message and dialed the number.

"It's been a while," the man said.

"Yes, it has been too long. What can I do for you?"

"I hate to inconvenience you," he said.

Bevan rubbed his forehead.

"What do you need?"

"I've been called for a review at the Company. I'm flying into Reagan tomorrow afternoon."

Bevan paused for a moment.

"I…"

"It's fine Bevan. I'll just take a cab."

"No, it's fine. I can pick you up. What flight and time?"

"I can't thank you enough. It'll be good to see you again."

Bevan took the information and disconnected. He made a quick text to Lane.

Message: Unexpected errand to run Thursday afternoon. Will be later than planned.

CHAPTER FORTY-THREE

The two large paper bags Gordon carried swayed as he walked down the long hallway to his suite. The original report from Boston indicated the plan had failed and all involved had been killed. Gordon had been relieved when Declan called to confirm Caren had been saved. Their loss of contact and information from the destruction of the home in Maine forced them to take action to find them.

The past year had not been pleasant, but they would never stop until Caren was in their safe keeping. Gordon shuffled the bags to another hand to use the key card. He waited a moment then opened the door.

"Doc!"

Marcus called out.

"Put your weapon away," Gordon told him.

"Smells like Italian."

Gordon waited for Marcus to come out of his room.

"Marcus, grab some plates and silverware, please."

"Wine?"

Marcus held up two bottles.

"Yes, red please." Gordon said, and removed two hot meals from the bags.

"I hope you bought extra garlic bread, Doc."

"I remembered your request, Marcus. Lasagna or stuffed shells?"

"Shells."

Marcus met Gordon at the table.

"To your health, Doc."

Gordon raised his glass.

"Salute."

Both men ate and drank in comfortable silence. Gordon removed a shell from Marcus's plate and added it to his.

"How's the jet lag?"

Marcus stopped eating and leaned back in his chair.

"Are we leaving?"

"Friday, we are to pick up two men to assist us."

"They must be close to us, Doc."

"We'll need air transportation."

"I'll arrange it. Is the location north or south of here?"

"South."

Marcus began to choke and cough. Gordon rose and moved to him.

"Are you okay?"

Marcus nodded, raised his hand, and took a drink of wine. Gordon returned to his chair.

"Doc, are we going to Mathews Virginia?"

"Yes, I think that's the name of the town, why?"

Marcus refilled his wine glass.

"Mathews is the last place I saw Caydon alive."

"You were the only person to make it out of that job, weren't you?"

Marcus nodded.

"I lost a number of good friends."

"Did you go out to the house with him?"

"No, I dropped him at the small airport. He paid me, shook my hand, and said goodbye."

"Was there anyone else with him?" Gordon asked.

"I was the only one of his men in the chopper. I remember a van at the airport. I can't say for sure if there was anyone in it."

"It has been a guess to what truly happened to him that night," Gordon said.

"I've heard rumors and stories that cannot be substantiated. I heard one story that he was an agent for the CIA and faked his death. Another indicated he was living in a foreign country. There are so many floating out there, take your pick, Marcus said."

"If Aaron is alive, he will be in plain sight and living well."

Gordon began to laugh.

"Why are you laughing?" Marcus asked.

"Aaron did work for the CIA years and years ago, but he left for bigger opportunities," Gordon said.

"That's information I didn't know. I cannot find anyone who has seen him in ten years," Marcus said.

"My guess, he's dead."

"I don't want to believe that Doc. It will be of interest to discover the association of these men to our situation."

"Agreed."

"Doc, you seem to have been closer to him or have known him longer. Did Caydon ever mention another team to you?"

"I may have known him longer, but he didn't share business affairs with me."

"I know of only one individual who was close enough to Caydon to know if there was another team."

"Who would that be?" Gordon asked.

"Daniel Dejongh."

"I understand a Ouija Board will be needed if we wish to have that conversation."

"Caydon was a master when it came to organization. It wouldn't surprise me, if he had another team," Marcus said.

"I assume you will know these men we are going to meet."

"I may not know their faces or names, but they will have an identifier."

"What do mean by an identifier?" Gordon asked.

"They will have a tattoo. It will be unique to their country and the specialized unit they served while in the military. Mine is from the Special Forces."

Gordon waited as Marcus rolled his sleeve up to display his.

"This type of tattoo will be their identification?"

"Yes," Marcus answered.

Gordon handed his plate to Marcus and waited until he returned from the kitchen.

"What if they don't have a tattoo?"

"I'll kill them."

CHAPTER FORTY-FOUR

Lane had not slept and paced the house which caused tension to grow among the three that worried about Bevan's absence. He continued to check for any answers from the multiple texts and voice messages that had been sent. When Bevan announced his intentions to remain at home overnight, he was concerned, but the added errand seemed a bad omen.

"Lane, stop your pacing and talk to us," Declan said.

"Where is Bevan?"

Lane rubbed the back of his neck and ignored Caren's question.

"Damn, Lane, tell us!"

Lane reached in his back pocket, pulled out a PayDay, tore open the wrapper and faced them.

"Lane, sit down, please," Caren said.

He finished the candy bar in two bites and found a chair.

"Where is Bevan?"

"For the last six months I've been working full time in the office."

"I knew it, prepping ye for a permanent desk job."

"No, and don't get your hopes up. I was temporarily assigned to Bevan's position."

Lane leaned forward and bowed his head.

"He's ill, isnt he?" she asked.

"No, the man looks fit," Declan said.

"I agree, Bevan does look fit now. He and Laura are runners. They have accomplished a number of marathons together. He loves to tell how fate intervened one day and forced them on the same running path. Seven months ago, they went for their morning run, and he had a massive heart attack. If Laura hadn't been there, he would've died."

"Bloody hell," Declan said.

Caren closed her eyes.

"Our arrival has caused added stress."

"He is scheduled to come back to the office in a couple of weeks."

"Lane, we need to go and check the house," Declan said.

"Give me ten minutes."

Caren left the room.

Lane leaned in close to Declan

"I don't feel this is health related."

"Ye believe he's been taken by the people chasing us."

"If he has been taken, it involved the errand, and it is someone he knows."

"Do ye have any idea?"

"No, and we are limited on man power," Lane said.

Caren entered the room with two duffels.

"Lane, I am quite capable of protecting myself."

"Caren, I'm sure you are…"

Lane never finished. He jumped up and ran full force towards her.

"Lane, don't," Declan said.

Caren took Lane to the floor with a hard kick to his chest and pulled her weapon. Declan began to laugh when Lane moaned and turned to his side.

"Ye could've just asked me."

"Lane needs proof, not words, correct?"

"Yes, yes, you proved you are a most capable team member."

Declan offered a hand and continued to laugh.

"Any more tests before we leave?" she asked.

Lane held both hands up.

"We won't be coming back here."

"Back to Reston," Declan said.

"Yes."

"Lane, we must see he is returned to his family," Caren said.

They arrived to the sight of a dark house; not the welcome they had hoped for after the drive from Fredericksburg.

"We'll go through the front. Declan go to the back," Lane said.

His phone stopped them from leaving the Jeep.

"Bevan?"

He nodded to Declan, and placed the cell on speaker.

"Boss, where are you? I've been kind of worried."

"I had to run into the office."

Lane shook his head.

"Anything I can do for you?"

"I'd appreciate it if you'd run by the house, feed General Lee, and take him for a walk."

"I can do that. Where's your family?"

"An overnight field trip for Sarah's homeschool's group. If you have the time, I need you to meet me in Mathews on Saturday."

"What time, boss?"

"Twelve-thirty would be fine and bring the three packages I left on the table with you."

The call abruptly ended.

"The dog is with Bevan's wife and child in Waynesboro," Caren said.

"Do you know what he meant about Mathews?"

Lane hesitated.

"Lane," Caren said.

"There is a house in Mathews. It's the last place Aaron was seen."

They exited the Jeep. Declan disappeared around the side of the home as Lane and Caren entered the house. He reached to deactivate the alarm.

"Shit!"

"What's wrong, Lane?" Caren asked.

"The house alarm wasn't activated."

They continued to clear the house room by room.

"Caren, open the back door and let Declan inside."

She touched his arm and walked toward the kitchen. He walked into the home office and checked for any information Bevan might have left for them. He entered the kitchen where Caren held a large envelope, and Declan drank a beer.

"It's empty," she said.

"Make yourself at home, Declan."

"Aye, I will."

Declan emptied the bottle.

"Have you found anything to help us?"

"No, but I believe since Bevan didn't set the alarm, he intended to return," Lane said.

"Do you know what the contents of this was?" Caren asked.

"One of the items is a photograph of your mother."

"Anything else?"

"I'm not sure, but it appears Bevan took them," Lane said.

"What can ye tell us about the location in Mathews?"

"It's a two-story antebellum home with a cellar. I'll make a sketch of the interior for us."

"We need to plan for a small group of four to six men," Declan said.

"No, there are only three," Lane said.

"Jesus, I missed Bevan's message," Declan said.

"What message?" Caren asked.

"The three packages meant three men at the house in Mathews," Lane said.

"Lee and two more," Declan said.

"Very clever," Caren said.

"Yes."

"Do ye have access to something besides sidearms?"

Lane smiled.

"I think I'll be able to find us a few things."

"Do you have a plan?" Caren asked.

"I'm working on something I think will work."

"Will it keep us all alive?"

"Declan, that I can't promise."

CHAPTER FORTY-FIVE

Cobb Creek, Virginia
October 19th
8:00 am

Declan returned to the small cabin after his check around the area. Lane still had the knack for collecting favors and called in one for this location. Their long conversation at the condo and his promise placed him in a dilemma. He prayed the lass would not force him to lie to her. The thought of any additional sorrow wasn't acceptable to him. Caren waited outside the front door.

"Anything we should worry about?" she asked.

"Lane did well. This is a good area."

"He seems to be a man of many talents. The weapons we have are impressive."

"Yes, he was that way back home."

They both turned as Lane walked outside.

"The house is about ten to fifteen minutes from here."

Lane handed both of them a warm breakfast burrito.

"Where did ye get these?"

"I found them in the freezer. Guess the last visitors left them," Lane answered.

Declan wasn't sure leftover frozen food would be safe to eat. He turned to warn Caren, and watched as the last piece of hers was devoured.

"Are ye driving?"

"No, we're walking. Declan are you going to eat that?"

"I'm fine, thank ye,"

Lane held out his hand for the burrito. He prayed neither would die from food poisoning.

"I guess you aren't worried about being seen," Caren said.

"Shortly, no one will be able to see us," Lane said.

Five minutes later, they entered a path off the main road and in ten minutes were in view of the antebellum home.

"This will be interesting tomorrow," Declan said.

Lane took a piece of paper from his pocket and gave it to Declan.

"I'll be back in a minute," Lane said.

They watched as he disappeared down the hill. Declan opened the paper.

"Sketch of the interior?" she asked

"I believe it is."

He handed it to Caren. A moment later he pushed her face forward in to a pile of leaves.

"Was that necessary?"

He pointed towards the house at a tall man.

"Donovan O'Shea," Declan said.

"He's the man I saw in Maine," Caren added.

"Lee must be inside."

He reached in his pocket, removed a spyglass and extended it.

"Where did you get that?"

"I borrowed it from the mantle at Bevan's," he said.

"I hope that isn't an heirloom," she said.

"I'll give it back. I see Bevan."

He gave her the spyglass and pointed to the top corner window.

"I'm relieved to see him," she said.

"Lass, tomorrow…"

"Declan, regardless the outcome tomorrow. I appreciate everything you've done for me."

Caren took his hand and squeezed it. He nodded and turned toward the noise Lane caused coming back to their location.

"Ye sound like a damn elephant coming through the trees."

"Who came outside?"

"His name is Donovan O'Shea."

"I presume an old work buddy," Lane said.

"Aye, a little surprised he'd be part of this, which means the price tag is high."

"We saw Bevan," Caren said.

"Where?"

Declan handed the spyglass to him.

"Oh shit. Why did you take this? Oh shit!"

"It's an heirloom, isnt it?" Caren said, and gave Declan a harsh look.

"This belonged to one of Bevan's ancestors from the Civil War," Lane said.

"Jesus, Mary and Joseph, I'm not stealing the damn thing."

"God in heaven just don't break it. Which corner?"

"Upper right," Caren answered.

Declan chuckled as Lane tenderly used the glass.

"Lee and Bevan just walked out the side door," Lane said.

"Anyone else?" Declan asked.

"There's a SUV behind the house. Didn't see anyone in it."

"I suggest we head back and discuss a strategy for tomorrow," Caren said.

The return trip to the cabin was delayed by a stop at the small store for supplies. Declan remained outside as guard, but the cool air forced him to enjoy the fall day. Lane exited the store eating a bag of chips and shoving two PayDays in his pocket.

"Caren?"

"She had a few more things to purchase," Lane said.

Declan smiled.

"Lane, I don't want the lass hurt tomorrow. She's been through enough."

"I believe she'll be able to hold her own in a fight. I've got the bruise to prove it."

He rubbed the center of his chest and grimaced.

"Aye, she is a formidable force for her size."

"You know it's going to get bloody regardless."

Declan nodded.

"She knows to leave if either of us go down."

"We'll have to do our best to make sure that doesn't happen to any of us."

"Go raibh maith agat." (Thank you)

Declan could see Caren through the screen door. He took the paper bags as she exited.

"This should get us through the rest of the day and breakfast."

Declan allowed them to walk ahead. He felt the need to lag behind and check for anyone that might be curious. As they took the left fork at the intersection, the arrival of two vehicles behind him caused a slower pace. He stepped to the side of a building to observe the two extended cab pickups loaded with camping equipment. Lane's whistle kept him from remaining to observe the occupants.

"Problem?"

"No."

"Declan, what's up? You're acting odd this morning," Lane asked.

"Do ye usually camp this time of year?"

"Camp, hunt, some guys like this time of year, to fish. Why?"

"A couple of trucks pulled into the store after we left. Both were loaded with a lot of gear in the back," Declan said.

"That's going to be pretty normal this time of year."

They approached the cabin. He opened the door for Caren and left Declan outside.

"Lane! Can ye open the door? These bags are heavy."

Declan placed the bags on the counter.

"Who has the sketch?" Lane asked

Caren took it from her pocket and handed it to Lane.

"Declan, I need…"

"A beer?"

He passed out three bottles.

"You two will arrive without me," Lane said.

"You want them to be focused on us," Caren said.

"Aye, but not for long. I'm sure everyone involved listened to Bevan's conversation. Donovan will know something isn't right."

"I'll enter through the kitchen. The biggest threat should be removed first," Lane said.

"That will be Donovan. I'll take him," Declan said.

"Lee will fold like wet paper," Caren said.

"I'll take the leader," Lane said.

Declan began to laugh.

"Did ye bring your bat, lass?"

"I have something better this time."

Caren placed the Glock on the table.

"Declan, they will disarm both of you," Lane said.

"Aye. They'll all but strip me naked for my knives."

"Then, I should find a way to carry them for you," Caren told him.

"She's right," Lane said, before Declan could protest.

"This is not a bad plan unless Bevan was wrong, and there are more," Declan said.

"In that case kill as many as you can."

●

October 20th
Noon

Caren checked the Glock even though she knew it would be removed once they entered the house. The two knives she carried had been placed, so when needed, accessible for Declan. She prayed that their location on her belt would be overlooked.

She entered the main room of the home to the sight of Declan adjusting Lane's tactical vest. They filled every holder with magazines and three of Declan's knives were being held with Velcro. Caren smiled as he opened his last PayDay.

"Declan, I have another vest."

"Did ye forget what I said about being stripped naked?"

"That is not a sight I want to be part of, sorry," Lane said.

"I seem to remember some parts of ye I'd like to forget when we were kids."

"Fair enough. Any questions or last-minute suggestions we haven't discussed?" Lane asked them.

"Are ye ready, lass?"

"We need to get Bevan out of there; for his family," Caren said.

"I need thirty minutes," Lane said.

They walked outside and watched as he disappeared through the trees.

"I regret involving Bevan in my search for Aaron," she said.

"He didn't have to help us. It was his choice, lass."

"All I wanted was information and direction."

"I'm sure it wasn't his plan to be kidnapped."

"Declan, who is this individual that wants me dead?"

"Caren, I can't answer that, but I will not let anything happen to ye."

"Declan, we can't fail here."

"Lass, could ye go get our bags?"

Caren walked inside, grabbed their duffle, and began to look for Lane's when she heard the motor on the Jeep.

"No!"

Caren dropped the bags, ran outside to find Declan and the Jeep gone.

"Declan! Declan, no!"

Caren turned as he ran from behind the cabin weapon drawn.

"Lass, are ye okay?

"Where did you go?"

"I moved the Jeep for…"

"I thought you'd left me. You promised you wouldn't leave me."

Declan watched the tears run down her face. He hadn't thought his actions would be taken in a wrong context. He took her in his arms.

"Lass, I'll never leave ye."

Caren nodded and wiped the tears away.

"Please don't ever do that again."

"Aye, I'll not. I swear."

They entered the home, retrieved the duffels, and locked the door leaving the keys under the doormat. She began to think about the man that had promised multiple times to never lie, or leave her. If they survived, she would make an effort to know more about the man who could have left her to die, but chose to remain. They approached the Jeep where Declan threw the duffels in the back.

"Do ye need a hand, lass?"

"Yes, just this once."

CHAPTER FORTY-SIX

evan stood at the window of his room concerned about the numerous outcomes and of his present situation. He hoped Lane understood the context of their brief conversation. He touched the side of his neck. Bevan wasn't able to recall anything after he arrived at Reagan airport. He assumed; the two puncture wounds were from a taser used to subdue him. He turned when the lock on his door was released.

"Alex thought you might like some clean clothes."

Bevan took the shirt and pants from Lee. Their introduction came after he regained speech.

"Speaking of Alex, where is he?"

"He's waiting downstairs for us. Thought we could have lunch before our guests arrive," Lee answered.

Bevan exited the room, walked down the creaking wooden stairs and into the dining area.

"Please sit down," Alex said.

"You do realize today is not going to end well for some of you," Bevan said.

Lee went into the kitchen, obtained several dishes and was followed by Donovan who held a platter of meat. He couldn't understand why they seemed to be unconcerned about the situation about to take place.

"Bevan, I am here for one person. Once I have her, we'll leave," Alex said.

"I'm not leaving until Declan is dead. I owe Beck that much," Lee said.

"What about you, Donovan? Can I really expect you not to kill all of us?" Bevan asked.

"I took this job for the money. I have no vendetta or revenge to fulfill just my pockets."

"If you will work with us this afternoon, I see no reason you won't be able to return home to your family," Alex said.

"If you are successful, I will never rest until you have been captured and brought to justice."

"I look forward to that," Alex said.

"The woman has been through enough. You've done enough!" Bevan said.

"What about you? Did you tell her about Caydon?" Alex asked.

"It wasn't my place to tell her," Bevan answered.

"If not your responsibility then whose?"

"Relax everyone, and enjoy your lunch," Donovan said.

"Bevan, play your part, and you'll see your daughter grow up," Alex said.

He attempted to eat, but thoughts of his family left him picking at the meal. Bevan had never questioned his mortality until he suffered a heart attack. He now faced the possibility he would not return home. The hands on the clock which sat on the buffet didn't seem to move, time had stopped. Today a choice would be made and Bevan hoped they would be proud of his decision.

●

Truths

The sound of a Jeep caused Bevan to rise and walk to the window. He watched as two individuals approached the house, which meant Lane had understood and another plan was in play. The standard protocol would be for local officers to be called in to assist. He knew in this situation it would only be the four of them. Bevan locked eyes with Donovan who followed him to the door as the bell rang. Two hard knocks followed.

"Don't get brave. Remember your family."

"They're exactly who I am thinking of."

Bevan opened the door and motioned for both of them to enter.

"It's good to see you. We were worried," Caren said.

The moment they entered, Lee walked out of the shadows and Donovan locked the front door.

"Good to see ye, Declan," Donovan said.

"Go to hell, Donovan."

"You'll be going before me."

"Maybe we should just go together," Declan said.

"Let's see how many knives ye brought."

Lee began to search him.

"One gun and four knives? You're getting sloppy," Donovan said.

"We were expecting someone else."

"Who would that be?" Donovan asked.

"My brother," Caren answered.

"Sorry to disappoint ye," Lee said.

Donovan walked over to Caren.

"Lass, do ye want to give me your weapon, or shall I take some time to search for it?"

Caren began to reach in her jean jacket.

"Slow lass," Lee said.

She removed her weapon and handed it to Donovan.

"This is the bitch that almost killed me."

"A little something my son taught me. The one you murdered."

Caren started toward him, but Declan stepped in front of her.

"Lass, don't."

"I suggest everyone calm down and have a seat," Donovan said.

"Who hired ye?" Declan asked.

"Why don't ye ask Bevan," Lee said.

They turned to face him.

"Bevan, what is he talking about?" she asked.

The sound of a bottle breaking and a thud in the kitchen brought everyone to their feet.

"Alex, do ye need some help?" Donovan asked, but kept his focus on Declan.

Alex walked into the main room where everyone stood.

"I apologize for my delay. An issue presented itself outside. Lee, there is a large problem in the kitchen, please move it to the cellar."

"Any other instructions?"

"Secure him, nothing more," Alex said.

"Back to your seats," Donovan said.

"You knew Lane was out there," Bevan said.

Alex nodded.

"Standard protocol to have a backup plan, and I knew there wasn't enough time to contact local authorities. I thought your reference to us as packages was quite cleaver."

"You let him approach you," Bevan said.

"Yes, he wanted to know why I was here? I told him you had invited me." Alex began to laugh.

"What's so funny?" Bevan asked.

"Lane's concern for my safety. He demanded I remain outside and call the state police."

"You didn't have to hit him with a bottle," Bevan said.

"I tasered him, he broke the bottle when he fell."

Declan turned to Bevan.

"Who is this shaking little bastard?"

"Yes, please do the introductions," Alex said.

"This little bastard is Blain Alexander Benjamin, my nephew," Bevan said.

He could see the shock and disbelief on their faces.

"No, I don't believe you," Caren said.

"Bloody hell, how did this happen?" Declan asked.

"In Bevan's defense, he didn't betray you. Until two days ago, he had no knowledge of my plan."

"The text message I sent in reference to an errand. He asked to be picked up at Reagan, when I arrived, I was tasered, and brought here," Bevan explained.

"You have my attention," Caren said.

"You're a much stronger woman than I expected," Alex said.

"The destruction of everything you love will do that to you."

"You are correct. Would you like to hear about the complete destruction of my life?"

"This isn't necessary, Blain," Bevan said.

"Oh, but I believe it is. I was an agent, a damn good agent with the CIA," Alex said.

"What happened to you?" she asked.

"Aaron Caydon happened to me. I was injured in an altercation when I was sent to protect Bevan's soon-to-be-wife."

"You're lucky he didn't kill ye," Declan said.

"I wish he had, because in the beginning, the physicians didn't believe the injuries were serious. I was expected to make a full recovery and return to duty. A year of painful physical therapy yielded little improvement, but they kept telling me to give it more time. I began to notice the shaking, and loss of balance, which the neurologist diagnosed as early Parkinson's. The combination of injuries and disease has led to this."

Alex held out his arms.

"I don't understand how you can believe Aaron is responsible for your condition," Caren said.

"He blames me," Bevan said.

"What has happened to me is a direct result from the injuries I sustained from Aaron Caydon. The job I loved gone, my health gone, any chance for a future gone!"

"You're the one that has been providing information to Donovan," Declan said.

"How is that possible?" Caren asked.

"He still holds a clearance," Bevan said.

"I'm medically retired."

"He is still allowed access to the building," Bevan said.

"I have limited access, but I have friends that are willing to do a favor or two for someone injured in the line of duty. If that fails, family is a great source. Grandmother thinks very highly of you two, and sent me pictures."

Alex held his cell phone up with a picture of Caren.

"Ye led us on a merry chase, but it's over," Donovan said.

"I killed a few of ye bastards along the way," Declan said.

"Yes, you did. I have wished many times I had hired you instead. You have cost me a lot of money and too many headaches."

"What now?" Declan asked.

"Caren and I are going on a trip," Alex said.

"You murdered my family and destroyed my life to get back at my brother?"

"I'm going to destroy any vestige that Aaron Caydon ever existed on this earth," Alex said.

"What do you mean?" she asked.

Bevan stood up and stepped forward. He then realized the belt Caren had been wearing was now on the chair.

"No further," Donovan said.

"That's enough, Blain!" "Don't call me that! Blain Benjamin died ten years ago when Kyleigh McNeil shot Caydon here in the cellar."

"Blain, no!"

Bevan lunged causing Donovan to fire his weapon. He fell to the floor with a wound to his right leg.

Caren screamed, turned and fell face forward into the chair. Declan fell over her as a shield and took both the knives.

"I'm sorry, lass. Get out of here."

"Donovan, it's time to leave," Alex said.

"Declan, back away from her."

Donovan reached down and took him by the shoulder.

"Ye bloody bastards," Declan said.

He stood, turned, and cut Donovan across the chest. The force caused him to fall back and discharge his weapon. Declan grabbed his left arm, and kicked the gun from his hand.

"Now, Caren go!"

Caren ran toward the kitchen as they continued to fight.

"Lee! Stop her! Lee!"

Alex started towards her when he felt a grip on his leg.

"Let it go, Blain," Bevan said.

"This is the last time I'm going to tell you not to call me that."

Bevan watched as his brother's son, the boy he had held and loved as a child, pull the trigger.

CHAPTER FORTY-SEVEN

Marcus and the rest of his team waited at the campsite for Javier to return. It had been a long time since he had camped out, but Doc had made it bearable with decent food. The last time he slept in a tent was on an island that last assignment with Aaron and his teammates. They had information Caren and Declan would be at the Antebellum home, so it was now a waiting game for them.

"Heads up, Marcus," Gordon said.

"We've got a problem," Javier said.

"Do we need everyone?" Marcus asked.

"No, but we need to go now."

"Doc, watch for my text," Marcus said.

Gordon held up his phone.

"Try not to get shot."

Marcus took his weapon and followed Javier to the edge of the tree line.

"What's happened?"

"There's been activity all morning; men in and out. Lane Brigham showed up just before I left to come get you."

"Lane Brigham, you're sure about that?" Marcus asked.

"Lane and I have history, it's a long story for another time. He came prepared, tactical vest, military grade automatic weapon."

"Did you see anyone else?"

"A tall man being guarded. At one Caren and Declan arrived."

"The tall man is probably Bevan Benjamin. What's the problem?"

"Shortly after they entered the house, Brigham approached but stopped. He began to wave at one of the men from inside the house," Javier said.

"Waved like he knew him?"

"Lane shook hands with the man and had him stand behind him as he entered the side door."

"Jesus, he didn't know," Marcus said, then sent a message for Doc to come towards the house.

"No, the person he thought was a friend is involved in this mess."

"We need to get in there now."

The two men hurried from their position and prepared to enter the house. Marcus turned back towards Javier.

"Who is yelling?" Marcus asked.

"This doesn't sound good."

They entered and positioned themselves in the kitchen where they waited for the opportunity to take control of the house. The scream of a woman and gunfire set their plan into motion. Marcus motioned for Javier to move to the side as Caren ran towards them, then stopped.

"Who the hell are you?" she asked.

Marcus was prevented from identifying himself due to a second gunshot and the arrival of a man from the cellar. He raised his gun, but the man attacked Caren preventing a clear shot.

"Where are you going?"

Marcus watched as the man wrapped his arms around Caren. He started to intervene when she raised both feet, and used the kitchen island to push the man into the door of the cellar. His grasp was released which allowed her to grab a wine bottle sitting on the counter. As she raised the bottle to strike, Marcus stepped forward and pushed her behind him.

"Get her out of here," Marcus said.

Their footsteps and the slam of the screen door assured her safety.

"Who the bloody hell are ye?"

Those were his last words spoken before he died on the floor. Marcus backed slowly out of the house and located Caren standing with Doc Morres.

"Caren are you hurt?" Gordon asked.

"No."

Marcus walked up and motioned for Javier to stand at the door.

"Where is Declan?"

"He's still inside. Who are you people?"

Doc Morres took her hands.

"Who else is inside?"

"Bevan Benjamin, his insane nephew, Alex, and Donovan."

Javier glanced back.

"What about Lane?"

"In the cellar," Caren answered.

"We have to go," Marcus said.

Caren reached out and took his arm.

"Until you tell me who you are, I am not going anywhere!"

"Aaron sent us," Gordon said.

"If my brother sent you, he would not leave the others behind. You have to help them."

"Our objective was to remove you to safety," Javier said.

"No! I'm not leaving them."

She moved quickly and removed Marcus's sidearm from his holster. Then she pointed the weapon at all of them.

The three men held their hands up and backed away.

"Caren, we're not your enemy," Gordon said.

"The men in there are in trouble, and I will not let them die. Are you coming?"

"I don't believe you need us," Marcus said.

"Cowards!"

Caren backed away from them and reentered the house.

"Did she call us cowards?" Javier asked.

"You did refuse to go back inside with her," Gordon said.

Marcus took his cell phone out and sent another text.

"She's covered."

CHAPTER FORTY-EIGHT

Answers

The house had become silent. The only sound was Caren's footsteps and the pounding of her heart. She cautiously avoided the blood pools, focused and prepared to end this nightmare. Donovan's lifeless body laid in the dining room, his blood had begun to congeal from the multiple cuts on his arms, chest and throat. Bevan's body was visible from where she stood in the dining room and she knew the gunshot to his chest meant he was dead or dying. She placed the weapon in the small of her back.

"Lee! Lee! Where are you?" Alex called.

"Lee isn't coming," Caren said.

"Stay back, Caren," Declan said.

She was glad to hear his voice. There was still a chance if she stayed calm.

"No, come in and join us."

Caren positioned next to the frame of the entry, and held her hands out where they could be seen by Alex. He stood above Declan, who was bloodied and bruised on the floor. He'd been shot. She shook her head, but he attempted to move, and Alex knocked him unconscious.

"We can finish our conversation without further interruption."

"There's a team of men outside waiting for me to call them inside." Alex began to laugh.

"Nice try, but if you had anyone to help you, they would be here."

"I have a question before I allow them to kill you," Caren said.

"Ask away. We have plenty of time," Alex responded.

"Where is the information Bevan brought with him?"

"The photograph of your mother and true birth certificate?"

"What do you mean by true birth certificate?"

She watched as he walked over to Bevan's body and used a foot to nudge him.

"Bevan was always good at holding back information for his own purpose."

Caren crossed her arms and leaned against the opening.

"Enlighten me and please be specific."

"Aaron Caydon was a genetic anomaly, a wondrous science project the government used for their benefit for years."

"I don't believe you."

"You seem like the type of person that needs proof, and proof I have."

"What did the government do to him?"

"It wasn't the government that did anything to him other than use him."

"Who was responsible?"

"His father."

"Our father?"

"No, you stupid bitch!"

Caren watched as he became enraged, and increased his pace towards the doorway. She reached behind for the weapon but was pushed to the floor by a strong hand. The last thing she saw was the expression on Alex's face as the back of his head exploded. She suspected one of the men outside took exception to being called a coward and had come to help. She turned her face up and found a familiar one looking back.

"I was tired of listening to him."

"Aaron."

●

The Reunion

Aaron reached down and pulled her from the floor, and into his arms. He surveyed the scene, turned and motioned for his men to advance. She pulled back and ran a hand across the long scar on his face. The sudden movement and sound caused him to stiffen, turn and raise his weapon at the man on the floor covered in blood.

Caren grabbed his arm.

"No, don't, he's a friend."

"Marcus check him."

Gordon entered the main room.

"Jesus H. Christ, Aaron! What a mess. Where do you want me to start?"

Aaron pointed towards Bevan.

"See if he's alive."

"Where have you been?" Caren asked.

"Hidden."

Javier entered the room.

"We're clear outside. Time will not be an issue."

"Aaron, I need you over here."

"Caren, are you okay?"

"Yes, Aaron save him, please."

He acknowledged her request, walked over, and knelt down next to Gordon who worked to save Bevan.

"Is all this blood his?"

"You tell me. With all the bodies, it's difficult to say," Gordon said.

"He looks bad."

"I can't believe he's still alive. I'll do my best, but he may need a higher power. It'd be better if I could get him out of here."

Aaron stood, took his phone out and made a call.

"Everyone is needed now."

He walked into the kitchen, removed a bottle of wine from the cabinet, opened and allowed it to breath. The constant pounding on the cellar door and profanities had become entertaining.

"Open the fucking door! Bevan! Declan!"

Aaron filled two glasses with the deep red liquid that resembled the blood pools in the main room. The back door opened, and six men entered and stopped for orders.

"The body in the kitchen, and the two in the front room are to be removed and permanently disappear. I need it done now."

"Aaron," Caren called.

He joined her in the main room and handed her the glass of wine.

"I think you could use this."

"He'll be fine, but Doc will need to remove the bullet," Marcus said.

"Caren, I need a moment.

Aaron motioned for Marcus to follow him back into the kitchen.

Marcus panned the kitchen floor.

"That didn't take long."

Aaron pointed to the cellar door. They watched as it vibrated with each hit.

"Listen for a moment."

"Open the fucking door!"

"Who's locked in the cellar?" Aaron asked.

"Lane Brigham."

They looked at the door as it vibrated again.

Aaron laughed.

"I should've known he'd be here."

"Any chance he'll break through it?" Marcus asked.

"Not unless he blows it off with an explosive."

"What do you want us to do with him?"

Aaron took a long drink from the glass.

"Did he see any of you?"

"No."

"Leave him."

"You sure about that?"

"I cannot think of anyone better qualified to explain this mess than him," Aaron said.

"We should be finished in two hours."

"An anonymous call to the state police will be appropriate once we're gone."

"You realize he isn't going to be able to give them any information?"

"As I said, he is the best one to leave alive. Marcus, there is information in the house I want located and brought to me. A photograph and birth certificate."

Caren walked into the kitchen.

"My friend wishes to speak to you."

Aaron followed her back into the main room where his men prepared to remove Donovan and Alex's bodies. He could see Caren had removed the blood from the man's face and placed a wet rag on his swollen eye. The injuries he had sustained would take time to abate. He smiled as the man attempted to stand.

"Stay put. It's not necessary for you to stand up," Aaron said.

"Aaron this is…"

"Declan Carrick Mallone."

"I guess introductions aren't necessary," she said.

"Ye know me, sir?"

"Your reputation and Ferrell," Aaron answered.

"Ye know my uncle?"

"I do."

Aaron could see Declan was physically shaking. He was unsure if it was due to being injured or speaking with a ghost.

"You wish to ask me something?"

"I thought ye were…"

"Dead?"

"Aye."

Aaron looked at Caren and lowered his head.

"I was, but that piece of refuse my men just drug out of here caused my resurrection."

Two men entered with a stretcher, and Aaron pointed across the room. The three watched as Bevan was moved and secured for transport.

"I need to check on Bevan."

He approached the stretcher and looked at the blood running through intravenous tubing.

We're ready to go," Gordon said.

"Stable?"

"I think that word will not be used for a while. He's critical, but not dead," Gordon said.

Aaron turned toward Declan.

"Can you travel?"

"Aye."

"Doc, take them with you. Declan has a bullet that needs to be removed."

"How long before you'll meet us?"

"A couple of hours," Aaron said.

"The house is a mess," Gordon said.

Aaron turned, viewed the devastation, and nodded his head.

"It's worse than last time."

He walked away to help Declan stand.

"Aaron," Caren said.

"I'll be with you in a couple of hours," Aaron said.

"What about Lane?" she asked.

"The man truly helped us, sir," Declan said.

"I'll make sure he is released in a few hours after we're gone. I hope eventually he'll stop pounding on that damn door," Aaron said.

He followed them outside where a van stood. His men stood guard as Bevan was placed inside. He shook Declan's hand and hugged Caren. When the lights disappeared, he turned towards Javier.

"One hour."

He walked back into the kitchen and poured another glass of wine, as his team moved quickly to meet the deadline. Aaron walked into the main room of the house, where Marcus met him with the information he'd been asked to find.

"I have one more project before we leave."

Aaron walked away and, motioned for Marcus to follow.

"I don't hear Lane. Did he give up? Marcus asked.

"It appears he did."

"What's left for us to do, Aaron?"

"I need all the wine labeled Brushy Creek Vineyards removed from the house and leave this empty bottle on the island."

CHAPTER FORTY-NINE

The Rescue

L ane walked to the bottom of the cellar, slid down the wall and accepted his fate for the moment. He assumed Blain tasered him and had Lee or Donovan shove him downstairs. He ran a finger over the cracked crystal on his watch. He assumed it was damaged due to his unconscious trip down the stone stairs or the hours of pounding against the impregnable door.

He was positive of one gunshot after his brain unscrambled, but nothing afterwards, no voices or, vehicles, just silence. He could see that it was almost nine and wished for a PayDay. The sound of shrill feedback made him stand up.

"This is the Virginia State Police. Come out of the cellar with your hands above your head," a male voice announced.

"Dammit, and they're using a bullhorn. Wonderful."

He walked to the top of the stairs.

"I'm Federal Agent, Lane Brigham. I have proper identification."

"You know the procedure then," a female instructed.

"Yeah, I know," Lane said.

He took a deep breath and began to prepare for the action of the officers once he exited the cellar. The door was unlocked, and two officers had weapons drawn on him.

"He's got a vest on!" announced the female.

"Take it slow," the male officer instructed.

"These fucking steps are steep. If I go any slower, I'll be going backwards," Lane said.

"He's a comedian," she said.

Lane walked through the door and was immediately tackled by two large officers. He was handcuffed, the vest removed and the officers continued to check him for weapons in places he'd never thought of until now. He would demand a cigarette once they finished. They moved him into the small dining area and placed him in a chair. Four officers stood guard over him, weapons at the ready. An hour past before their Sergeant made his appearance.

"Stand down and release him," Sergeant James said.

"Thank you. Before I answer any questions, I need to use the restroom," Lane said.

He walked out the back door and into the first stand of trees. He didn't wish to contaminant evidence in the house. When he returned four officers stood in the kitchen.

"I appreciate your cooperation while we checked your credentials," Sergeant James said.

"Your officers were quite thorough with their search. I need to call my doctor on Monday and cancel my prostate exam."

Lane walked towards his equipment.

"What happened here?"

Lane stopped and turned around to see if the man was serious.

"Are you really going to ask me that question? I've been locked in the fucking cellar for eight hours."

"Agent Brigham, can you explain what you were doing out here?"

"I was on a rescue mission."

He heard laughter from the kitchen.

"Is there anything you can tell me?"

"Unfortunately, I am not at liberty to discuss it further."

They walked into an area not covered in blood. Lane took a moment and viewed the carnage.

"My people cleared the house," Sergeant James said.

"How many have been through here?"

"Two."

"Did they find anyone alive or any bodies?"

"Agent, you are the only body we have found. I would have to say with all the blood on the floor, you were lucky to have been locked in the cellar."

"Sergeant James, I do not wish to step on anyone's feelings here or overstep my authority."

"Agent if this is a government operation, I have been advised to step down."

"I would appreciate it if your officers would secure the perimeter. I need to contact a unit to meet me here."

Sergeant James and his officers left the house while Lane called for a unit with an investigator. Where were all the bodies? There had been six adults in the house at one point. A battle had taken place, and all he could see were two spent rounds on the floor. He began to run scenarios through his mind most ended with people dead or dying. He entered the kitchen and froze.

"Sergeant!"

Sergeant James reentered the house.

"What can I do for you Agent Brigham?"

"Sergeant, was this bottle here when your officers arrived?"

"As I explained, we cleared the house. My officers have not touched or moved anything."

"Thank you, I'll be out in a moment."

Lane wanted to deny what stood on the island. A cold chill ran down his back as he read the name of the wine, Archidamus from Brushy Creek vineyard. The last time he had seen a bottle of wine with the name of that vineyard an entire family had been eliminated.

He walked back outside and waited for his people to arrive. The lights of a van and two sedans pulled into the drive of the home. Lane walked out to meet the investigator.

"Lane, are you hurt?"

"Deena Lyles, thank you for coming. I was tasered and shoved down a flight of stairs."

"After you walk me through. You know the routine."

"Trip to the emergency room to be checked out and start my report."

"Are any of our people missing?"

"Bevan Benjamin."

"What was he doing out here?"

"Come in. I'll fill you in on Bevan. The information I have on what occurred inside the house will be limited."

CHAPTER FIFTY

Bevan could hear the crackle of a fireplace and smell the scent of the wood that burned. He had difficulty opening his eyes and thought someone had said it was raining. The rattle of the windows left him with a sense winter had arrived. He longed to see Laura, and knew she sat at his side each night. He would rest and grow strong in order to hold his family once again.

"Laura," Bevan called.

"He's been doing that frequently," Caren said.

"I'm pleased to hear him speak," Gordon said.

There was a light knock on the door, then it opened to allow Aaron and Declan entry.

"Caren, it is not necessary for you to sit in here night after night. I installed monitors so he could be constantly observed," Aaron said.

"I'm aware of the monitors, but this man nearly died to save me. What I am doing is a simple thing, and the least I can do, to make sure he knows someone is here."

"Doc, when do you believe I can have a short conversation with your patient?"

"I'm going to decrease the dosage of pain medication starting tonight, maybe tomorrow or Sunday."

"Excellent!"

"Aaron, if there is one moment of your conversation that endangers him, I will end it. The man shouldn't be here. Let's not mess things up," Gordon asked.

"I want to do what is best for him. Declan come with me to the office?"

"Yes, sir. Caren, I'll be back to relieve you in a few hours."

"Take your time, I'm good here. Aaron, I would like a glass of wine."

"Of course, Declan will bring it to you shortly."

Gordon took his stethoscope and listened to his patient's heart and lungs.

"Aaron is correct. You don't have to keep sitting in here night after night. It will take some time, but he will recover."

"Doctor Morres, you must understand this has become very personal for me. All I can see is another family mourning, their lives changed forever. If my presence will help in any way to make sure he returns home, I must to do it."

"I'll be back in a few hours to lower his medication. Caren, I want you to rest too. The last thing I need is another patient."

"Declan will relieve me shortly. I promise to go and rest."

•

November 3rd

Bevan slowly opened his eyes and began to view the strange surroundings. The soft beep of machines made him raise slightly and touch the bandages on his chest. He traced the wires and closed his eyes as it brought back painful memories from his heart attack.

The sound of furniture being drug across the floor made him think Laura was present. The footsteps were heavy, and he waited to hear Lane's voice or the sound of a candy wrapper. He turned his head slightly and began to breathe rapidly, the alarms on the monitors rang out. He could not accept what the eyes said was true.

"Jesus Christ, I told you this wasn't a good idea," Gordon said.

The man who had spoken walked to the bed and placed a small tube in his nose which allowed oxygen to assist his breathing.

"No!"

"Bevan, take some slow breathes. I want you to calm down."

The man gave him a small sip of water. Pale hands shook as they grabbed hold of the man's arm at his bedside. Bevan shook his head back and forth.

"No, no."

"I want you to listen to me. You are safe, and in my care. I will not allow anyone to hurt you. Bevan, you must slow your heart rate down, do you understand?"

"This can't be! It just isn't possible."

"Bevan."

Caren called to him as she entered the room.

The alarms ceased, the monitors paced normally and his breathing became regular. He smiled as she touched his hand which caused him to release the doctor.

"Please listen to the doctor. I'll be back later to sit with you," she said.

Bevan nodded his head.

"Thank you," Gordon said.

"He'll be fine."

She left the room.

Bevan closed his eyes, attempted to relax, but jerked as a cork exited the bottle. He turned to see Aaron pour a glass of wine and lean back into the rocker. The slow methodical back and forth movement added to the surrealness of the moment. He watched as a dead man raised a glass of red wine to his lips and smiled.

"Bevan, did you truly believe it would be that easy to kill me?"

"I…, I buried you, ten years ago."

"Yes, you did, and it was quite touching, thank you."

"How is this possible?"

He began to cough, and pointed towards the cup of water.

"Just a sip."

Gordon helped him.

"Bevan. I have access to some of the best geneticists, plastic surgeons and physicians money can buy," Aaron said.

Bevan's heart rate increased.

"Aaron, I would appreciate it if you didn't undo all my work."

"It seems I am causing unnecessary stress upon you. One more question until you're feeling better," Aaron said.

"Declan?"

"He survived and has been taking turns with Caren sitting up through the nights with you. I know you are concerned about Brigham. He was left unharmed in the cellar. The state police were contacted and he was rescued a few hours after we left."

Bevan grimaced and reached for his chest.

"Aaron that's enough."

Gordon picked up a bottle, filled a syringe and began to push medicine through the tubing.

"Have a good rest, Bevan. We'll have plenty of time to catch up when you're better," Aaron said.

Bevan could feel the warmth of the medication as it flowed into his body. His eyes began to blur, sounds muffled, and the terrible nightmare disappeared along with the pain.

CHAPTER FIFTY-ONE

CIA
November 4th

L ane entered the office and, stopped in shock at the mountain of
paperwork that had appeared since Friday. His respect for Bevan
had grown over the last year with the acknowledgement of what this
job required on a daily basis to function. He knew there would be
a least a hundred emails to read and answer. He just didn't give a
damn about any of it.

He had one purpose, to find and bring his boss home. The light on
the desk phone lit up as he sat down, which made him grab a PayDay
from his desk drawer instead of the breakfast taco from the sack.

"Brigham!"

"Checking in with you," Deena said.

"Are you here?"

Yes, I picked up a few lab results and information from the agents
in Wyoming."

"Head this way."

"I'm coming through the door."

Lane was pleased when Deena Lyles had arrived in Mathews as
the lead investigator. She served with the FBI in New York and was
picked up by the Company three years ago. The past two weeks had
yielded little information and fewer clues. He hoped for better news
this morning. He held up a large sack.

"Breakfast taco?"

"Yes, bacon please."

The two ate in silence for a few moments. Three tacos later, and a
quart of chocolate milk, Lane was ready to talk.

"I hope you brought something we can work with this morning."

"Which of the bad news do you want first?" she asked.

"Dammit, I knew it. I want the report from Wyoming."

"Blain bought an old motor court in the middle of nowhere. A place called Moose," she said.

"Are you talking about those similar to the 1940's and 50's?"

"Yes, these were individual cabins instead of one connected unit. It appears he renovated several and dismantled the rest. The agent reported the three renovated cabins had two sets of bunk beds, no double or queen size beds."

"A perfect place to house a fair number of men, train them, and not draw notice from local residents."

"The large cabin was Blain's dwelling. Lane it's filled with classified information."

"How did he get all those copies?"

"They weren't copies. Every box was filled with originals files."

"Christ! This is going to mean another major investigation into the office."

"What do you mean another investigation?"

"Ten years ago, information was flying out of here like birds going south. Several arrests were made, and a major change in policies."

"The agents believe some of the information is at least eight maybe nine years old," she told him.

Lane shook his head.

"The little bastard removed it before he retired. Blain knew there wouldn't be a way to get it out once his clearance and movements became limited."

"I checked the computer logs. He did make a number of visits before the move to Moose."

"We will never know what those visits detailed. I can imagine those little perks for retirees will be changing in the future. How long before the information from Wyoming will be here?"

"It should arrive around mid-week. Did you know Blain's neurological deterioration had advanced?"

"Bevan had mentioned that he had become withdrawn and irritable at family gatherings. He was extremely upset with the final evaluation of the physicians which gave the brass no option. He was medically retired."

"It took a few days to obtain all his medical information. The reports indicate he was diagnosed with Parkinson's. Unfortunately, it was advancing rapidly. He would have been an invalid within two years."

"What about his psychological evaluations?"

"Positive reports," she answered.

Lane looked at the ceiling.

"It appears someone didn't ask the appropriate questions."

"Lane, he was an agent. Blain knew how to give the answers that were expected, to those type of questions."

"What about the scene in Mathews? Do you have a report on the blood?"

Deena turned on the iPad, pulled up the scene, and turned it towards Lane.

"In the main room, there are four donors and one in the kitchen. We found your blood on the cellar door of course."

"Blood in the kitchen? Where?"

She took the stylet and made a circle.

"A small amount was located at the base of the island. It was nearly missed. The wine bottle on the island had no prints."

"Of course, it didn't."

"We believe it was brought to the house."

"Are you saying there wasn't any more wine in the house?"

"No, there's an extremely nice selection of wines, but none from that particular vineyard."

Lane leaned over the desk.

"At some point, while I was locked in the cellar, a person or persons unknown entered the house. They removed the bodies, did a partial clean up and left an empty wine bottle."

"It appears that is exactly what happened. The evidence or lack of, indicates no other scenario is possible," she said.

"I can see the brass now, reading your report and demanding a drug screen on both of us. Why would you clean one room?" Lane asked.

She took the bag and removed another taco.

"Why would you leave one specific empty bottle?"

Lane shrugged his shoulders.

"What was the blood type in the kitchen?"

"Male."

"What about the samples from the main room?"

"All of the blood in the main room is male, Blain and Bevan's have been identified. I'm waiting for the locations of Donovan and Lee, leaving one unknown."

"An unknown male in the main room?"

"Yes, do you have any idea who that fifth individual may have been?"

"Locked in the cellar remember?"

"Lane, why would Blain kidnap his own family?"

"My guess is revenge."

"Revenge for what?" she asked.

"A sociopath named Aaron Caydon had threatened a number of agents ten years ago. Our boss was at the top of his list. Bevan's fiancé was a possible target so he sent an agent as protection."

"Blain."

"The injuries he sustained in an altercation with Caydon resulted in a year of treatments and finally a medical retirement."

"Tell me more about the injuries."

"They didn't appear at first to be serious, but nerve damage would have doomed him to a permanent desk job," Lane explained.

"The Parkinson's diagnosis left no alternative for Blain."

"Bevan had no option but to agree with the decision of his superiors. It did not set well with Blain."

"I'll need the file number for my report."

Lane took a piece of paper and wrote down a number, then slid it to her.

"What else did you find?" he asked.

"We collected three spent shells and brain tissue from the floor."

"I saw two. Where was the third?"

"It was found next to the wall under some broken glass."

"I'm almost afraid to ask, any prints?"

"Donovan's prints were on two from a Beretta, and the third from a Glock 22, was clean. No spent shells were recovered in the kitchen."

"Do you have a report on the brain tissue?"

Deena reached in her pocket for the phone.

"It belongs to Blain. Just a minute that's the lab calling."

"You have full confirmation?"

Deena nodded her head, made a few notes, and ended the call.

"The lab has now confirmed the blood in the kitchen is a match to Lee. Donovan's was in the dining area."

"What about the main concentration in the main room?"

"The largest concentrations of blood belonged Bevan."

"Scenarios."

"First, you understand we are working with an enormous number of unknowns here. All I can do is speculate on what might have possibly happened."

"Deena, tell me what you believe based on the evidence found."

"One unknown male in main room is believed to have survived. I'm unable to give a decision either way on Lee due to the single drop of blood. Donovan is presumed dead due to the amount of his blood found. It's my belief Blain is dead due to the amount of brain tissue discovered."

"Bevan?"

"Lane, if he was not treated immediately, I see no possible chance of survival."

"Where are the damn bodies?"

"The search of the area has produced no evidence. The only tire marks were those of the SUV in the back, your Jeep, and the team's vehicles."

"You're not serious."

"I have never seen a crime scene like this before. Bodies removed, a possible partial clean up, and removal of physical clues."

"The evidence left in the house was to serve a purpose, and that included not killing me."

Lane rose from his chair and walked to the window. He exposed his back and the knives he carried. He turned back towards Deena and lowered his head.

"When did you start carrying knives?"

He smiled.

"You've never been in the field with me. I carry and use them frequently. A good friend once taught me how to use them."

"Lane, we're flying blind here. Is there anything you left out?"

"It's all in my report."

"I read the report. I want you to walk me through it."

"Again?" he asked.

"Yes, again."

"Laura contacted me concerned Bevan hadn't made it home from my apartment."

"Did he visit you often?"

"No, I had some issues with all the damn reports that are due daily. He agreed to come and walk me through them."

"I understand, this office is unbelievable when it comes to reports being generated on a daily basis."

"I don't believe Bevan was ever late or behind even one day. The man is amazing."

"He came for how long?" she asked.

"I think two hours, then left. I never heard from Laura so figured he'd made it home. The next day, I received anonymous information Bevan was being held hostage in Mathews. I arrived to recon the location and discovered Blain behind the house."

"Were you concerned when you saw him?"

"Surprised, actually, and concerned for his safety. Blain advised he was in town for a meeting at the office, and Bevan had contacted him to come to Mathews. At this time, I felt whoever had Bevan intended to take Blain as a hostage."

"I checked, and Blain had no such meeting scheduled. Bevan does meet once a week with the President and would have information valuable to foreign enemies. Blain has had access to sensitive materials in the past so your concerns were valid."

"I advised him to remain outside and contact the state police."

"Why didn't you take a backup team with you?"

"My initial plan was to arrive, observe the situation and call for assistance. Blain's arrival was cause for immediate action."

"You realize your action was improper and could have resulted in your death."

Lane pointed to his butt.

"The boys from internal affairs have thoroughly chewed my ass and advised of a pending suspension. While I was stuck in the cellar the constant thought of dying from hunger and dehydration was ever present. I will be happy to any amount of time they give me once we have answers and bodies."

"Lane, I'm trying to understand why this happened. You aren't one to enter an unknown situation without support. I've read your records and this is out of character."

"We all screw up, Deena. I let my concern for Bevan override protocol, and it cost me. It may have cost Bevan."

"Can you tell me what happened after you entered the house?"

"I reached the kitchen and was apparently tasered by Blain. I don't believe he was capable of moving me, so it was Lee or Donovan."

"How many gunshots did you hear?"

"One and nothing else. No conversation, no movement."

"Did you note the time of the gunshot?"

"No, I had begun to wake up from the tumble downstairs. Lane touched the back of his neck.

"I had concerns about your story of not being able to hear through the door. We discover the door was abnormally wide and did a number of experiments for sound. Individuals that stood inside the cellar at the door yelling could be heard in the kitchen. If you were standing at the door or down in the bottom of the cellar you could hear nothing from the kitchen or any area of the house. I'm surprised you heard the gunshot. My guess is you heard the shot that killed or injured Lee."

"I heard that damn bullhorn."

Deena laughed.

"I heard about the state police take down."

"The cellar is basically soundproof."

"An entire army could've come in and removed the bodies. You heard one gunshot out of three that we can prove."

"Deena, I refuse to tell Laura Benjamin her husband is dead without proof."

"How is she handling all of this?"

"She is reacting the exact way I expected; strong and with a resolve that if Bevan is alive, he will come home to them."

"Lane, this is one case there may not be a positive resolution."

Lane smiled at Deena.

"You don't know Bevan Benjamin."

CHAPTER FIFTY-TWO

Alvord, Texas
Brushy Creek Vineyards
November 11th

The gray skies had changed into blue which allowed sunshine to brighten the room. As Bevan's drug induced fog began to dissipate over the last week, the sounds on the other side of the locked door became more of an interest. What he first believed was as an unorthodox hospital, took shape into a family dwelling. The confinement did have some bright moments with visits from Caren and Declan. His improved condition allowed the uncomfortable catheter to be removed and the intravenous fluids to cease.

The large chaise positioned next to the huge window in his room had beckoned Bevan for days. Today, he had accomplished the short walk from his bed to the lounger. He was impressed with the view and noted the isolated location of the house. When the lock on the door released, he expected someone other than Aaron, who entered with a bottle of wine and two glasses.

"Good afternoon. I've been informed you have improved enough for wine and my visit."

Bevan noticed a folder under Aaron's arm.

"Is there any chance for something other than soup today?"

"I'll see if it's a possibility for this evening's meal."

Bevan stood and slowly began to move back towards the bed.

"The fire could use wood."

Aaron started towards the fireplace then turned back to Bevan.

"Do you need assistance?"

"I need to do this. Just add the wood as it's the one amenity of this prison I have enjoyed."

He watched as Aaron stoked the fire and arranged the furniture for a face to face conversation.

"I apologize for the locked door. I can't have you attempting to escape until you are well enough to travel back home."

Aaron poured two glasses of wine.

"I'd like to thank you for saving my life."

"My pleasure."

"Do you have any word on my wife?"

"My contact advised she is concerned, but has refused to accept any suggestion you will not be returning home. Laura is a resilient woman and you are a fortunate man."

"Yes, yes I am. What's the word on the investigation in Mathews?"

Aaron laughed.

"You never believed the house cleaning ten years ago would stop the flow of information, did you?"

"I had some trepidations."

"Lane and Agent Deena Lyles are fumbling through an unexplainable scene."

"I assume you did some cleaning and removed all the bodies."

"You know my methods well."

"To your health."

Bevan held his glass up.

"And to your continued improvement."

"It's taken some time for me to admit this situation was real and not my mind playing a bad joke or the drugs causing hallucinations."

"Our first encounter proved to be too much for you and your physician. I was forbidden to come back until now."

"I have questions."

"I'm sure you do."

"How have you remained unnoticed all this time?"

"No one searches for a dead man."

"Interesting point, and you're correct."

"You know how easy it is working for the Company, to disappear if you truly wish. I would have remained deceased, but your nephew felt the need to resurrect me."

"Could you be more specific?"

"Blain began to siphon money out of my retirement account with the Company. I had not been reported deceased, so the money was a nice savings which grew and would be obtained at a later date. In the beginning, it was small amounts easily overlooked or explained if someone checked. This last year, the amounts increased substantially."

"Large amounts of money leaving an account should have alerted a check on where it was being sent, especially yours."

"It appears Blain became quite skilled in his computer abilities since retirement. I could no longer ignore the theft of my money. You know how I feel when things are taken from me?"

"Yes."

"You haven't forgotten the punishments for those infractions."

"My memory serves me well on your methods of handling such violations. I can assume Blain will no longer be at family gatherings."

"My judgement was final in his case."

"Will there be the possibility of a funeral in the future?"

Aaron leaned back in the rocker.

"No, and I would remind you, who it was that placed you into my care."

Bevan touched his chest.

"I'm painfully aware."

"The money in that account was for Caren's children, so they would have a financially secure future."

"What was your plan to obtain it, with all the alerts?"

"Simply time and the continued improvement in technology. I have discovered hackers love the opportunity to screw with the government. The ones I have dealt with in the past do it for the thrill; others required a small fee, and it would be an easy fix. The yearly audit would find the account empty and any information connected with the theft untraceable."

"If you are a patient man all things will come to you."

Aaron nodded.

"Blain was a greedy, little bastard. I was content to send my own people to handle him and remain a ghost. When he placed the large bounties on my family, I was forced to return from dead."

"You were never truly out of the game, were you?"

"What do you mean by game?"

"You continued to run your business from the grave."

"I've had backup plans in motion since before the first fiasco in Mathews. The individuals who are indebted to me were expected to pay whether I was alive or dead. The constant rumors over the last ten years have caused a few issues. Some hesitated to provide payment, and one thought it possible to not pay at all. More wine?"

Bevan placed his glass on the table between them.

"Please, so what you are telling me is you had more individuals like Daniel Dejongh."

"Yes. I've tried to prepare for all possibilities in every aspect of my life, but never expected anyone to discover my family."

"How did he discover her? The only information I had is now in your possession."

"I have shared my personal information with only a small intimate group of individuals. It became obvious one of those men committed the unforgivable sin."

"He betrayed you."

"Betrayed the confidence brothers share in combat, and used it for another purpose."

"Money?"

"No, leverage should something happen, and he be caught. The name of Caydon's family was priceless. I have not discovered who sold the information to Blain but he will not go unpunished."

"I have no doubt."

"I was one step behind Blain since the contract was first discovered."

"Did you intend to send Caren to me?"

"No, not originally. I called payment due on an old debt."

"Declan."

"I needed a soldier, someone who still had a sense of morality. I made the right decision. He has honored his family's debt to me."

"What is going to happen to him?"

"Yet to be decided."

"How is Caren?"

"She takes long walks alone, returns with red swollen eyes. My failure to oversee the mission caused the death of her family."

"She's a strong woman."

"Strong enough to follow the clues, stay alive, and locate you."

"You knew I would be intrigued by her story about the boxes left in Maine."

"Their arrival at your front door left a puzzle. You had to know what information she had, and I needed the information in your possession."

He held up the file. Both men heard voices and doors slamming. Aaron walked over to the window.

"Caren and Declan?"

"She seems quite fond of him."

"Is that the reason he is still alive?"

Aaron never answered his question, simply returned to the chair and emptied the bottle into their glasses.

"I read your medical records last night. You had a severe heart attack a few months ago."

"You never cease to amaze me with the knowledge you can procure. I've been on medical leave due to the attack. Laura and I were on a run. If it hadn't been for her, I wouldn't be here. I guess I can say the same about you."

"I believe you'll be around for a long time, Bevan."

"I thought the heart attack was bad, but when Blain pulled the trigger, I knew it was over for me."

"My people are extremely good at what they do, especially your physician."

"I would like to know who died in Mathews ten years ago."

"Have you ever wished you could be in two places at once? I'm aware of how your office runs, being pulled in multiple directions at the same time. I became divided between business and…"

"Kyleigh."

"I located an individual with similar characteristics of mine and made the offer of a lifetime. He became my very expensive double; one so close, my own men didn't know. Imagine a life where you were feared, and lived as a king."

"He didn't mind it was all a lie?"

"No, not at all."

"The perfect solution to your dilemma."

"Yes, even when I wasn't with Kyleigh. I was able to accomplish a number of operations that required me to be in multiple locations."

"A very powerful and unnatural image to present to your allies and enemies."

"I had been satisfied with our arrangement."

"What happened?"

"He became careless and difficult to control. Kyleigh saved me the trouble of killing him. I do wish to tell you how much I appreciated your thoughtfulness at the cemetery in Texas."

Bevan shook his head.

"The only individuals in that cemetery were the caretakers and myself."

"You missed what was in front of you. I had to remove his remains to keep you or someone else going back and checking DNA."

They ceased their conversation as the door opened.

"Bevan, it's so good to see you're improving," Caren said.

"It's good to be here."

"Aaron, you're needed outside," Caren said.

"Bevan and I are almost finished."

"I'm pleased to see this conversation is going better than the first time."

Caren smiled and left the room.

Bevan watched Aaron pick the envelope up and open it. He took the photograph Aaron offered.

"Caren deserves to know the truth. You should tell her."

"Vanora was a beautiful, intelligent and funny woman, who gave those traits to her daughter. Did you know that sociopaths are incapable of loving or caring for anyone but themselves? There was a time in my life when Vanora changed what many believed I had become. I loved her with all that was still human inside, but when she was taken from me, it all died."

"What about Caren? Do you love her?"

"I have adapted at displaying emotions when necessary. The truth will continue as it always has. You do not take what belongs to me."

Bevan watched as he took the original copy of Caren's birth certificate and placed it in the fireplace.

"Aaron, please don't."

"I believe my daughter has been through enough. How do you think she would react to the knowledge of who I truly am, of her longevity, and possible immortality?"

Bevan handed the photograph back to him.

"Why did you save me? You could've let me die, and no one would have ever known you were alive."

"We have an interesting history, don't you think? Many years as friends and many as foes. The reason you are alive is because Caren begged me to save you."

"A couple more questions before you leave."

"Of course, anything you wish to know."

"Where am I?"

"Texas, in a bed and breakfast."

"Who owns this place?"

"I do."

Aaron smiled at Bevan and left the room.

CHAPTER FIFTY-THREE

Brushy Creek Vineyards
November 28th
Thanksgiving Day

Bevan had been awakened by the sounds of laughter and the smell of bacon cooking. This seemed like an unusual wakeup call at five in the morning. He turned on the light and walked to his locked door. He could hear a conversation between Declan and Caren.

He knocked on the door and found it opened to his touch. A robe was donned, and he entered a large room to discover a large contingency of men and weapons. He had interrupted their discussion as all conversation ceased.

"Please don't stop on my account," Bevan said.

Aaron turned towards Caren.

"Would you set the table for us, please?"

Declan walked away from the group of men.

"Coffee?"

"Yes, that would be nice."

The three walked to a built-in breakfast nook.

"I guess you're wondering about all of this," Declan said.

"When Aaron is involved, I have stopped asking."

Aaron slid into the corner next to Bevan.

"We're leaving."

Caren began to set family style dishes of food on the table. He could feel his mouth salivating.

"I hope my physician has released me to eat this."

"You can have scrambled eggs and one serving of biscuits and gravy," Caren said, and passed a basket to him.

"Bevan, I'd like to take a walk this morning after breakfast if you are up to it."

"Will I be coming back?"

He regretted the comment immediately as he saw hurt and concern in Caren's face.

"Of course. I'm not in the habit of destroying something I have taken time to repair," Aaron said.

"Declan is leaving with the men. I'll follow with Aaron," Caren said.

"I regret we cannot take ye back home to your family," Declan said.

"I'll find my way eventually," Bevan said.

"Thank you, for helping us when you could've said no," Caren said.

"I believe, I'm the one who should be thanking you."

"I am going to give credit to your physician," Aaron said.

"You should give me his name. I'll need it for payment of services."

"Your bill has been paid," Aaron told him.

Bevan took in the view of the large home. The multiple windows gave a true vision of this land.

"Bevan, aren't you hungry?"

"Sorry Caren, I am impressed with all of this and the spectacular view."

"Eat, so you'll be able to enjoy the day," Declan said.

Bevan was watchful of the men who never spoke during their meal. They didn't seem to be concerned they were seen by him.

"Any nausea?" she asked.

"I am pleased to say what has been devoured is remaining where it should," Bevan answered.

"Caren, why don't you see Declan and the men off."

Declan reached out and shook Bevan's hand.

"I wish ye well, but hope to never see ye again."

"Bevan, there are some clothes in your room," Aaron said.

"I placed them in the wardrobe. I hope they fit," Caren said.

"I'm sure they will be fine. Do I have time for a shower?"

"Take all the time you'd like," Aaron said.

"Then I will head back and clean up."

Bevan reentered the room and expected to be locked inside, but no one followed to close the cell door. He turned on the shower and could not wait to be totally bathed instead of sponged off. He looked at his wounds as the water ran over his body. The marks of the taser were gone and his leg had improved. He was thankful the bullet missed the bone, or he would've been in a cast for weeks.

The chest wound and long scar from his heart surgery would be a constant reminder that death had no warning. It felt wonderful to shave and have the opportunity to wear clothes again. The warm up suit, running shoes and jacket felt natural to him. Caren had done a nice job. Bevan walked out into an empty and silent room.

"Bevan, I'm in the office down the hallway."

He entered a simple room with a number of awards lining a shelf. He remained silent as Aaron appeared to be signing some type of paperwork at the desk.

"Is this a vineyard?"

"What's really bothering you, Bevan?"

"Have you been growing grapes and making wine for the last ten years?"

Aaron looked up from the desk and smiled.

"Does that seem odd to you?"

"Actually, it does. I never believed you were capable of anything but death and destruction. The past weeks have proved I've been wrong on a number of things."

"I bought the vineyard, two years after my death, as a silent partner. In the beginning, I made several trips to check on my investment. It was suggested I might want to think about building a bed and breakfast."

"This is all very interesting. You said something about a walk."

Aaron opened the small fridge behind his desk and obtained two bottles of water.

"I was given orders you were to stay hydrated."

They walked outside where Bevan observed three large SUV's drive away leaving a dust trail behind them. Caren turned, waved, and disappeared into another building.

"What is that?"

"The tasting room."

"Out here? You have people who come to taste the wine?"

"The vineyard is off the beaten track, but yes. I have many visitors that stop, drink and buy the wine."

Aaron pointed to the golf cart.

"Seriously?"

"It's this or a long walk. I don't believe you are physically ready."

Bevan sat down and opened the bottle of water as they drove away from the house. They drove quite a distance before they stopped. He stood and looked back at the house to see where his room was located. He walked out to where Aaron stood inspecting vines.

"I imagine this place is beautiful in the spring."

"Spring, summer, fall. The only time I dislike it is when everything is dormant and the snow. It is an enormous amount of work year-round and there are no guarantees you will have a good harvest. I will miss this place."

"Will I be dining alone tonight?"

"I would have enjoyed another meal and conversation together for old times' sake."

"I didn't notice a phone in the house."

Aaron reached in his pocket and handed Bevan two cell phones.

"They both need to be charged. I wouldn't use your personal phone until you and Lane have spoken."

"I would imagine there is some type of alert on my personal cell."

"I have someone arriving this afternoon to stay with you. They will have two chargers."

"I assume this individual will wait until you've been given a few hours head start before giving them to me."

"Always thinking like the officer, you were in Atlanta. Bevan, who are you going to tell besides Lane that I'm alive? You destroyed all my files when you took them home. How many witnesses did you have in Mathews, that will confirm Aaron Caydon died ten years ago on a cold cellar floor? You are going to have enough issues with the current situation. I would suggest you follow the story Lane has presented."

"If there were a body or two it would make the explanation less difficult and my story more believable."

"I will unfortunately be unable to accommodate you this time."

The conversation ceased with the buzz of Aaron's phone.

"Your ride must be here."

"Time for us to return to the house. I wouldn't want you to over-exert yourself on your first day out."

Bevan could see Caren on the porch as they drove up. He stepped out of the cart, but his feet began to feel heavy and a wave of dizziness made him stumble. Aaron placed his arm around him to prevent a fall.

"I felt fine earlier."

"Aaron, you kept him out too long," Caren said.

"I'll see to him."

Bevan could barely sit long enough for Aaron to remove his shoes.

"I think Caren is correct. I need to lay down."

"I know your family will be pleased to see you," Aaron said.

His eyes were heavy and couldn't seem to speak clearly. The last thing he remembered was Caren's kiss on his forehead.

"Good bye and thank you, Bevan," she said.

"Have a good rest."

Aaron held the water bottle up and shook it.

"Bastard."

CHAPTER FIFTY-FOUR

Lane was cocooned in his Irish flag blanket on the living room sofa, snoring to the white noise of the television. The twelve empty bottles of Guinness were lined up like bowling pins waiting to be scored upon with the yellow nerf ball.

His thirty-day suspension would begin Monday, and he felt there was no need to wait to celebrate. He dedicated two rounds to the brass in their wisdom to cancel any furthers search for Bevan after January first. He should've thanked Deena for pulling him out of the conference room when the decision was announced or the punishment could've been extended or a permanent situation.

Fred, the iguana, had been happy to rest on his owner's chest until the snoring began. He slipped slowly away into the bedroom and found peace in a pile of dirty clothes. The cell phone on the floor began to ring and was pushed further beneath the sofa as Lane attempted to reach it. The next five rounds of calls forced him out of the blankets and on his knees until it was located.

"Jesus Christ, it's Saturday!"

He looked at the unknown number and started to block it when two words stopped him.

"I'm alive!"

Lane became angry at this sick joke and threw the phone back on the floor. He had covered his head when the ringing began once more. He picked up the phone again.

"That's it. This bastard is going to pay for screwing up my weekend. Stop fucking calling me, you prick!"

Lane waited in silence for a response.

"Not the proper response to your boss."

Lane stood up and knocked over all the bottles on the table. He had prayed to the virgin for weeks, lit fifty candles at his church, almost offered to give up beer in order to hear Bevan's voice again. His voice cracked when he began to speak.

"It's good to hear your voice, boss."

"Are you crying?"

"No, no, just clearing my throat. I had a few friends over, to tell lies and drink last night."

"My guess is you've been suspended and decide to celebrate. This means you're free for a few days."

"I don't know. My calendar is pretty full."

"Let me guess. You, Fred, and the couch for thirty days."

"Pretty much."

"I need a chauffeur."

"I'm your man."

"I understand there are a number of issues left over from the Mathews incident."

"Where do I begin. The main room looked like a slaughter house, three spent shells recovered, but four bodies missing and a fifth unknown. Yes, it has not been fun. Oh, did I mention the cavity search from the Virginia State Police?"

"I regret I wasn't there to be of some assistance to you."

"It's actually better you came up missing. Why didn't you use your phone?"

"I thought it might be more advantageous to have some time together before I am questioned by, I believe it's Agent Deena Lyles."

"You seem to know a lot for someone who is presumed dead. What can I do for you?"

"Call Laura. Have them drive to Waynesboro and rent the Big House at the Long-Bowe for the next month. Advise them Santa is arriving early this year."

"I assume that will mean something to her?"

"It's private, but yes."

"Bevan, where are you?"

"I'm getting there. You need a one-way ticket to Dallas."

"Why are you in Texas?"

"Lane, I need you to stop asking questions. Once you arrive, rent a large SUV. Something comfortable for a long drive. I prefer to discuss what transpired out of my wife's presence."

"They've been strong through all of this, and it has been difficult, the Company searched your home. I have some pressing questions."

"You mean more than what you've already asked?"

"I'm serious, boss,"

"I'll do my best to answer them all."

"Are you the only one that made it out alive?"

"Declan was injured, and Caren is alive. Everyone else is dead."

"I'm almost afraid to ask the next question."

"Why don't you wait until I see you, then."

"We found an empty wine bottle. I know it isn't possible, but the bottle had a Brushy Creek label on it.

Lane waited for Bevan to speak.

"You're not going to believe where I am."

•

December 1st

Lane wasn't positive Deena would place surveillance on him, but he could not make that assumption. His sweet, elderly neighbor was pleased to keep Fred and promised her total silence for two hundred dollars and his Netflix codes. When he arrived at Bevan's home, a lone candle flickered in the window. Laura had placed this for her husband when she was first advised he was missing. She said it would remain there until he returned home. He walked to the front door and knocked.

"Laura, it's Lane."

The door opened, and she appeared with a weapon at her side.

"Are you alone?"

"It's just me."

"Come in."

She locked the door behind him.

"I heard they searched the house. I'm sorry that's all on me."

"Searched is a mild word. They did five thousand dollars' worth of damage."

"Did they take anything?"

"My phone, computer and Sarah's computer. Bevan had taken his with him There wasn't much else, but they tore the house apart. I was so angry I decided if I didn't leave, I'd be going to jail."

"I'll see what can be done when I'm off suspension."

"Why are you here?"

"I've some news to give you."

Laura placed her weapon on the entry table.

"I've been preparing myself, come back to the family room."

"Is Sarah here?"

"No, she's at a sleepover at a friend's house. I wanted her to have some semblance of a normal life."

"I've been instructed to tell you that, Santa is arriving early this year."

Lane waited for a moment and began to smile. He watched as tears flowed down her face, and then, she threw herself in his arms. He could see she was going to ask a question, but he stopped her and pointed to his ear.

"Are you sure?"

He shook his head no.

"Can I buy you a coffee.?"

"I'll get my coat."

Lane drove them down the street to the local coffee shop and found a location where he could observe the customers that entered.

"Where is he?"

"In Texas, and that's all I can say. I have instructions for you."

Lane passed a piece of paper to her.

"I'll make the reservation on our way back to the house. I'd appreciate it if you would stay a while, so I can pack. When I pick up Sarah tomorrow, we'll leave. What about you?"

"I'm on the first flight tomorrow morning out of Reagan. It may take us a few days to arrive."

"Why so long to get there? Lane, was he injured?"

"I can't answer that, but he sounded well. He said for you not to worry. We have a few matters to discuss, work related."

"Promise me, you'll drive safe."

Lane held up three fingers.

"Promise. Did you buy another phone?"

"It's a burner phone. Damn thing doesn't work half the time. I'll put my number in your phone."

Laura put the contact information in his phone.

"Lady Law?"

"I figure if someone checks your phone, they'll believe it's a new flavor of the week for you."

"Hey, that's not nice."

"Lane, when is the last time you've dated anyone longer than six months?"

"Fair enough. If you should get a text from an unknown number, it will be us. I hope you'll forgive me for involving you in all of this."

"Right now, they are welcome to come back and tear it down to the foundation. The knowledge my family will be whole again makes what happened insignificant and meaningless."

"I need to take some of Bevan's clothes, something comfortable."

"I'll take care of it when we return."

When they arrived back at the house, he waited as she quickly packed and loaded the family car. She placed Bevan's clothes in a paper grocery bag with a loaf of bread where it could be seen at the top.

"Are you and General Lee in for the evening?" Lane asked, and rubbed the dog's head.

"Yes, we're going to open a bottle of wine and watch, *It's a Wonderful Life*. I'll pick Sarah up tomorrow around nine. She will be sad to have missed you."

"I'll see her in a few days. Do me a favor."

"Anything."

"Make sure there's batteries in that candle, and don't turn it off."

Laura hugged Lane tightly.

"Not a chance. Until he's home with us."

He took the paper bag, waited for Laura to lock the door, and left. Lane made numerous circles around different neighborhoods and stopped at his favorite burger joint. He added Bevan's items to his bag then Ubered from his apartment to the Motel 6 close to Reagan. When the Do Not Disturb sign was placed on the door, he decided the only surveillance had been his own.

CHAPTER FIFTY-FIVE

Alvord, Texas
December 2nd

Lane arrived in Dallas on time and was pleased the rental agency was able to honor his request. The GMC Yukon Denali was available. He was grateful the inflatable car mattress was blown up and in place according the agent. He located the Denali, placed his luggage in the back, and eased into the leather seat. The location of Brushy Creek Vineyards was placed in his phone's GPS. He was pleased with only an hour's drive ahead of him and the bright sunny day with a temperature of sixty. As he stopped at the first light, his phone rang. The caller was Lady Law.

"Lane, where are you?"

"Dallas."

"I picked Sarah up early. We are on our way."

"Be safe, and we'll see you in a few days."

Lane listened to the instructions of the GPS. The hour drive seemed longer to him, maybe due to all the emotions he was feeling. The huge sign indicating he had arrived at the vineyard made him shiver. The photographs of the family Caydon had murdered flashed forward. An entire generation ended, because a case of Brushy Creek Wine had been taken from him. Bevan's description of the bed and breakfast's location further back away from the road was perfect. Lane stood next to the driver's door, took his weapon from the bag, and chambered a round.

"You won't need that."

Lane jumped and stumbled backwards.

"Jesus, I almost shot you."

He grabbed Bevan and hugged him.

"It's good to see you, too."

"I had to make sure you weren't my imagination. Good God, you're pale as a ghost. Are you sure it's safe to travel?"

"The physician that was here yesterday released me to travel with limitations."

"What type of limitations?"

"We need to break the trip up in several days. We need to go inside."

"Is there anyone here?"

"A very nice housekeeper who has made an outstanding brunch for us."

"Your family will be waiting for us."

"Thank you."

"We are going to have some sensitive material to discuss. Is it safe to talk in her presence?"

"You're joking, right?"

They walked into a warm and cozy home, with a huge fireplace. Lane warmed his hands and bent down to scratch the huge calico cat that circled his legs. He watched Bevan walk slowly to the breakfast nook. The woman had placed food on the large center island and smiled.

"The food is ready. Please eat," she said.

"Coffee?" Lane asked.

Bevan held up a carafe.

"On the table here."

"I have juice and champagne if you wish," she said.

"We'll be fine, thank you."

"I have work to do. Just leave the plates in the sink. Bevan will you two be here for dinner?"

"I will be ending my stay today. It has been nice to meet you."

They watched as she nodded to them and left the house. Lane fixed a plate for Bevan then two for himself.

"Bevan, what is this place?"

"A vineyard, with this functioning bed and breakfast."

"This is an outstanding set up, and the food is seconds worthy."

"Were you able to get the mattress for the back seats?"

"Yes, all set up, but it needs sheets and a couple decent pillows."

"I'll be able to find what we need here. I want to talk for an hour before we leave this place."

"I brought some personal items and clothes from home. The tank on the Denali is full. We can go now if you'd like."

"In an hour. I need to know what happened to your plan?"

"I sent Declan and Caren ahead without me. I was to enter through the kitchen and take control, but discovered Blain outside the house. He said you had called him to meet you. I believed his lie and ended up in the cellar, with two punctures in the back of my neck."

Bevan touched the back of his neck.

"He tasered me too, terrible experience."

"At least you didn't get shoved down a flight of stairs."

"I would take the stairs over the bullet to my chest."

"When my brain unscrambled, I made it to the door where I heard one gunshot. Eight hours later, the Virginia State Police found me, and that was another unpleasant experience. What about you?"

"The last full memory I have is watching Blain pulling the trigger of his weapon. I have no idea of the time that passed before waking up the first time here."

Lane stood up and walked over to the window.

"Bevan, you already know my next question."

"The answer is yes, Aaron Caydon is alive. He said he had been here for eight years."

"What do you mean here?"

"He bought this vineyard, built the bed and breakfast, and has been making wine."

Lane's hands were shaking when he returned to the table.

"How is it possible?"

"I asked the same question."

"What was his answer?"

"No one looks for a dead man."

Lane thought for a moment.

"The attack on Caren brought him out."

"Yes. That and Blain removing money from his Company retirement."

"Who did Kyleigh kill then?"

"A double."

"A damn good one. It convinced me. I don't suppose you have an idea of where they went?"

"They left yesterday right after he sedated me. The resources he has I would imagine they are probably halfway across the world. We have enough problems to deal with than being concerned with his resurrection."

"Speaking of problems, I should explain my story to the Company. Bevan, I have to apologize for involving your wife. It caused a major search of your home and damages."

"I'll handle that issue once I've returned to the welcoming arms of the Company. I know you wouldn't have involved her unless it was necessary. I need the information you gave Agent Lyles."

Lane abbreviated his story in order to meet the hour deadline and get them on the road. He walked through the kitchen and filled a bag full of goodies. Bevan appeared in a pair of his favorite sweatpants and long-sleeved t-shirt.

"I thought a snack would get us down the road."

He watched as Bevan kept smelling the sleeves of his shirt.

"Boss, is there something wrong with your shirt?"

"I wasn't sure I would ever smell home again."

"Are you sure you feel up to leaving?"

"I'll be fine. No more than five hours on the road today, maybe less. I think we have some holes to fill on the story, more so on my side."

"You tell me when you're ready to stop. We'll have time to go over everything again."

He helped Bevan into the front seat, then set Google Maps on his phone to the Long-Bowe Bed and Breakfast.

"We should arrive Wednesday."

"I don't care Lane. I just don't want to be here."

Lane nodded and drove away.

CHAPTER FIFTY-SIX

Waynesboro, Georgia
Long-Bowe Bed and Breakfast
December 7th

Lane awakened to the hard knock on his door, and knew a certain young girl was playing alarm clock. The seventeen-and-a-half-hour drive was drawn out for Bevan's comfort, and continuous review of information. They arrived late Wednesday night at the Big House of the B&B, where Laura had allowed Sarah to stay up late for Santa's arrival.

He would never forget the sounds of happiness through tears and excited voices at their arrival. Lane had given them as much time to be a family as possible, with long walks and visits in town. The next knock on his door was lighter.

"Lane, breakfast is ready," Laura said.

"I'll be down shortly."

He dressed quickly before he headed down the stairs into the kitchen. His mouth salivated at the feast Laura had prepared again.

"I am moving in with you and Bevan when we get back to Virginia. Where is he?"

"He left at dawn to go for a walk."

"Alone?"

"The General went with him."

"How's he doing?"

"He slept well last night, but refused to take any pain medication."

"Where is Sarah?"

"Here."

She poked Lane in the back. He turned and grabbed the child swinging her around.

"You are growing way too fast."

"Thank you for bringing my Daddy home."

Sarah hugged Lane's neck, which caused a few moments to pass before he could speak.

"It was my pleasure young lady."

"The door opened, and General Lee ran into the kitchen wagging his tail begging for a treat.

"Bevan!" Laura called.

"Let me put my coat up," Bevan said.

"Good morning, boss."

He turned and dropped his cup on the floor.

"Lane, did you burn yourself?"

Laura handed him a paper towel.

"What's wrong?"

"Did you look in the mirror this morning?"

"Laura, do I look different today?"

"The only difference is you no longer look like the ghost that arrived three days ago," she said.

"Bevan do you feel any different?"

"I feel stronger, but it will be two months the nineteenth, since Mathews. I would hope my body would have begun to recover."

"You're probably right. I'm just surprise how good you look."

"I'd like to believe his wife and child put the color back in his face."

Laura winked at Lane.

"After breakfast, we should probably make contact with Deena. How do you feel with the story?" Lane asked.

"I'm good. I don't want to wait until they are about to stop the search. It would raise more questions."

"Sarah and I will go over to your mom's after breakfast and check on her. She wasn't feeling well last night when I called. I hated to lie when you were missing but didn't feel she needed the stress."

"No, you did the right thing. Tell her I'll be over later."

Lane finished off the last of the blueberry pancakes and bacon while Bevan walked out with his family. He cleaned the table, loaded the dishwasher and poured the last of the coffee in two cups for them.

"Let's get this over with."

Bevan took the cup and followed Lane.

"It's Saturday. Will she be at home or the office?" Bevan asked.

"I'd say office with the search about to be called off, and you declared dead. If there is no answer there, I'll call her personal cell."

"When do you think the team will arrive?"

"If she can gather a crew together, probably tomorrow. If not it will be Monday."

"Make the call and put it on speaker."

Lane turned on his cell and pressed the number to the office.

"Agent Deena Lyles."

"Working on the weekend, are you?"

"My parents are coming for the holidays. I don't want to have this case hanging over me until the first of the year. How's the suspension going?"

"It's actually been rather productive."

"Lane don't lie. I have an idea of your productivity. You and Fred watching reruns, and drinking beer with a lot of cold pizza."

"I have something that will change your opinion."

"Let me guess. Beer bottle bowling with old friends," she said and laughed.

"I left town."

"That was a bold move with a thirty-day suspension hanging over your bank account. Where'd you go?"

"Waynesboro, Georgia."

They heard her phone drop on a hard surface.

"Why are you in Waynesboro?"

"I'm here because Bevan called me."

"Bevan Benjamin, alive, in Waynesboro?"

"Yes, recovering from the injury he suffered in Mathews."

"Who else knows he's alive?"

"He contacted his wife and child, which I would've done first, too."

"I'll put a team together, and we'll be there tomorrow. You haven't questioned him, have you?"

"It wouldn't matter if I had. I'm on suspension remember, but no I haven't questioned him. He's happy to be alive."

"Do you think he can travel? It would be nice if he could return with us."

Bevan shook his head.

"I don't believe that would be wise due to the injuries he has sustained."

"Do we need to bring medical assistance for him?"

Lane looked at Bevan for approval. He nodded.

"Deena, it's been a few days since he was seen. Go ahead and bring someone with you for an official check."

"I'll contact medical. We will do the interviews there and continue to allow him to convalesce. I'll see you tomorrow," she said, and ended the call.

"That went better than I expected," Lane said.

"I would have preferred to wait on the medical evaluation until I returned, but it looks good for them to be here."

"Do you have the physician's name from Texas?"

"Yes, they will have fun interviewing him."

"Why is that?"

"He's about a hundred years old. I'm sure Aaron probably paid him enough money to forget anything but what he was told to say."

"I'm sure he only has paper records that will be misplaced."

Lane's phone buzzed with a text.

"You need to turn in the rental before they arrive for our story to gel. Lane are you listening to me?"

"We need to leave now."

Lane handed the phone to Bevan.

"Bevan needed, his mother is very ill, ambulance on the way, hurry."

CHAPTER FIFTY-SEVEN

Bevan placed a black overcoat on, wrapped a scarf around his neck and walked out of the Big House to say his goodbyes to the investigators from the Company. Deena and her team loaded their luggage into two SUVs and prepared to drive to the local airport. The interviews and interrogation had gone as they had planned. He played the part, answered all the questions and agreed to take a polygraph, which was a formality. As a critically injured victim, he would never be subjected to this, but the offer would read well in the report to his superiors.

The death of his mother, which coincided with the arrival of Agent Lyles, had made the week tedious. He made notifications to family, and final arrangements between the interviews. Bevan moved his family to the main Benjamin home and left Lane with the team at the Big House. He walked down the stairs and shook hands with the team.

"Bevan, I believe we have everything that will be needed to complete the report and this case," she said.

"My plan to return to the office will be delayed for at least another month for obvious reasons."

"I'll have my report finished in a few days. You are extremely lucky to be alive."

Bevan nodded his head.

"You will inform me should Blain's body be located. My brother and his wife are very distraught. It makes closure impossible for them."

"Yes, of course, and please accept our deepest sympathy for the loss of your mother."

"Thank you."

He watched as the car disappeared from the drive. Lane joined him at the bottom of the stairs.

"I'm happy to see them leave, boss."

"As am I."

"Laura called and said everyone is waiting for us at your folks' house."

"Were you able to obtain what I asked for?"

"It's in the car."

They drove to his parents' house and joined the rest of the Benjamin family. His mother had requested a simple graveside service when her time came. They drove to the Bowen Cemetery where his father had been buried. The Bowen, Long, and Benjamin families had been associated for many years. It seemed appropriate they be among their friends. When the services had ended, Bevan's brother walked up and hugged him.

"Bevan, could I speak to you for a moment?"

He could see the dark circles beneath his brother's red and swollen eyes. He placed a brotherly arm around his shoulder as they walked to a far corner of the cemetery. He observed the tears that ran down Barton's face.

"What can I do for you?"

Barton lowered his head.

"I don't know what to say to you. We worried when Blain isolated himself in Wyoming and stopped calling us. I'm so sorry you were injured."

"Brother, we all missed the signs."

"Brooklyn and I are leaving from here to return home. Will you keep us informed?"

Bevan hugged his brother.

"Yes, of course."

He waited until they left the cemetery then motioned for Lane to join him.

"How are they doing?"

"Embarrassed, heartbroken. They need closure, something tangible."

"You told him?"

"I told him there was a possibility his body might not be recovered. I will never be able to tell them a dead man killed their son."

Lane removed a small, white stone cross from his coat.

"Where would you like me to place this?"

Bevan could hear shovels of dirt beginning to fill his mother's grave. He took the cross from him.

"I'll take care of this before we leave Waynesboro."

"Laura told me you are the executor."

"Yes. It's one of the reasons you'll be covering for me for another six weeks, maybe longer."

"Any chance your brother or sister will come back here to live?"

"No, it was difficult to get them here for reunions once a year. Laura and I are the only ones that truly enjoy the peace and solitude of my parents' home."

"Boss, your family has been through enough this year. Go buy some lottery tickets. You need to take a long look at the people who love and care about you."

"We should head back to the house, any chance you can stay a few more days?"

"I believe another week of your wife's cooking will be just what my suspension ordered."

The short ride back to his parents' house had given Bevan enough time to think about the conversation with Lane. He stepped out of the car, took a deep breath of cold air, and enjoyed the smell of wood burning.

Lane stood at the front door of the house.

"Boss, is something wrong?"

"No, I'm just thinking."

He removed his coat, and began to listen as those who knew his mother speak of the great loss the community will feel. The stories from family and friends brought laughter among the tears. He waited in the doorway that led to the kitchen and smiled as Laura pointed to a glass of wine. He motioned for her to follow him.

"I was about to send a search party out for you and Lane."

"We needed a moment after everyone left."

"Barton and Brooklyn have left; all of this seems too much for them."

"He spoke with me in the cemetery. I wish I could do something to relieve their grief."

"I guess we'll be here a little longer."

Bevan put his glass down and pulled her into his arms.

"What would you say if we make it permanent?"

"You're serious."

"Yes, think you could live here away from the big city?"

"I have always loved this house and the peace it brings, but there's another person we need to ask."

"We'll discuss it as a family, tomorrow."

CHAPTER FIFTY-EIGHT

Bevan stood in his father's home office and smiled as Laura waved on her way to meet the school bus. This had become an everyday occurrence since Sarah had been enrolled in public school. She would listen to all the new and exciting events of the day on their walk back to the house. The last six months had been a whirlwind of activity for the three of them.

He had felt Laura would be happy to move and live in Waynesboro. They worried about uprooting their daughter from the only home she knew, and neighborhood friends. The day after the funeral, they suggested a move from Reston to Waynesboro. They were both surprised when Sarah didn't hesitate to say yes. She even ran upstairs and picked out her room. He turned towards the desk when his cell phone began to ring.

"Good afternoon," Bevan said.

"How's life in the very slow lane these days?" Lane asked.

"Life is wonderful thanks to a good friend's advice."

"I have a file to mail out."

"The final outcome of Agent Lyles' investigation?"

"I thought you would like it for your personal collection," Lane said, then laughed.

"I'll use it to start my first fire come winter. Are you cleaning out my desk to make room for more PayDays?"

"No, I turned down the offer. I'm not a report writing desk jockey and will never be the diplomat you were. The meetings with the President caused me to keep a box of Zantac next to the PayDays."

"I had to give you the opportunity. No one deserves the job more in my opinion. I didn't think you were ready to be locked in an office."

"I appreciate it, but in three weeks, this mess will be a headache for someone else. I'll be back in the field where I belong."

"Why so long before the change?" Bevan asked.

"The brass expected me to accept your headache of a job. When I turned the offer down the battle for your office began. They have finally cut the list down to three candidates. The final interviews and background checks are to be completed in the next three weeks. I can't wait to give the keys to the coffee maker to someone else."

Bevan began to laugh.

"You should take a week off and come by here. We have plenty of room."

"Mark the date, three weeks and I'll be there."

"I'll have Laura increase the pantry. Sarah will be happy as always to see you."

"They do have Guinness there, right?"

"See you soon."

Bevan heard the front door open and small feet ran towards the office.

"Daddy, look what I did today in school."

Bevan took the drawing, held it up, and placed it on the wall with the others.

"You are improving every day."

"Bevan, the painters are coming next week. We have a few more decisions on where the personal items should go," Laura said.

"Mom's will made all of this less complicated, but I do want to get the bigger items gone. I'll make another call to the church to see if they can take them," he said.

"Did you send the checks to Barton and Belinda, for their share of the inheritance?"

He held up two envelopes.

"I'll place these in the mailbox for the postman tomorrow."

"Belinda called, and said they were happy we decided to buy the property. I still can't believe our house in Reston sold the first day on the market."

"I'm just glad we're not still waiting for it to sell. Lane called while you were gone."

"He didn't take the job, did he?"

"No, I didn't think he would, but Lane was my first choice. He will be out to see us in three weeks then back to field work."

"It's where he belongs," she said.

"Can you spare me for about thirty minutes? I need to run out to the cemetery and check on mom's headstone."

"We can find something to do like make cookies while you're gone."

"Chocolate chip!" Sarah said.

Bevan kissed his wife and child, then walked out into a beautiful Georgia afternoon. His first purchase after their move was a Jeep with removable doors and roof. Open air driving was enjoyable most of the time, but he had made the mistake of ignoring weather reports which caused several soggy drives home.

The two close handshakes with death had caused him to realize what had nearly been lost. He pulled up to the small gate at the Bowen Cemetery and stopped. The stone marker had waited long enough to take its place with family. He walked to his parents' grave and placed the small cross between their markers.

"I hope you've found peace."

This small simple act was out of love and respect for his brother. *Blain Alexander Benjamin, beloved son, missing.*

CHAPTER FIFTY-NINE

New Zealand
Vanora Vineyards
June 1, 2014

Aaron stood on the large balcony of his home in Wairapapa. The vineyards here had been purchased five years ago and renamed while he remained in Texas. The Vanora Vineyards was his retreat from the world with a full complement of workers for the fields and staff for the house.

This location was where he would conduct all business, rebuild his teams, and a safe place for Caren to call home. The extra crews for the upcoming harvest had been hired, and the report from the fields indicated the production would double over the previous year. He closed his eyes and thought of Texas and Brushy Creek where he would return one day. He never moved when Declan called from the doorway.

"Ye called for me, sir?"

"I did. Come out on the balcony with me Declan."

"This is a lovely place."

Aaron gave Declan a glass of wine.

"We have business to discuss."

"Thank ye, sir."

"Have a seat Declan."

"Yes, sir."

"First, I would prefer you call me Aaron when Caren is present. She needs to believe there is a connection between us other than strictly business. In the presence of my men or others, you will refer to me as Caydon."

"Yes, sir."

"You have questions?"

"With your permission, there are some things I need to address with ye."

"I have never been one to answer questions from individuals. Bevan was one of the exceptions. I am not blind to the fact my daughter has feelings for you; something I had not expected. I'll allow you ten minutes to ask all the questions you wish. Once you have finished, we will not speak again on those subjects."

"May I remain in your service?"

"I can always use a man of your talents. I need men I can trust, who follow orders. It was one of the reasons you were chosen."

"When the lass is ready, I wish to marry her, with your permission."

Aaron stood, walked to the banister of the balcony and motioned for Declan. They could see Caren on a small scooter headed towards the house.

"She rides out every morning to check the fields."

"Caren has fallen in love with this place."

"I've seen her in the library, on the computer, absorbing all the information possible on vineyards and their management. Declan, you understand her happiness and safety is all that matters."

"Aye, sir."

"I hand-picked you for the job in Boston."

"I will live with my mistake…"

Aaron held up his hand and stopped him.

"You saved her, and for that, I am in your debt. The one time I was not in control, the plan failed and the cost was great. I will allow you to remain, and the rest will evolve over time."

"Thank you."

"You are aware and have seen the consequences of those who fail or displease me?"

"Aye, my life and blood are yours."

Aaron was pleased to hear those words.

"I received information that your uncle passed in his sleep two days ago. I apologize for the late notification."

"I cannot return for his funeral, but appreciate ye informing me."

"Come inside. I have an errand you need to accomplish for me."

They walked inside to a large desk. Aaron took his seat and viewed the photographs of Vanora and Caren in silver frames. He removed an envelope from the drawer and gave it to him.

"Do ye need me to deliver this to someone?"

"You are to go to the infirmary and give that to Doctor Morres today."

"Will there be a reply for ye?"

Caren ran through the door and wrapped her arms around Aaron's neck.

"Good morning, big brother."

Aaron placed his hands over hers and raised his eyes to Declan.

"Caren, would you wait for me on the balcony. We have business to complete. It will not take long."

"The only business you need to talk about is how we're going to harvest all the grapes," she said.

"It's taken care of, but we'll discuss it further. There is a new Pino Noir on the balcony," Aaron said.

"Sounds nice," she said.

Both men watched as she almost skipped out of the room and into the sunlight.

"The information in the envelope is in regards to a treatment for you."

"He cleared me weeks ago."

"This has nothing to do with the present, but everything to do with your future."

"I'll go now."

"You might be in the infirmary for a few days. I'll make any apologies necessary to Caren for you."

"The treatment will make me unwell?"

"Everything will be explained to you. Declan, should you refuse this treatment, there will be no consideration on any future with my daughter."

"Understood."

Aaron walked out into the sunlight, and joined Caren. He refilled their empty wine glasses.

"Where did Declan go?"

"I sent him on an errand. Caren, I have one more item of business that must be tended to before the day is yours."

"I'll be here enjoying this wine and sun."

He returned to the desk and removed a large piece of cloth parchment from the top drawer. He reached for the quill and began to write. Twenty minutes later, the letter was secured in wax. He opened his cell and sent a text message. A courier entered the room a few moments later and collected a plain tube that he had placed the letter in for delivery.

"Your shipment of wine to the States arrived safely," she said.

"Excellent, I would like this to be delivered in person," Aaron said.

The courier took the tube and an envelope from him.

"As always, a pleasure to be in your service," she said.

Caren walked into the room.

Aaron, do I need to make an appointment to talk to you?"

"It seems that way today doesn't it? My apologies."

Caren held up the glass of wine she was drinking.

"You were right. This is an excellent wine."

"I thought you would appreciate it."

"Declan and I are going to the pool this afternoon. Will you join us?"

"The errand he was sent on will cause him to be away for a couple of days. I will be happy to join you."

"I do have something I'd like to discuss with you."

"As I said, the day is now yours."

"Is there any possibility to obtaining something from the lock box in Boston?"

"I believe it's possible. You would be referring to the cashier's check you never cashed."

"Stephen's idea to leave it. He always worried that much money would cause problems for us."

"What do you have in mind for the money?"

"I'd like to see it go to charity or a scholarship in my family's honor, but I'm unsure how to accomplish that without causing questions."

"I believe I have a solution if you will trust me."

"Of course, I trust you. What a silly statement."

"If you will head to the pool, I'll arrive shortly."

"Bring another bottle with you."

"Texas or Vanora?"

"Surprise me. See you downstairs."

Aaron turned his cell on and pressed a number.

"One United Bank of Boston, can I help you?" the man asked.

"Yes, I need to speak with the manager please."

CHAPTER SIXTY

The call from Hawaii this morning caught Bevan off guard as he couldn't remember changing the tone on the cell phone alarm. He didn't wish to disturb the rest of the family and advised Taylor twenty minutes would be required on a return call. He stumbled into the kitchen and made a single cup of coffee, let General outside, and made his way into the office. He returned the call.

"This is an unexpected surprise, Taylor."

"Bevan, I wasn't sure who I should contact. I knew since you had retired, I was safe from official inquiries."

Bevan wasn't sure what to make of this unusual, cryptic conversation.

"Taylor, what has happened?"

"I received a cashier's check yesterday for ten million dollars."

Bevan nearly knocked his coffee cup over.

"What bank?"

"A bank out of Boston, and it came with some very specific stipulations."

"The money I couldn't locate for you. Tell me about these stipulations."

"The letter attached requests one million be given to five listed charities."

"What about the rest?"

"A scholarship is to be set up in the name of the Johnson Family for special needs children. Bevan, that's the family that was killed two years ago. The mother is still missing."

"Yes, was there anything else?"

"A warning."

"Let me guess, I will not forgive or forget," Bevan said.

"I thought this was all behind us. What should I do?"

"Honor the request and never tell anyone you called me."

"I'll take care of it Monday, and Bevan, don't be a stranger," Taylor said.

"We have plenty of room here, too."

The sounds of pans in the kitchen indicated the house was awake, and the General would need to be fed. He entered the kitchen and made another cup of coffee in the Keurig.

"Who called so early?"

"Taylor Shaw. It appears Aaron returned the ten million dollars to him."

Laura stopped and faced her husband.

"You're serious."

"Every last dime. There were of course stipulations attached with the return."

"What type of stipulations?"

"The money goes to charities and a scholarship."

"What did you tell him?" she asked.

"Honor it."

"Daddy!"

"Good morning, princess."

"Are we going to carve the pumpkins today?" Sarah asked.

"Sounds like a good idea," Bevan said.

●

Bevan picked up two pumpkins from the kitchen island and followed his daughter out of the house.

"Daddy, I can carry it."

Bevan handed the smaller one to her.

"I'm sure you can."

He stopped and watched as she ran to the small table in the front of the house. Laura waited for them with stencils and knives to make the scariest jack-o-lanterns possible, for their first Halloween in their

Waynesboro home. One year ago, today, he nearly lost everything important in his life. The scars had faded and his strength returned.

"Bevan, what are you doing?"

"Lost in thought."

"These pumpkins are not going to carve themselves," Laura said. "Hurry, Daddy."

As he reached the table outside, Sarah chose the stencils to be carved. He smiled, and began to gut the first pumpkin.

"Bevan, we have company."

A black town car pulled into their drive and stopped. They moved their daughter behind them. A driver exited, then opened the back door of the vehicle. A tall, slender woman with dark sunglasses, was assisted from the car and given what appeared to be a small packing tube. Bevan knew this individual had been sent by Aaron. He moved, but Laura grabbed his arm and stopped him.

"Laura, I don't believe we are in any danger. Stay here."

He met the woman away from his family.

"Bevan Benjamin?"

"Yes, may I help you?"

"I have a delivery for you."

She handed him the tube with a gloved hand.

"I assume an explanation is inside."

He held up the tube.

"I'm simply the courier."

She returned to the town car and left the property.

He walked back to his family.

"I'm going to put this inside and look at it later."

"Caydon."

"Probably, but I refuse to allow him to take another moment away from my family."

He placed it on the entry table inside the door. The rest of the day was spent in laughter and slimy pumpkin guts. As evening approached, Sarah placed tea light candles inside each jack-o-lantern.

"Our home is now protected," Sarah said.

"I think a young lady needs a bath," Laura said.

"Daddy, will you read to me?"

"Just like last night and the night before."

Reading to his daughter and knowing she felt safe would always be his favorite part of being a father. He entered the master bedroom to a peaceful scene of his wife reading and General Lee ever on guard at the end of their bed.

"Is she asleep?"

"Within the first ten minutes of the story. I have something to do in the office before coming to bed."

"Bevan, do me a favor and burn it when you're finished."

He nodded and walked to the entry table where the item had remained untouched since its arrival. This was a typical delivery from Aaron, no identification or indication of origin.

He eased into the leather chair behind his father's desk and opened the tube. The cloth parchment eased out on the desk. He turned it over to observe a wax seal with a crest and the words Werner. He broke the seal, watched as the parchment unfurled without assistance, and Bevan shook his head as he began to read.

Bevan,

It is with great sadness that I write this letter ending our lengthy relationship. You have been an admired adversary over the years, but all good things must end as I have been told for almost a century.

I send my deepest sympathy at the loss of your mother. She was a lovely, intelligent woman and the perfect hostess when I visited your parents years ago.

I celebrate your retirement and say "Bravo!" on the complete and total deception at Mathews. I have always been impressed with your duplicity and where it took you over the years with the Company.

Your move to one of my favorite places in Waynesboro was unexpected, but I'm pleased to know your family will remain there for many years. I took the liberty of restocking the wine cellar while the house was repainted. You will enjoy the Pino

Noir. It was an excellent year.

I must now address the main reason for my letter. At one point during our conversations in Texas, I mentioned that you would be with us for a long time.

My friend, you will outlive your wife, child and probably all of your grandchildren.

I have given you the gift of unknown longevity.

In most cases, a small amount of my blood will cure or heal even the severest of injuries. Your near fatal condition required several units of blood, which concerned your physician, who felt you might not survive. I never had a doubt as family means everything to us.

I say farewell and toast your long life.

Archidamus

Bevan leaned back into the chair, closed his eyes, and wanted to deny the words. He tried to pretend this was another of his lies. He opened the file on his desk and removed the unopened letter with the results from the cardiologist in Atlanta. His new family physician had referred him for follow up and baseline testing for future references. He opened the letter and read the report.

No signs of heart disease or indication of any previous myocardial infarction as stated in the records. Subject has the heart of a young man possibly in his twenties.

It is suggested a possible mistake on testing and mislabeled bloodwork has occurred. Mr. Benjamin should be rescheduled for testing, and bloodwork will need to be retaken as all samples have been misplaced or destroyed.

Bevan now understood the request for a conference by the local physician. He was unsure where all of this would lead, but he would never become a guinea pig or freak for the medical community. He could never explain how this transformation had taken place and would forever be avoiding anyone that questioned his health. Caydon had played his best hand and won.

He walked to the fireplace and burned the letter. As he entered the kitchen Laura stood with a bottle of wine.

"Bevan, I found this in the wine cellar."

He took it from her and read the label.

"Pino Noir, Vanora vineyards, New Zealand."

"There must be five cases down there. I guess you mother ordered them before she passed. I'll get the glasses."

Bevan opened the bottle and motioned for her to follow him. They stopped at their daughter's door, and Laura wrapped her arm around him. "Have you ever imagined what she'll become in the future?"

"I hope a good person like her father."

"Do you want to fix her covers?"

She straightened a duvet of fairies and unicorns, then left a tender kiss before leaving the room.

"Bevan, she is so happy here."

"What about you, Laura? Are you happy?"

"Why are you asking now?"

"I need to know that we made the right decision to come here."

"You will never know what this life means to me, to us. The time you were missing was difficult, but I never gave up. I knew you would do anything to come back home to your family."

They entered the master bedroom where the wine was left untouched until physical needs were fulfilled. In the silence of their room, Bevan closed his eyes, and held the woman he loved. He waited patiently for the next words she would speak to him.

"Bevan, what did the letter say?"

He pulled Laura close and kissed her.

"There was nothing in the letter, that the future can't handle."